Thomas Taylor

Student´s Hand-Book of
Mushrooms of America

Outlook

Thomas Taylor

Student´s Hand-Book of Mushrooms of America

1. Auflage | ISBN: 978-3-73262-722-6

Erscheinungsort: Frankfurt am Main, Deutschland

Erscheinungsjahr: 2018

Outlook Verlag GmbH, Frankfurt.

STUDENT'S HAND-BOOK OF MUSHROOMS OF AMERICA

Part 1.
    Introduction.
    Cryptogams.
        Fungi.
    Classification.
    Structural Characteristics of the Agaricini.
        Mushroom Gills.
        The Volva.
        The Mushroom Veil.
        Mushroom Spores and Mycelium.
        Mycelium.
    Etymology of the Word "Mushroom."
    Food Value of Mushrooms.
    Cautionary Suggestions.
    Descriptions of Genera and Species.
    Appendix A.

Preserving and Cooking Mushrooms.
Receipts.
Appendix B.
Glossary of Terms used in Describing Mushrooms.
Authorities Consulted.
Part 2.
Ascomycetes.
Discomycetes.
Descriptions of Genera and Species (continued).
Receipts For Cooking.
Mushroom Growing.
Directions for Preparing the Compost for the Beds.
Compost for Mushroom Beds.
Mushroom Culture in Canada.
Cultivation of Mushrooms in Japan.
Manufacture of Spawn.
"Brick   Spawn."
"Mill   Track"   Spawn.
Spawn Produced in a Manure Heap.
Appendix A.
Continuation of Glossary of Terms used in Describing
Mushrooms.
Appendix B.
Part 3.
Descriptions of Genera and Species (continued).
Analytical Table.
Polyporei.
Descriptions of Genera and Species (continued).
Recipes for Cooking Mushrooms.
List of the Genera of Hymenomycetes.
Brefield's Classification of Fungi.
Coniomycetes and Hyphomycetes.
Hyphomycetes.
Phycomycetes or Physomycetes.
Bibliography.
Continuation of Glossary of Terms used in Describing Mushrooms.
Part 4.
Gasteromycetes.   Descriptions
of Genera and Species (continued). Myxomycetes
or Myxogasters.—"*Slime Fungi.*" Genera of
Gasteromycetes, according to Saccardo.
Bibliography.

2

Descriptions of Genera and Species (continued).
Appendix.
Part 5.
Descriptions of Genera and Species (continued).
Alkaloids of the Poisonous Mushrooms.
Muscarin.
Phallin.
The Poisonous Alkaloid of Gyromitra Esculenta Fries
(Helvella Esculenta Pers.)
Helvellic Acid.
Poisonous and Deleterious Mushrooms of the Lactar, Russula,
and Boleus Groups.
Poisonous Boleti.
Recent Instances of Mushroom Poisoning.
Bibliography.   Fungi.
Bibliography. Toxicology ofMushrooms.
Index to Illustrations.
Correction of Plates.
Transcriber's Notes.

STUDENT'S HAND-BOOK

OF

MUSHROOMS OF AMERICA

EDIBLE AND POISONOUS.

BY
THOMAS TAYLOR, M. D.

AUTHOR OF FOOD PRODUCTS, ETC.

3

Published in Serial Form—**No. 1**—Price, 50c. per number.

WASHINGTON, D. C.:
A. R. Taylor, Publisher, 238 Mass. Ave. N.E.
1897.

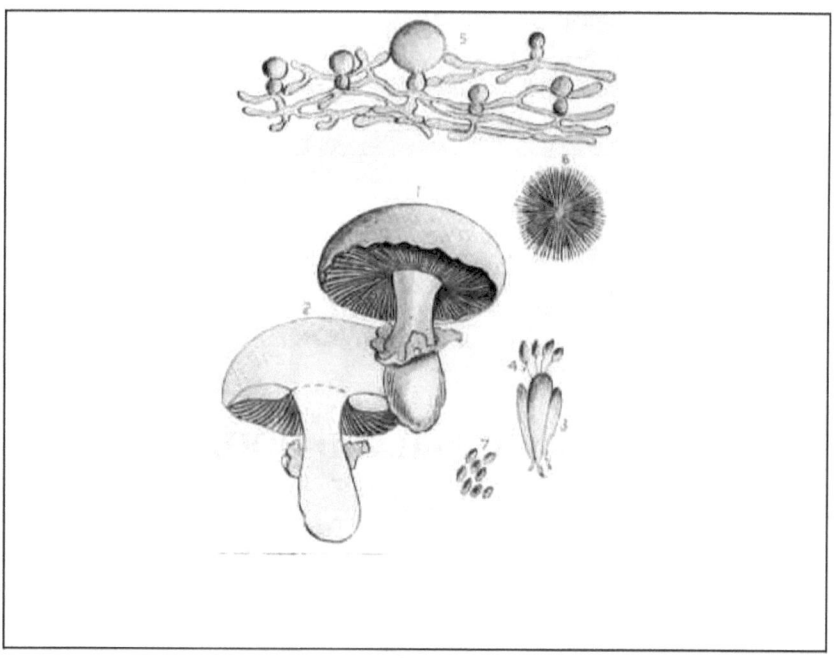

Plate A.

In Plate A is presented a sketch of the common field mushroom, Agaricus campester. Fig. 1 represents the mature plant; Fig. 2, a sectional view of the same; Fig. 3, the basidia, club-shaped cells from the summit of which proceed the slender tubes called sterigmata, which support the spores—highly magnified; Fig. 4, the sterigmata; Fig. 5, the mycelium, highly magnified, supporting immature mushrooms; Fig. 6, the spores as shed from an inverted mushroom cap; Fig. 7, spores magnified.

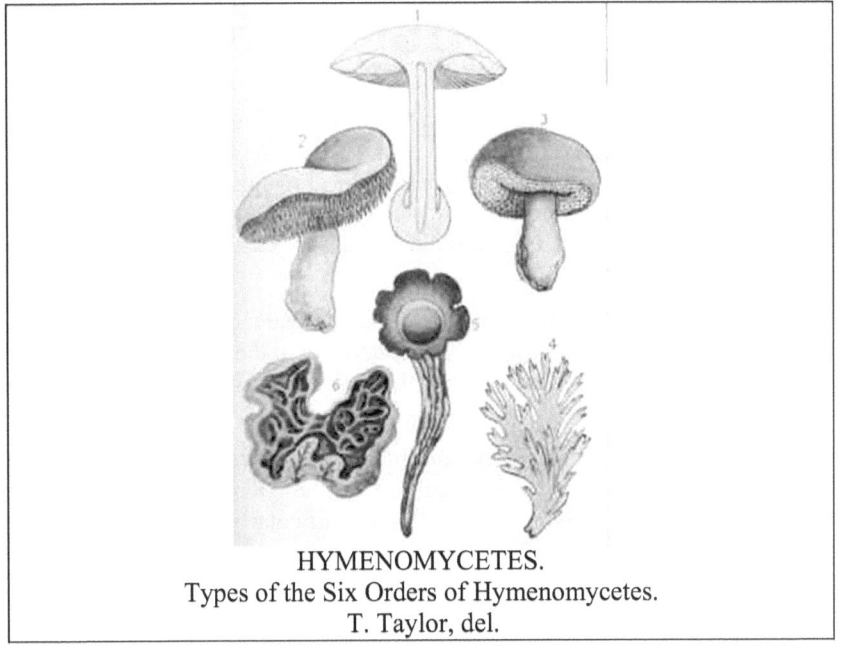

HYMENOMYCETES.
Types of the Six Orders of Hymenomycetes.
T. Taylor, del.

PLATE B.

In Plate B is represented a leading type of each of the six orders of the family Hymenomycetes:

Fig. 1. Cap with radiating gills beneath. Agaricini.
Fig. 2. Cap with spines or teeth beneath. Hydnei.
Fig. 3. Cap with pores or tubes beneath. Polyporei.
Fig. 4. Cap with the under or spore-bearing surface even. Thelephorei.
Fig. 5. Whole plant, club-shaped, or bush-like and branched. Clavarei.
Fig. 6. Whole plant irregularly expanded, substance gelatinous. Tremellini.

INTRODUCTION.

In the year 1876, as Microscopist of the Department of Agriculture, I prepared, as a part of the exhibit of my Division at the Centennial Exhibition at Philadelphia, a large collection of water-color drawings representing leading types of the edible and poisonous mushrooms of the United States, together with representations of about nine hundred species of microscopic fungi detrimental to vegetation.

In the preparation of the first collection I had the valuable assistance of Prof. Charles H. Peck, State Botanist of New York, and in the second the hearty cooperation of Rev. M. J. Berkeley and Dr. M. C. Cook, the eminent British mycologists.

The popular character of this exhibit attracted the attention of the general public, and many letters were received at the Department showing an awakening interest in the study of fungi, particularly with regard to the mushroom family, as to methods of cultivation, the means of determining the good from the unwholesome varieties, etc.

My first published paper on the subject of edible mushrooms, entitled "Twelve Edible Mushrooms of the U. S.," appeared in the annual report of the Department of Agriculture for 1885. This was followed by others to the number of five, and as the demand for these reports increased, reprints were made and issued, by order of the Secretary of Agriculture, in pamphlet form, under the general title of "Food Products." Numerous editions of these reprints were issued by the Department up to 1894. During the year 1894, and the first half of 1895, 36,600 of these reports were sent out by the Department, and the supply was exhausted. They have been out of print for more than two years. It is in view of this fact, and in response to a great and constant demand for these publications, that I have undertaken to publish a series of five pamphlets on the edible and poisonous mushrooms of the United States, which shall embody the substance of the five pamphlets on "Food Products" above alluded to, supplemented by new matter relating to classification, general and specific, analytical tables of standard authors, and a continuation of the chapters on structure, etc. Additional plates, representing leading types of edible and poisonous mushrooms, will also be inserted in each number.

In the compilation and extension of this work I have the assistance of my daughter, Miss A. Robena Taylor, who has given considerable attention to the study of fungi, and who has been my faithful coadjutor in the work of collecting specimens, etc., for a number of years.

For valuable suggestions as to structural characteristics and methods of classification I am especially indebted to Prof. Chas. H. Peck, of Albany, New York, Dr. M. C. Cooke, of England, and Prof. P. A. Saccardo, of Italy.

The colored plates in pamphlet No. 1, together with a few of those which will appear in the succeeding numbers of this series, are reproductions of those prepared, under my direct supervision, for the pamphlets entitled "Food Products" published by the Department of Agriculture and referred to above.

THOMAS TAYLOR, M. D.

MAY 7, 1897.

CRYPTOGAMS.

The cryptogamic or flowerless plants, *i. e.*, those having neither stamens nor pistils, and which are propagated by spores, are divided, according to Dr. Hooper, into the following four classes:—Pteridophyta or vascular acrogens, represented by the ferns, club-mosses, etc.; Bryophyta or cellular acrogens, represented by the musci, scale-mosses, etc.; Algæ, represented by the "Red Seaweeds," Diatomacæ, etc.; Fungi or Amphigens, which include the molds, mildews, mushrooms, etc. The lichens, according to the "Schwendener Hypotheses," consist of ascigerous fungi parasitic on algæ.

FUNGI.

Botanists unite in describing the plants of this class as being destitute of chlorophyll and of starch. These plants assume an infinite variety of forms, and are propagated by spores which are individually so minute as to be scarcely perceptible to the naked eye. They are entirely cellular, and belong to the class Amphigens, which for the most part have no determinate axe, and develop in every direction, in contradistinction to the Acrogens, which develop from the summit, possessing an axe, leaves, vessels, etc.

Fungi are divided by systematists into two great classes:

1. Sporifera, in which the spores are free, naked, or soon exposed.
2. Sporidifera, in which the spores are not exposed, but instead are enclosed in minute cells or sacs, called asci.

These classes are again subdivided, according to the disposition of the spores and of the spore bearing surface, called the hymenium, into various families.

The sporiferous fungi are arranged into four families, viz:

1. *Hymenomycetes*, in which the hymenium is free, mostly naked, or soon exposed. *Example, "Common Meadow Mushroom."*
2. *Gasteromycetes*, in which the hymenium is enclosed in a second case or wrapper, called a peridium, which ruptures when mature, thus releasing the spores. *Example, Common Puff Ball.*
3. *Coniomycetes*, in which the spores are naked, mostly terminal on inconspicuous threads, free or enclosed in a perithecium. Dust-like fungi. *Example, Rust of Wheat.*
4. *Hyphomycetes*, in which the spores are naked on conspicuous threads, rarely compacted, Thread-like fungi. *Example, Blue Mold.*

Of these four subdivisions of the Sporifera, only the Hymenomycetes and the Gasteromycetes contain plants of the mushroom family, and these two together constitute the class known as the Basidiomycetes. The chief distinction of the Basidiomycetes is that the naked spores are borne on the summits of certain supporting bodies, termed basidia. These basides are swollen, club-shaped cells, surmounted by four minute tubes or spore-bearers, called sterigmata, each of which carries a spore. See Figs. 3 and 4, Plate A.

These basides together with a series of elongated cells, termed paraphyses, packed closely together side by side, and intermixed with other sterile cells, called cystidia, constitute the spore-bearing surface or hymenium of the plant.

To the naked eye this hymenium appears simply as a very thin smooth membrane, but when a small portion of it is viewed through a microscope with high powers its complex structure is readily observed and can be carefully studied.

The *Sporidiferous* fungi are represented by the families Physomycetes and Ascomycetes. The first of these consists wholly of microscopic fungi.

Ascomycetes.—In the plants of this family the spores are not supported upon basidia, but instead are enclosed in minute sacs or asci formed from the fertile cells of a hymenium. In this connection it would be well to state that Saccardo does not recognize the divisions *Sporifera* and *Sporidifera* by those names.

They are nearly the equivalent of Basidiomycetes and Ascomycetes.

What Cooke names Physomycetes, Saccardo calls Phycomyceteæ, introducing it in his work between Gasteromyceteæ and Myxomyceteæ, which some mycologists consider somewhat out of place.

Saccardo calls its asci (sacs which contain the spores) sporangia. He does not regard them as genuine asci, but as corresponding more to the peridium of the *Gasteromyceteæ* and *Myxomyceteæ.*

Peck says that this group seems to present characters of both Hyphomycetes and Ascomycetes, with a preponderance towards Hyphomycetes.

It is a small group, however, and since it consists wholly of microscopic fungi, need not be farther considered in this work.

In the Ascomycetes are included the sub-families Discomycetes, Pyrenomycetes, and Tuberacei. Of these the Discomycetes and the Tuberacei are the only groups which contain any of the mushrooms, and but few of these are large enough or sufficiently tender to possess value as esculents. A good example of the first (Discomycetes) is found in the Morel, and of the second (Tuberacei) in the Truffle.

In the Discomycetes or "disk fungi," the spores are produced in minute membraneous sacs, each sac usually containing eight spores. These spore sacs are imbedded in the flesh of the exterior and upper surface of the mushroom cap.

In the four classes, Hymenomycetes, Gasteromycetes, Discomycetes, and Tuberacei, therefore, are included all of the plants which are here designated under the generic term of "mushrooms."

Some idea of the relative numerical value of these classes may be obtained from the following figures given by the distinguished British mycologist, M.

C. Cooke:

"Hymenomyceteæ— total number of described species 9,600
Gasteromycetæ—   "   "   "   "   "   650
Discomyceteæ—   "   "   " known   "   3,500"

(The Tuberacei comprise a very small group of subterranean fungi, and comparatively few of the species are described.)

Saccardo in his Sylloge gives a total of 42,000 described species of fungi of all classes, including the most minute. Of these the Hymenomycetes include by far the largest number of edible mushrooms.

The family Hymenomycetes is divided into the following six orders: Agaricini, Polyporei, Hydnei, Thelephorei, Clavarei, Tremellini.

In the order Agaricini the hymenium is found on the under surface of the mushroom cap, covering pleats or gills, technically called lamellæ. These gills vary in character in the different genera, being "persistent in such as the Agaricus, Russula, and Lentinus, deliquescent (melting) in Coprinus, Bolbitius, etc. The edge of the gills is acute in Agaricus, Marasmius, etc., but obtuse and vein-like in Cantharellus, longitudinally channelled in Trogia, and splitting in Schyzophyllum."

In the Polyporei, pore-bearing mushrooms, the gills are replaced by tubes or pores. The tubes are little cylinders, long or short, pressed one against another, forming by their union a layer on the under surface of the cap, and the sporiferous membrane or hymenium lines their inner walls. Their upper end is always closed, while the lower extremity is open to permit the outward passage of the spores. The tubes are generally joined together and are not easily disunited. They are free, i. e., separable, in the sole genus *Fistulina*. As regards their attachment to the cap, the tubes may be firmly adherent as in the genus Polyporus or easily detached in a single mass as in Boletus, the fleshy form of the order Polyporei. They frequently leave a circular space of greater or less dimensions around the stem, or they adhere to or are prolonged upon it in such a manner that the orifices rise in tiers one above another. The color of the tubes, although not offering as characteristic varieties as that of the gills, changes nevertheless according to species and according to the age of the plant. The tubes may sometimes be of a different color from their orifices, as in *Boletus luridus*. In some of the Boleti the color of the flesh is changed on exposure to the air and the tubes often assume the same tints. The tubes, generally called pores, are sometimes closely adherent to the substance of the cap, which is often hard, corky, or coriaceous, as seen in most of the *Polyporei*.

In the Hydnei, spine-bearing mushrooms, the hymenium is seen covering the spines or needle-like processes which take the place of gills in this order, and which project from the under surface of the cap. These spines may be divided or entire, simple or ramified, and are formed of the substance of the cap. In the early stages of development they appear like small projecting points or papillæ, those on the margin of the cap and at the apex of the stem being always less developed, frequently remaining in this rudimentary state. They are rounded in the species Hydnum imbricatum, sometimes compressed in Hydnum repandum, sometimes terminating in hairs or filaments, as in Hydnum barba Jovis, or very much divided, as in Hydnum fimbriatum.

In the Clavarei, the whole plant consists of solid fleshy masses without any stem of a distinct substance, sometimes club-shaped, sometimes branched with the hymenium smoothly covering the entire surface, never incrusting or coriaceous.

In the Thelephorei, the lower surface of the cap presents neither gills, pores, nor spines, but instead the hymenium covers an uneven or slightly wrinkled surface, partially striate, sometimes obscurely papillose. The plants of this order assume a great variety of shape, from that of a perfect cup with a central stem to an irregularly and much branched frond. They are generally dry and tough. Very few are recommended as edible. Prof. Peck says of this order that probably no edible species will be found in any of its genera outside of the genus Craterellus.

In the order Tremellini we have a great departure from the character of the substance, external appearance, and internal structure of the other orders of the Hymenomycetes. The substance is gelatinous; the form is lobed, folded, or convolute, often resembling the brain of some animal. It is uniformly composed throughout of a colorless mucilage, with no appreciable texture, in which are distributed very fine, diversely branched, and anastomosing filaments. Towards the surface the ultimate branches of this filamentous network give birth to globular cells, both at their summits and laterally, which attain a comparatively large size. These cells are filled with a protoplasm, to which the plant owes its color. The fertile threads are not compacted into a true hymenium.

Representative types of the above-described orders of the Hymenomycetes are shown in Plate B. The various genera, and species of these orders, will be described more in detail in connection with the species illustrated.

CLASSIFICATION.

Owing to the fact that botanists of various countries, writing in diverse languages, have for more than a century been engaged in describing the fungi of their respective countries, with their work frequently unknown to one another, it is not surprising that there has been constant revision, or that many changes have been made in the way of classification and nomenclature which to the amateur student are often confusing.

The classification by the pioneer mycologist, Elias Fries, as presented in his several works on fungi, ignored all microscopical characters, and Saccardo's classification, as presented in his *Sylloge Fungorum*, was the first complete system offered in its place.

Saccardo, in 1882, commenced his Sylloge, of which not less than twelve volumes have been published. In Saccardo's system of classification the six orders of the Hymenomycetes are not essentially different in their arrangement from that of Fries, although Saccardo has raised all the subgenera of Agaricus to the rank of genera, and then altered their sequence so as to bring them into four sections, distinguished by the color of their spores. Having raised the old subgenera of Fries to generic rank, Saccardo found it necessary to limit the application of the term Agaricus to the group of fungi to which it was originally applied by Linnæus, viz., the common field mushroom Agaricus campester, and its allies, represented by Agaricus arvensis, Agaricus Rodmani, etc., or, as Prof. Peck more definitely states it, "to those of the gilled mushrooms which have brown spores, free gills, a stem bearing a ring, gills generally pink-colored in the early stage, and brownish black when fully matured." M. C. Cooke, the distinguished English mycologist, prefers to retain the *genus Agaricus* with its original subgenera intact, succeeded by the other genera of Agaricini, as in the Hymenomycetes Europei of Fries, giving as his reason the belief "that for purposes of classification features should be taken which are present and evident in the specimens themselves, and are not dependent on any of their life-history which cannot be presented in the herbarium."

In a work such as the present, which is designed to be popular in character rather than purely technical, it is deemed advisable to select as a basis for classification that system which is most accessible to reference by the general reading public. Saccardo's Sylloge, while exhaustive in character and of inestimable value to the mycologist, is written in Latin, and is, moreover, a very expensive work—facts which render it practically unavailable to the general public.

In the compilation of this series of pamphlets I have adopted the classification of M. C. Cooke, which, as regards the Hymenomycetes, the family containing most of the fleshy fungi, is, with exceptions noted, in accord with that of Saccardo. M. C. Cooke's hand-book of fungi is of convenient size and form for ready reference.

For the convenience, however, of those who may wish to familiarize themselves with both systems, a synopsis of *Saccardo's Genera* of Hymenomycetes will be given later.

STRUCTURAL CHARACTERISTICS OF THE AGARICINI.

By far the greater number of the Agaricini have both cap and stem. The form of the cap, as well as that of the stem, varies somewhat in the different genera and species. Those which are terrestrial in habit are generally of an umbrella-like shape, while those which grow upon trees and decayed tree-stumps are apt to be one-sided or semi-spherical.

In many of the parasitical mushrooms the stem is absent. Where the stem is present it is either an interrupted continuation of the hymenophore or fleshy substance of the cap, or else is supported separately as a pillar on which the cap rests, a more or less distinct line of demarcation showing where the fibers terminate. Sometimes it is quite easily detached from the cap socket, as in the Lepiota procerus. It may be hollow or stuffed, solid or fibrillose. It varies in length and thickness. In some species it is smooth and polished, in others rough and hairy, reticulated, etc., sometimes tapering, sometimes distinctly bulbous at the base.

The spores of the species differ in color and are usually globular or oblong in shape. All of these characteristics assist in determining the species.

MUSHROOM GILLS.

Mushroom gills, or lamellæ, anatomically considered, are composed, first, of a central portion, a prolongation of the hymenophore or flesh of the cap, more or less dense, sometimes so thin as to be scarcely perceptible; second, the hymenium or spore-bearing membrane covering the surfaces of this prolonged hymenophore. They are vertical, simple, equal, respectively, or more frequently alternating with shorter gills. They are often evanescent and putrescent, sometimes liquefying altogether. Their color is usually different from the upper surface of the cap, not always similar to that of the spores borne upon them, at least in youth; with age, however, they usually assume the color of the mature spore. The change of color of the gills according to the age of the plant is very important in the study of the Agaricini; it accounts for the white gills of certain species in youth, the pink in maturity, and the brown when aged.

The end of the gill nearest the stalk of the plant is termed the posterior extremity; the opposite end, the anterior extremity. In most of the Agaricini the gills are unequal. Some extend from the margin to about half the space between it and the stem; others are still shorter.

THE VOLVA.

The volva is a membrane which envelops the entire plant in embryo, giving it the appearance of an egg. It originates at the base of the mushroom and furnishes it, during its fœtal life, with the means of support and nourishment. Its texture is so delicate that it generally disappears, leaving very little trace of its existence on the adult plant. In many of the volvate species this organ exists only so long as they are under ground, and some mycologists restrict the term "volvati" to such only as retain it afterwards. As the young plant expands it breaks through the top of this volva or wrapper, and, emerging, carries with it patches of the membrane on the upper surface of the cap. These are more or less prominent, numerous, and thick, sometimes irregularly disposed, sometimes regularly in the form of plates, warts, etc. At the base of the stem of the mushroom the remains of the volva are seen in the form of a sort of wrapper. This is more or less ample, thick, and ascending. It is called *free* when it is loose or easily detached from the stem, and *congenital* when it cannot be separated from it without laceration. In some species it is distinctly membranous, and in others floccose, and friable in character, sometimes appearing in ridges as a mere border, at others broken up into scales, and, as the plant matures, wholly disappearing. The volva is a feature of great importance in the study of the Agaricini, of the subgenera Amanita, Volvaria, etc.

THE MUSHROOM VEIL.

The veil is not a constant feature in the Agaricini, at least it is not always visible. When present it consists of a membrane which extends from the margin of the cap to the stem, veiling or protecting the gills. This membrane, called the cortina, has given its name to a numerous and important class of mushrooms (the *Cortinarias*). It is generally white, soft, slightly spongy, cottony, at times fibrillose or even slightly fibrous, again in texture comparable to the spider's web, and may be even powdery or glutinous. It exists intact only in the youth of the plant. It is not visible in the developing mushroom, at least while the cap is closely pressed against the stem, but as the cap expands the membrane extends and finally breaks, leaving in some species its remnants upon the margin of the cap and upon the stem in the usual form of a ring or a mere zone. When the stem is not ringed the veil rises high upon the stalk, stretches across to meet the edges of the cap, and is afterwards reflected back over its whole surface.

MUSHROOM SPORES AND MYCELIUM.

The spore is the reproductive organ of the mushroom. It differs from the seed of the flowering plant in being destitute of an apparent embryo. A seed contains a plantlet which develops as such. A spore is a minute cell containing a nucleus or living germ, the reproductive cell germ called by some authors the germinating granule. This in turn throws out a highly elongated process consisting of a series of thread-like cells branching longitudinally and laterally, at length bifurcating and anastomosing the mass, forming the vegetative process known as mycelium or mushroom spawn.

On this mycelium, at intervals, appear knob-like bodies, called tubercles, from which the mushrooms spring and from which they derive their nourishment. See Fig. 5, Plate A.

Where the conditions have been unfavorable this mycelium has been known to grow for years without bearing fruit.

Mushroom spores are very variable in size, shape, and color, but are generally constant at maturity in the same genus. Their shape, almost always spherical in the young plant, becomes ovate, ellipsoidal, fusiform, reniform, smooth, stellate, sometimes tuberculate, or remains globose. This feature, varying thus with the age of the plant, should be studied in the mature plant.

MYCELIUM.

De Leveille has thus defined mycelium: "Filaments at first simple, then more or less complicated, resulting from the vegetation of the spores and serving as roots to the mushroom."

The mycelium of mushrooms or the mushroom spawn is usually white, but is also found yellow, and even red. It is distinguished by some writers as nematoid, fibrous, hymenoid, scleroid or tuberculous, and malacoid. The nematoid mycelium is the most common. Creeping along on the surface of the earth, penetrating it to a greater or less depth, developing in manure among the débris of leaves or decayed branches, always protected from the light, it presently consists of very delicate filamentous cells more or less loosely interwoven, divided, anastomosing in every direction and often of considerable extent.

Its presence is sometimes difficult to detect without the use of the microscope, either on account of its delicacy or because of its being intermingled with the organic tissues in which it has developed.

Sometimes mycelium unites in bundles more or less thick and branched. This has been called the fibrous mycelium. Where the filaments intercross closely, are felted, and inclined to form a membrane, it is hymenoid mycelium. Where the filaments are so small and close that they form very compact bodies, constituting those solid irregular products called sclerotium, it is scleroid or tuberculous mycelium. With malacoid mycelium we have nothing to do in this paper. It is a soft, pulpy, fleshy mycelium.

Systematists have divided the Agaricini into groups according to the color of their spores. These groups are defined as follows by various authors:

According to—

Elias Fries, 5 groups: *Leucosporus*, white; *Hyporhodius*, pink; *Cortinaria*, ochraceous; *Derminus*, rust; *Pratella*, purplish black.

Rev. J. M. Berkeley, 5 groups: Very frequently pure white, but presenting also pink, various tints of brown, from yellowish and rufous to dark bister, purple-black, and finally black; *Leucospori*, white; *Hyporhodii*, salmon; *Dermini*, ferruginous; *Pratellæ*, brown; *Coprinarius*, black.

Dr. Badham, 6 groups: Pure white or a yellow tinge on drying; brown; yellow; pink; purple; purple-black; some pass successively from pink to purple and from purple to purple-black.

Mrs. Hussey, 11 shades: White; rose; pale ocher; olivaceous-ocher; reddish-ocher; ochraceous; yellowish olive-green; dull brown; scarcely ferruginous; snuff-color; very dark brown.

Hogg & Johnson, 5 groups: *Leucosporei*, white; *Hyporhodii*, salmon; *Dermini*, rusty; *Pratellæ*, purplish-brown; *Coprinarii*, black.

C. Gillet, 7 shades: White; pink; ochraceous; yellow; ferruginous; black or purplish black; round, ovate, elongated, or fusiform, smooth, tuberculate or irregular, simple or composite, transparent or nebulous, etc.

Jules Bel, 5 groups: White; pink; red; brown; black.

Dr. Gautier, 5 shades: White; pink; brown; purplish-brown; black.

Constantin & Dufour, 5 groups: White; pink; ochraceous; brownish-purple; black.

J. P. Barla, 7 groups: *Leucosporii*, white; *Hyporhodii*, pink; *Cortinariæ*, ochraceous; *Dermini*, rust; *Pratellæ*, purplish-black; *Coprinarii*, blackish; *Coprini* and *Gomphi*, dense black.

L. Boyer, 5 groups, 11 shades: White to cream yellow; pale pink to ochraceous yellow; bay or red brown to brown or blackish bister; rust color, cinnamon or light yellow.

W. D. Hay, 5 groups: White; pink; brown; purple; black.

C. H. Peck, 5 groups: *Leucosporii*, white; *Hyporhodii*, salmon; *Dermini*, rust; *Pratellæ*, brown; *Coprinarii*, black.

Saccardo divides the Agaricini into four sections, according to the color of their spores, as follows: Spores brown, purplish brown or black, *Melanosporæ*; spores ochraceous or rusty ochraceous, *Ochrosporæ*; spores rosy or pinkish, *Rhodosporæ*; spores white, whitish or pale yellow, *Leucosporæ*.

Dr. M. C. Cooke, 5 groups: *Leucospori*, white or yellowish; *Hyporhodii*, rosy or salmon color; *Dermini*, brown, sometimes reddish or yellowish brown; *Pratellæ*, purple, sometimes brownish purple, dark purple, or dark brown; *Coprinarii*, black or nearly so.

These shades are somewhat different from the colors of the mushrooms' gills, so that, when it is of importance to determine exactly the color of the spore in the identification of a species, we may without recourse to the microscope cut off the stem of an adult plant on a level with the gills and place the under surface of the cap upon a leaf of white paper if a dark-spored species, and upon a sheet of black paper if the spores are light. At the expiration of a few hours we will find, on lifting the cap, a bed of the shed spores which will represent their exact shade. These may be removed to a glass slide and their size and form determined by means of the microscope.

In the present work Dr. M. C. Cooke's grouping of the spore series is adopted.

ETYMOLOGY OF THE WORD "MUSHROOM."

Various opinions have been offered as to the derivation of the word "mushroom." According to Hay, it probably had its origin in a combination of the two Welsh words *maes*, a field, and *rhum*, a knob, which by gradual corruption have become *mushroom*. Some writers on the other hand regard it as a corruption of *mousseron*, a name specifically applied by the French to those mushrooms which are found growing in mossy places. But it seems to be of older usage than such a derivation would imply, and therefore the first explanation seems the more likely to be correct.

In England the term "mushroom" has been most commonly applied to the "meadow mushroom," that being the one best known; but English-speaking mycologists now apply it generically very much as the French do the term "champignon," while the name "champignon" is restricted in England to the Marasmius oreades, or "Fairy Ring" mushroom.

Berkeley says the French word "champignon" was originally scarcely of wider signification than our word "mushroom," though now classical in the sense of fleshy fungi generally. The German word *Pilz* (a corruption of Boletus) is used to denote the softer kinds by some German authors. Constant and Dufour, in their recently published Atlas des Champignons, include types of a great variety of mushrooms.

Hay contends that the pernicious nick-name "toad-stool" has not the derivation supposed, but that the first part of the word is the Saxon or old English "tod," meaning a bunch, cluster, or bush, the form of many terrestrial fungi suggesting it. The second syllable, "stool," is easily supplied. "The erroneous idea of connecting toads with these plants," says Hay, "seems to be due to Spenser, or to some poet, possibly, before his time." Spenser speaks of the loathed paddocks, "paddock" then being the name given in England to the frog, afterwards corrupted to "paddic," and once received, readily converted by the Scotch into "puddick-stool." It would seem, therefore, from the foregoing, that the term "toad-stool" can have no proper relation to mushrooms, whether edible or poisonous.

The three mushrooms illustrated and described in this pamphlet, Plates I, II, and III, are of the order Agaricini or gilled mushrooms. They are well-defined types and of wide geographical distribution.

FOOD VALUE OF MUSHROOMS.

Rollrausch and Siegel, who claim to have made exhaustive investigations into the food values of mushrooms, state that "many species deserve to be placed beside meat as sources of nitrogenous nutriment," and their analysis, if correct, fully bears out the statement. They find in 100 parts of dried *Morchella esculenta* 35.18 per cent. of protein; in *Helvella esculenta*, 26.31 per cent. of protein, from 46 to 49 per cent. of potassium salts and phosphoric acid, 2.3 per cent. of fatty matter, and a considerable quantity of sugar. The *Boletus edulis* they represent as containing in 100 parts of the dried substance 22.82 per cent. of protein. The nitrogenous values of different foods as compared with the mushroom are stated as follows: "Protein substances calculated for 100 parts of bread, 8.03; of oatmeal, 9.74; of barley bread, 6.39; of leguminous fruits, 27.05; of potatoes, 4.85; of mushrooms, 33.0."

According to Schlossberger and Depping, in 100 grams of dried mushrooms they found the following proportions of nitrogenous substances:

Varieties.	Grains.
Chanterelles	3.22
Certain Russulas	4.25
Lactarius deliciosus	4.68
Boletus edulis	4.25
Meadow mushroom	7.26

But all chemists are not agreed as to these proportions. For instance, Lefort has found 3.51 grains of nitrogenous matter in the cap of *Agaricus campestris*, 2.1 grains in the gills and only 0.34 of a grain in the stem. Payen has found 4.68 grains in *Agaricus campestris*, 4.4 grains in the common Morel (*Morchella esculenta*), 9.96 grains in the white truffle, and 8.76 grains in the black.

A much larger proportion of the various kinds of mushrooms are edible than is generally supposed, but a prejudice has grown up concerning them in this country which it will take some time to eradicate. Notwithstanding the occurrence of occasional fatal accidents through the inadvertent eating of poisonous species, fungi are largely consumed both by savage and civilized man in all parts of the world, and while they contribute so considerable a portion of the food product of the world we may be sure their value will not be permanently overlooked in the United States, especially when we consider our large accessions of population from countries in which the mushroom is a familiar and much prized edible. In Italy the value of the mushroom as an article of diet has long been understood and appreciated. Pliny, Galen, and Dioscorides mention various esculent species, notably varieties of the truffle, the boletus and the puff-ball, and Vittadini writes enthusiastically of the gastronomic qualities of a large number of species. Of late years large quantities have been sold in the Italian markets. Quantities of mushrooms are also consumed in Germany, Hungary, Russia, France, and Austria.

Darwin speaks of Terra del Fuego as the only country where cryptogamic plants form a staple article of food. A bright-yellow fungus allied to *Bulgarin* forms, with shellfish, the staple food of the Fuegians. In England the common meadow mushroom *Agaricus campestris* is quite well known and used to a considerable extent among the people, but there is not that general knowledge of and use of other species which obtains in Continental Europe.

In the English-speaking countries much has been done by the Rev. M. J. Berkeley, Dr. M. C. Cooke, Worthington G. Smith, Rev. John Stevenson, Prof. Hay, Prof. Chas. H. Peck, Prof. W. J. Farlow, and others, including the various mushroom clubs, to disseminate a more general knowledge on this subject.

Late investigations show that nearly all the species common to the countries of Continental Europe, and of Great Britain, are found in different localities in the United States, and a number of species have been found which have not been described in European works.

The geographical distribution of many species of the mushroom family is very wide. We have had specimens of the *Morel*, for instance, sent to us from California and Washington, on the Pacific coast, and as far north as Maine, on the Atlantic, as well as from the southern and the midwestern States, and the same is true of other species. The season of their appearance varies somewhat according to the latitude and altitude of place of growth. Mushrooms are rarely seen after the first heavy frosts, although an exception is noted in this latitude in the species Hypholoma sublatertium, which has been found growing under the snow, at the roots of trees in sheltered woods. Frozen mushrooms of this and closely allied species have revived when thawed, and proved quite palatable when cooked.

At the present time only two species, Agaricus campester and Agaricus arvensis, are cultivated in America. Some attempts have been made by an amateur mushroom club in Ohio to cultivate the Morel, but the results have not, so far, been reported. In the meantime, however, it is well to utilize the wild mushrooms as fast as the collector can satisfactorily identify them. The woods of all moist regions of this country abound with edible varieties. Prof. Curtis, of North Carolina, gives a list of over one hundred edible species found in that State alone, and nearly all of these occur in our Northern States as well. It is not contended that this list includes all the species which may be eaten, nor have all of these equal value from a gastronomic point of view. Some are insipid as to flavor, and others are too tough or too slimy to please the popular taste.

CAUTIONARY SUGGESTIONS.

Before collecting for the table mushrooms found growing in the woods or fields, it would be well for inexperienced persons to consult carefully some work on the subject in which the characteristics of edible and poisonous varieties are described and illustrated.

Considering that an opinion seems to prevail that the discoloration of the silver spoon or small white onions when brought into contact with mushrooms during the culinary process is an infallible test of the poisonous species, I quote from a French author on mushrooms the following in relation to this supposed test:

> * * * We may not dispute the fact that a silver spoon or article of brass, or onions, may not become discolored on contact with the poisonous principle, but this discoloration is not reliable as a test for deciding the good or bad quality of mushrooms. In fact, we know that in the decomposition of albuminoids sulphureted hydrogen is liberated which of itself discolors silver, brass, and onions.

I have deemed it advisable to publish this as one of the best means of answering those correspondents who have made inquiries as to the reliability of this test.

It is by some supposed that high colors and viscidity are indications of non-edible species, but there are numerous exceptions here. *Russula alutacea*—the pileus of which is often a purplish red—*Amanita Cæsarea*, and other species of brilliant coloring are known to be edible. As to viscidity, two very viscid species, when young, are among the highly prized esculents by those who know them, viz., *Fistulina hepatica*, or the ox tongue, and *Hygrophorus eburneus*, the ivory mushroom.

The method of deciding the character of mushrooms by their odor and flavor is not to be relied upon. Edible mushrooms are usually characterized by a pleasant flavor and odor; non-edible varieties have sometimes an unpleasant odor, and produce a biting, burning sensation on the tongue and throat, even in very small quantities, but several of the *Amanitas* have only a slight odor and taste, and certain species of mushrooms, acrid otherwise, become edible when cooked.

In fact there is no general rule by which the edible species can be distinguished from the unwholesome or poisonous ones. The safest as well as the most sensible plan, therefore, is to apply the same rule as that which we adopt in the case of the esculents among the flowering plants, viz., to learn to know the characteristics of each individual species so as to distinguish it from all others.

With regard to the mushrooms which have been designated as poisonous, it should be remembered that the term "poisonous" is used relatively. While some are only slightly poisonous, producing severe gastric irritation and nervous derangement, but without fatal results, others, if eaten in even very small quantity, may cause death. Happily, however, the most dangerous species are not numerous as compared with the number that are edible, and with careful attention on the part of the collector they may be avoided.

Since the Amanita group is made responsible by competent authority for most of the recorded cases of fatal poisoning, we would recommend the amateur mycophagist to give special study to this group in order to learn to separate the species authentically recorded as edible from the poisonous ones.

Some writers, as a measure of precaution, counsel the rejection of all species of Amanita. But this is, of course, a matter for individual preference. There would seem to be no good reason why the observant student should not learn to discriminate between the edible and the poisonous species of the Amanita as of any other group, and they should not be eaten until this discriminating knowledge is acquired.

Saccardo describes fifteen edible species of this group of mushrooms. We have tested three of this number, which, on account of their abundance in our locality and their good flavor, we would be loth to discard, viz., A. rubescens, A. Cæsarea, and A. strobiliformis.

A type of the Amanita group, which is named first in the genera of the order Agaricini, is shown in Fig. 1, Plate B.

By reference to this figure some of the special characteristics of the group can be observed. There are mushrooms in other genera which show a volva or sheath at the base of the stem, and which contain edible species, but in these the stem is ringless. The Volvariæ, for instance, show a conspicuous volva, a stem that is ringless, and pinkish spores. The Amanitopsis vaginata carries a volva, but no ring. The spores are white, as in the Amanita.

In gathering mushrooms either for the table or for the herbarium, care should be taken not to leave any portion of the plant in the ground, so that no feature shall be lost that will aid in characterizing the species. In the careless pulling up of the plant the volva in the volvate species is often left behind.

AGARICINI. Fries.

LEUCOSPORI (SPORES WHITE, OR YELLOWISH).

Genus Russula Fr. The *Russulæ* bear some resemblance to the *Lactars*, their nearest allies, but are at once distinguished from them by their want of milk.

They are very abundant in the forests and open woods. The genus is cited by some authors as the most natural of the agarics, but, as many of the species very closely resemble each other, it requires careful analysis to determine them. The plants of this genus are not volvate, and have neither veil nor ring. The hymenophore is not separate from the trama of the gills. Although some are pure white, the caps are usually brilliant in coloring, but the color is very susceptible to atmospheric changes, and after heavy rains the bright hues fade, sometimes only leaving a slight trace of the original coloring in the central depression of the cap.

The cap in youth is somewhat hemispherical, afterwards expanding, becoming slightly depressed in the centre, somewhat brittle in texture; gills rigid, fragile, with acute edge; stem thick, blunt, and polished, usually short. The spores are globose, or nearly so, slightly rough, white or yellowish, according to the species. In R. virescens the spores are white, while in R. alutacea the spores are an ochraceous yellow in tint.

A number of the species are of pleasant flavor, others peppery or acrid. Out of seventy-two described by Cooke, twenty-four are recorded as acrid. With some of these the acridity is said to disappear in cooking, and a few mycophagists claim to have eaten all varieties with impunity. We have recorded, however, some well authenticated cases of serious gastric disturbance, accompanied by acute inflammation of the mucous membrane, caused by the more acrid of these, notably *R. emetica* and *R. fœtens*, and in view of this fact it would seem a wise precaution for the *amateur* collector to discard or at least to use very sparingly all those which have an acrid or peppery taste, until well assured as to their wholesomeness.

The *genus Russula* has been divided into the following tribes or groups:— Compactæ, Furcatæ, Rigidæ, Heterophylla, and Fragiles. The species *Russula*

(Rigidæ) virescens, illustrated in <u>Plate I</u>, belongs to the tribe Rigidæ. In the plants of this group, the cap is absolutely dry and rigid, destitute of a viscid pellicle; the cuticle commonly breaking up into flocci or granules; the flesh thick, compact, and firm, vanishing near the margin, which is never involute, and shows no striations. The gills are irregular in length, some few reaching half way to the stem, the others divided, dilated, and extending into a broad rounded end, stem solid.

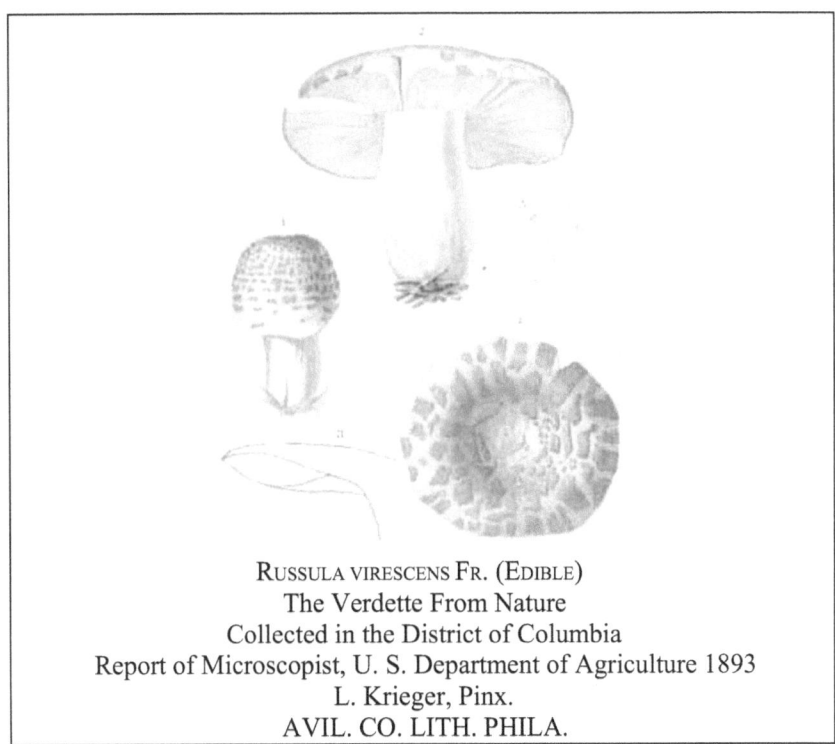

RUSSULA VIRESCENS FR. (EDIBLE)
The Verdette From Nature
Collected in the District of Columbia
Report of Microscopist, U. S. Department of Agriculture 1893
L. Krieger, Pinx.
AVIL. CO. LITH. PHILA.

PLATE I.

Russula virescens Fries. *"The Verdette"* or *"Greenish Russula."*

EDIBLE.

The cap of this species is fleshy and dry, the skin breaking into thin patches. The margin is usually even, but specimens occur which show striations. The color varies from a light green to a grayish or moldy green, sometimes tinged with yellow; gills white, free from the stem or nearly so, unequal, rather crowded; stem white, stout, solid, smooth, at first hard, then spongy; spores white, nearly globose.

One writer speaks of the "warts" of the cap, but the term warts, used in this connection, refers merely to the patches resulting from the splitting or breaking up of the epidermis of the cap, and not to such excrescences called warts, as are commonly observed on the cap of Amanita muscaria, for instance, which are remnants of the volva.

The *R. virescens* is not as common as some others of the Russulæ, in some localities, and hitherto seems to have attracted but little attention as an edible species in this country, although highly esteemed in Europe. It has been found growing in thin woods in Maryland and in Virginia from June to November, and we have had reports of its growth from New York and Massachusetts. The peasants in Italy are in the habit of toasting these mushrooms over wood embers, eating them afterwards with a little salt. Vittadini, Roques, and Cordier speak highly of its esculent qualities and good flavor. We have eaten quantities of the virescens gathered in Washington, D. C., and its suburbs, and found it juicy and of good flavor when cooked.

EXPLANATION OF PLATE I.

Plate I exhibits four views of this mushroom (*R. virescens*) drawn and colored from nature. Fig. 1, the immature plant; Fig. 2, advanced stage of growth, cap expanded or plane; Fig. 3, section showing the unequal length of the gills and manner of their attachment to the stem; Fig. 4, surface view of the cap showing the epidermis split in characteristic irregular patches; Fig. 5, spores, white.

AGARICINI.

COPRINARII (SPORES BLACK OR NEARLY SO).

Genus *Coprinus* Fries. Hymenophore distinct from the stem. Gills membranaceous, at first coherent from the pressure, then dissolving into a black fluid. Trama obsolete. Spores, oval, even, black. M. C. Cooke.

The plants of this genus have been divided into two tribes, viz., *Pelliculosi* and *Veliformis*. In the *Pelliculosi* the gills of the mushrooms are covered with a fleshy or membranaceous cuticle, hence the cap is not furrowed along the lines of the gills, but is torn and revolute. In this tribe are included the *Comati*, *Atramentarii, Picacei, Tomentosi, Micacio* and *Glabrati*. In the tribe *Veliformis* the plants are generally very small, and the cap much thinner than in those of the *Pelliculosi*, soon showing distinct furrows along the back of the gills, which quickly melt into very thin lines. The stem is thin and fistulose.

Cordier states that all the species of *Coprinus* are edible when young and fresh. This is probably true, but most of them have so little substance and are so ephemeral as to be of small value for food purposes. *C. comatus, C. atramentarius, C. micaceus,* and *C. ovatus* have the preference with most mycophagists, but even these soon melt, and should be gathered promptly and cooked immediately to be of use for the table.

COPRINUS COMATUS FR.(EDIBLE)
The Maned Mushroom from Nature
Collected in the District ofColumbia
Report of Microscopist, U. S. Department of Agriculture 1893
L. Krieger, Pinx.
AVIL. CO. LITH. PHILA.

PLATE II.

Coprinus comatus Fries. *Maned or Shaggy Coprinus.*

EDIBLE.

Cap at first oblong or cylindrical, then campanulate, the cuticle breaking into shaggy fibrous scales, color whitish, the scales generally yellow or yellowish, margin revolute and lacerated, soon becoming black. Gills linear, free, and close together, at first white, then pink or purplish, turning to black. Stem hollow or slightly stuffed, nearly equal, somewhat fibrillose, with bulb solid; the ring movable or very slightly adherent, generally disappearing as the plant matures. Spores oval, black, .0005 to .0007 in. long.

This species is found in abundance in different parts of the United States, generally in rich soil, in pastures, by roadsides, in dumping lots, etc. Of late years quantities have been gathered in the lawn surrounding the Capitol grounds, and in the parks of the District of Columbia, as well as in the débris of the wooden block pavements used for surface soiling gardens in vicinity of the capital. They have been offered for sale in open market as low as 25 cents per pound.

A correspondent from Rochester, New York, states that in a patch of his grounds which had been quarried out and filled with street sweepings the Coprinus comatus appeared in such quantities as to make it impossible to walk over the space without stepping upon them, and that he was able to gather from this small space from one to two bushels at a time in the spring and the fall. In flavor the C. comatus resembles the cultivated mushroom, though perhaps more delicate.

The *Coprinus ovatus*, "*Oval Coprinus*," a closely allied species, is similar to the comatus, but smaller, more ovate in shape and delicate in flavor, less deliquescent; stem usually ¾ of an inch long. The *Coprinus atramentarius* has a mouse-gray or brownish cap with irregular margin, slightly striated. It is not shaggy, but is spotted with minute, innate punctate scales. The stem is hollow, somewhat ringed when young. Spores elliptical, black.

Coprinus micaceus is a very common species, and is found generally in clusters on old tree stumps or on decaying wood. The cap is thin and of a reddish buff or ochraceous tint, often showing a sprinkling of glistening micaceous scales or granules; gills crowded, whitish. It is at first ovate or bell-shaped, then expanding; striated. The stem is white, slender, and hollow, not ringed. The spores in this species are a very dark brown, which is unusual in the genus *Coprinus*.

It is generally found in decaying wood or old tree-stumps, growing in dense clusters.

Prof. Peck says: "European writers do not record the '*Glistening coprinus*' among the edible species, perhaps because of its small size. But it compensates for its lack of size by its frequency and abundance. In tenderness and delicacy it does not appear to be at all inferior to the '*Shaggy coprinus*.'"

Explanation of Plate II.

Coprinus comatus Fr. *The Shaggy Maned Mushroom.*

Fig. 1. A young plant.
Fig. 2. A plant partly expanded, exposing the tender pink of the gills.
Fig. 3. A mature plant, bell-shaped and shaggy, with movable ring
    detached from the cap, and with stem unequal and rooting.
Fig. 4. A sectional view, showing hollow stem, thin cap, and broad, free,

linear gill.
Fig. 5. Spores black.

AGARICINI.

LEUCOSPORI (SPORES WHITE, OR YELLOWISH.)

Genus *Marasmius* Fries.—Tough dry shrivelling fungi—not putrescent, reviving when moistened; veil none. Stem cartilaginous or horny. Gills tough, rather distant, edge acute and entire. M. C. Cooke.

A characteristic of the species of this genus is their tendency to wither with drought and revive with moisture. This biological characteristic is of great importance in determining the true Marasmii. The plants are usually small and of little substance.

Cooke divides the Marasmii into three tribes, and these again into several subdivisions. In the division Scortei of this genus are classed three species which are described in the works of most of the Continental writers; the Marasmius oreades, which has recognized value as an esculent, Marasmius urens and Marasmius peronatus, which have the reputation of being acrid and unwholesome.

MARASMIUS OREADES FR. (EDIBLE)
The Fairy Ring Mushroom.
Report of Microscopist, U. S. Department of Agriculture 1893
L. K. after Gillet.

Plate III.

Marasmius oreades Fries. *"Fairy Ring Mushroom."*

Edible.

Cap fleshy, convex at first, then nearly plane, pale yellowish red, or tawny red when young, fading to yellow or buff as the plant matures, slightly umbonate, flesh white; gills broad, wide apart, rounded or deeply notched at the inner extremity, slightly attached to or at length free from the stem, unequal in length, whitish or creamy yellow in color; stem slender, solid and tough, whitish, generally one to two inches in length and one-fourth of an inch in thickness, showing a whitish down, easily removed, not strigose or villose, as in the Marasmius urens. Spores white.

This species is usually found in open grassy places, sometimes in rings, or in parts of rings, often in clusters, and writers generally agree as to its agreeable taste and odor. When properly cooked its toughness disappears.

Prof. Peck describes two mushrooms which are somewhat similar in appearance to the *"Fairy Ring,"* and which might be taken for it by careless observers, viz., the Naucoria semi-orbicularis, sometimes growing in company with it, and the *Collybia dryophila*, a wood variety which is sometimes found in open places.

The first of these may be distinguished from the *oreades*, by the rusty brown color of the gills, its smooth stem and rusty colored spores. In the second the gills are much narrower and the stem is very smooth and hollow.

The *Marasmius urens* as described by European authors has a pale buff cap, not umbonate but flat, and at length depressed in the centre, from one to two inches across. The gills are unequal, free, very crowded; cream color, becoming brownish. The stem is solid and fibrous, densely covered with white down at the base. It is very acrid to the taste. In habit of growth it is subcæspitose; sometimes found growing in company with the M. oreades.

Prof. Peck says of *M. urens* that he has not yet seen an American specimen which he could refer to that species with satisfaction. Our experience, so far, is the same as that of Prof. Peck.

Marasmius peronatus has a reddish buff cap, with crowded thin gills, creamy, turning to reddish brown; the stem solid and fibrous, with yellowish filaments at the base. It is acrid in taste and is usually found among fallen leaves in woods.

Explanation of Plate III.

In Plate III, Fig. 1 represents an immature plant; Fig. 2, cap expanding with growth; Fig. 3, cap further expanded and slightly umbonate; Fig. 4, mature specimen, cap plane or fully expanded, margin irregular and smooth, stem equal, smooth and ringless; Fig. 5, section showing gills broad, free, ventricose, unequal, and flesh white; Fig. 6, spores white.

APPENDIX A.

PRESERVING AND COOKING MUSHROOMS.

In Europe several species of mushrooms are preserved by boiling and afterwards placing them in earthern jars or tubs filled with water, which is renewed from time to time. This simple and economical method of keeping mushrooms affords the people considerable provision. With regard to the preparation of fresh mushrooms for table use, Dr. Roques, an eminent writer on fungi, gives the following excellent suggestions: "After selecting good mushrooms, remove the skin or epidermis, cutting away the gills, and in some cases the stem, which is usually of not so fine a texture.

"It is important to collect for use only young and well-preserved specimens, because a mushroom of excellent quality may, nevertheless, when overmature or near its decline, become dangerous for food. It then acts as does every other food substance which incipient decomposition has rendered acrid, irritating and indigestible. It is, moreover, rarely the case that mushrooms in their decline are not changed by the presence of larvæ."

In Geneva a very lucrative trade is carried on in the exportation of the "*Edible Boletus*," which is preserved for use in various ways, the simplest of which consists in cutting the caps in slices and stringing them, after which they are placed on hurdles in the shade to dry. They may also be dried in a stove or oven, but the former method is preferable, as the mushroom then retains more of its flavor or perfume. When the slices are perfectly dried they are put into sacks and suspended in a dry, airy place. Sometimes before the mushrooms are sliced they are plunged into boiling water for an instant, which treatment is said to preserve them from the ravages of insects. Several kinds of mushrooms are preserved in the following manner: After they have been properly washed and cleansed, they are boiled in salted water and afterwards wiped dry. They are then placed in layers, in jars, sprinkled with salt and pepper, and covered with pure olive oil or vinegar. *Lactarius deliciosus*, *Cantharellus cibarius*, *Morchellas*, *Clavarias*, etc., are thus preserved. Before using the dried mushrooms they are soaked in tepid water for some time and afterwards prepared as if fresh, with the usual seasoning.

RECEIPTS.

Broiled procerus.—Remove the scales and stalks from the agarics, and broil lightly on both sides over a clear fire for a few minutes; arrange them on a dish over freshly made, well-buttered toast; sprinkle with pepper and salt and put a small piece of butter on each; set before a brisk fire to melt the butter, and serve quickly. Bacon toasted over mushrooms improves the flavor and saves the butter.

Agarics delicately stewed.—Remove the stalks and scales from the young half-grown agarics, and throw each one as you do so into a basin of fresh water slightly acidulated with the juice of a lemon or a little good vinegar. When all are prepared, remove them from the water and put them in a stewpan with a very small piece of fresh butter. Sprinkle with pepper and salt and add a little lemon juice; cover up closely and stew for half an hour; then add a spoonful of flour with sufficient cream or cream and milk, till the whole has the thickness of cream. Season to taste, and stew again until the agarics are perfectly tender. Remove all the butter from the surface and serve in a hot dish garnished with slices of lemon. A little mace or nutmeg or catsup may be added, but some think that spice spoils the flavor.

Cottager's procerus pie.—Cut fresh agarics in small pieces; pepper, salt, and place them on small shreds of bacon, in the bottom of a pie dish; then put in a layer of mashed potatoes, and so fill the dish, layer by layer, with a cover of mashed potatoes for the crust. Bake well for half an hour and brown before a quick fire.

A la provencale.—Steep for two hours in some salt, pepper, and a little garlic; then toss them into a small stewpan over a brisk fire with parsley chopped and a little lemon juice.

Agaric catsup.—Place the agarics of as large a size as you can procure, layer by layer, in a deep pan, sprinkling each layer as it is put in with a little salt. Then next day stir them several times well so as to mash and extract their juice. On the third day strain off the liquor, measure and boil for ten minutes, and then to every pint of liquor add half an ounce of black pepper, a quarter of an ounce of bruised ginger root, a blade of mace, a clove or two, and a teaspoonful of mustard seed. Boil again for half an hour; put in two or three bay leaves and set aside until quite cold. Pass through a strainer and bottle; cork well and dip salt on the gills. Lay them top downwards on a gridiron over a moderate fire for five or six minutes at the most.

To stew mushrooms.—Trim and rub clean half a pint of large button mushrooms. Put into a stewpan 2 ounces of butter; shake it over a fire until thoroughly melted; put in the mushrooms, a teaspoonful of salt, half as much pepper, and a blade of mace pounded; stew until the mushrooms are tender, then serve on a hot dish. This is usually a breakfast dish.

Mushrooms à la crême.—Trim and rub half a pint of button mushrooms; dissolve in a stewpan 2 ounces of butter rolled in flour; put in the mushrooms, a bunch of parsley, a teaspoonful of salt, half a teaspoonful each of white pepper and of powdered sugar; shake the pan for ten minutes; then beat up the yolks of two eggs with two tablespoonfuls of cream, and add by degrees to the mushrooms; in two or three minutes you can serve them in sauce.

Mushrooms on toast.—Put a pint of mushrooms into a stewpan with two ounces of butter rolled in flour; add a teaspoonful of salt, half a teaspoonful of white pepper, a blade of powdered mace, and a half a teaspoonful of grated lemon; stew until the butter is all absorbed; then serve on toast as soon as the mushrooms are tender.

APPENDIX B.

GLOSSARY OF TERMS USED IN DESCRIBING MUSHROOMS.

Abortive, imperfectly developed.
Acaulescent, *acaulous*, having a very short stem or none.
Acetabuliform, cup-shaped.
Acicular, needle-shaped.
Aculeate, slender pointed.
Acuminate, terminating in a point.
Acute, sharp pointed.
Adnate, gills firmly attached to the stem.
Adnexed, gills just reaching the stem.
Adpressed, pressed in close contact, as applied to gills.
Æruginous, verdigris-green.
Agglutinated, glued to the surface.
Aggregated, collected together.
Alveolate, socketed or honeycombed.
Amphigenous, when the hymenium is not restricted to a particular surface.
Analogy, superficial or general resemblance without structural agreement.
Anastomosing, branching, joining of one vein with another.
Annular, ring-shaped.
Annulate, having a ring.
Annulus, ring round the stem of agarics.
Apex, in mushrooms the extremity of the stem nearest the gill.
Apical, close to the apex.
Apiculate, terminating in a small point.
Appendiculate, hanging in small fragments.
Approximate, of gills which approach the stem but do not reach it.
Arachnoid, cobweb-like.
Arboreal, *arboricle*, tree-inhabiting.
Arcuate, bow-shaped.
Areolate, divided into little areas or patches.
Argillaceous, clayey, like clay.
Ascending, directed upward.
Asci, *ascidia*, spore-cases of certain mushrooms.
Attenuated, tapering gradually to a point upward or downward.

Band, a broad bar of color.

Banded, marked with bands.

Barbed, furnished with fibrils or hairs.

Basidia, cellular processes of certain mushroom-bearing spores.

Bibliography, condensed history of the literature of a subject.

Bifurcated, divided into two, as in the gills of certain agarics.

Booted, applied to the stem of a mushroom when inclosed in a sheath or volva.

Boss, a knob or short rounded protuberance.

Bossed, bullate, furnished with a boss or knob.

Branched, dividing from the sides; also styled furcate and forked.

Brick, trade term for a mass of mushroom spawn, in dimensions the size of a brick of masonry.

Broad, wide or deep vertically.

Bulbous, having the structure of a bulb.

Cæspitose, growing in tufts.

Calcareous, chalky, chalk-like.

Calyptra, applied to the portion of volva covering the pileus.

Campanulate, bell-shaped.

Canaliculate, channelled.

Cancellate, latticed, marked both longitudinally and transversely.

Cap, the expanded, umbrella-like receptacle of the common mushroom.

Capillitium, spore-bearing threads, variable in thickness and color, sometimes continuous with the sterile base, sometimes free, dense, and persistent, or lax and evanescent, often branched; found in the Lycoperdons.

Carious, decayed.

Carneous, fleshy.

Cartilaginous, hard and tough.

Castaneous, chestnut color.

Ceraceous, wax-like.

Channelled, hollowed out like a gutter.

Chlorosis, loss of color.

Cilia, marginal hair-like processes.

Ciliate, fringed with hair-like processes.

Cinerous, ash-colored.

Circinate, rounded.

Clathrate, latticed.

Clavate, club-shaped, gradually thickened upward.

Close, packed closely side by side; also styled crowded.

Columella, a sterile tissue rising column-like in the midst of the capillitium, serving as a point of insertion for the threads which connect it with the peridium in the form of a network.

Concentric, having a common center, as a series of rings one within another.

Connate, united by growing, as when two or more caps become united.

Concolored, of a uniform color.

Confervoid, from the finely branched threads.

Continuous, without a break, of a surface which is not cracked, or of one part which runs into another without interruption.

Cordate, heart-shaped.

Coriaceous, of a leathery texture.

Corrugated, drawn into wrinkles or folds.

Corticated, furnished with a bark-like covering.

Cortina, a partial veil formed not of continuous tissue but of slender threads, which in certain mushrooms when young unite the stem with the margin of the cap. This membrane remains later as a filamentous ring on the stem, or threads hanging to the margin of cap. Applied to the peculiar veil of the Cortinarias.

Cratera, a cup-shaped receptacle.

Crenate, *crenulate*, notched at the edge, the notches blunt or rounded, not sharp as in a serrated edge, serratures convex.

Cribrose, pierced with holes.

Cryptogamia, applied to the division of nonflowering plants.

Cupreous, copper-colored.

Cuspidate, with a sharp, spear-like point.

Cyathiform, cup-shaped.

Cystidia, sterile cells of the hymenium, generally larger than the basidia cells, with which they are found.

Deciduous, temporary falling off.

Decurrent, as when the gills of a mushroom are prolonged down the stem.

Dehiscent, a closed organ opening of itself at maturity, or when it has attained a certain development.

Deliquescent, relating to mushrooms which at maturity become liquid.

Dentate, toothed, with concave serratures.

Denticulate, finely dentate.

Dermini, brown or rust colored spores.

Determinate, ending definitely; having a distinctly defined outline.

Diaphanous, transparent.

Dichotomous, paired by twos; regularly forked.

Dimidiate, applied to some gills of mushrooms which reach only
   halfway to the stem.
Disciform, of a circular, flat form.
Dissepiments, dividing walls.
Distant, applied to gills which have a wide distance between them.
Divaricate, separating at an obtuse angle.

Echinate, furnished with stiff bristles.
Echinulate, with minute bristles.
Effused, spread over without regular form.
Elongate, lengthened.
Emarginate, applied to gills which are notched or scooped out suddenly
   before they reach the stem.
Embryo, the mushroom before leaving its volva or egg stage; also any
   early stage of mushrooms which may have no volva.
Entire, the edge quite devoid of serrature or notch.
Epidermis, the external or outer layer of the plant.
Epiphytal, growing upon another plant.
Equal, all gills of the same, or nearly the same length from back to front.
Eroded, the edge ragged, as if torn.
Etiolated, whitened, bleached.
Even, distinguished from smooth: a surface quite plane as contrasted
   with one which is striate, pitted, etc.
Excentric, out of center. The stems of some mushrooms are always
   excentric.
Exotic, foreign.

Family, a systematic group in scientific classification embracing a
   greater or less number of genera which agree in certain
   characters not shared by others of the same order.
Farinaceous, mealy.
Farinose, covered with a white, mealy powder.
Fascia, a band or bar.
Fasciate, zoned with bands.
Fasciculate, growing in small bundles.
Fastigiate, bundled together like a sheath.
Favose, honeycombed.
Ferruginous, rust-colored.
Fibrillose, clothed with small fibers.
Fibrous, composed of fibers.
Filiform, thread-like.
Fimbriated, fringed.

Fissile, capable of being split.
Fistular, *fistulose*, tubular.
Flabelliform, fan-shaped.
Flavescent, yellowish, or turning yellow.
Flexuose, wavy.
Flocci, threads as of mold.
Floccose, downy.
Flocculose, covered with flocci.
Foveolate, pitted.
Free, in relation to the gills of mushrooms reaching the stem but not
     attached to it.
Fringe, a lacerated marginal membrane.
Fructification, reproducing power of a plant.
Fugacious, disappearing rapidly.
Furcate, forked.
Fuliginous, blackish or sooty.
Fulvous, tawny; a rather indefinite brownish yellow.
Furfuraceous, with branny scales or scurf.
Fuscous, brownish, but dingy; not pure.
Fusiform, spindle-shaped.

Genera, plural of genus.
Generic, pertaining to a genus.
Genus, a group of species having one or more characteristics in
     common; the union of several genera presenting the same
     features constitutes a tribe.
Gibbous, in the form of a swelling; of a pileus which is more convex or
     tumid on one side than the other.
Gills, vertical plates radiating from the stem on the under surface of the
     mushroom cap.
Glabrous, smooth.
Glaucescent, inclining to glaucose.
Glaucose, covered with a whitish-green bloom or fine white powder
     easily rubbed off.
Globose, nearly spherical.
Granular, with roughened surface.
Greaved, of a stem clothed like a leg in armor.
Gregarious, of mushrooms not solitary but growing in numbers in the
     same locality.
Grumous, clotted; composed of little clustered grains.
Guttate, marked with tear-like spots.
Gyrose, circling in wavy folds.

Habitat, natural abode of a vegetable species.
Hepatic, pertaining to the liver; hence, liver-colored.
Heterogeneous, of a structure which is different from adjacent ones.
Hibernal, pertaining to winter.
Hirsute, hairy.
Homogeneous, similar in structure.
Hyaline, transparent.
Hygrophanous, looking watery when moist and opaque when dry.
Hymenium, the fructifying surface of the mushroom; the part on which
    the spores are borne.
Hymenophore, the structure which bears the hymenium.
Hypogæous, subterranean.

Identification, the determination of the species to which a given
    specimen belongs.
Identify, to determine the systematic name of a specimen.
Imbricate, overlapped like tiles.
Immarginate, without a distinctborder.
Immersed, sunk into the matrix.
Incised, cut out; cut away.
Indehiscent, not opening.
Indigenous, native of a country.
Inferior, growing below; of the ring of an agaric, which is far down on
    the stem.
Infundibuliform, funnel-shaped.
Innate, adhering by growing into.
Inserted, growing like a graft from its stock.
Involute, edges rolled inward.

Laciniate, divided into flaps.
Lactescent, milk-bearing.
Lacunose, pitted or having cavities.
Lamellæ, gills of mushrooms.
Lanceolate, lance-shaped; tapering to both ends.
Lateral, attached to one side.
Latex, the viscid fluid contained in some mushrooms.
Laticiferous, applied to the tubes conveying latex, as in the Lactarias.
Lepidote, scurfy with minute scales.
Leucospore, white spore.
Ligneous, woody consistency.
Linear, narrow and straight.
Linguiform, tongue-shaped.

AUTHORITIES CONSULTED.

Fries, Saccardo, Kromholtz, Cooke and Berkeley, M. C. Cooke, Peck, Stevenson, Badham, Gillet, Boyer, Gibson, Roques, Hussey, Hay, Bel, Paulet and Leveille, Constantin and Dufour, Barla, Roze, W. G. Smith, Vittadini.

STUDENT'S HAND-BOOK

OF

Mushrooms of America

EDIBLE AND POISONOUS.

BY

THOMAS TAYLOR, M. D.

AUTHOR OF FOOD PRODUCTS, ETC.

Published in Serial Form—**No. 2**—Price, 50c. per number.

WASHINGTON, D. C.:
A. R. Taylor, Publisher, 238 Mass. Ave. N.E.
1897.

The ten mushrooms illustrated in the five plates contained in the first number of this series belong to the family Hymenomycetes. In the present number are presented illustrations representing three additional specimens of the Hymenomycetal fungi (Plates V, VI, and VII). There are also presented, in plates C and D, illustrations of nine species comprised in four genera of the sub family Discomycetes, of the family Ascomycetes.

ASCOMYCETES.

Fruit, consisting of sporidia, mostly definite, contained in asci, springing from a naked or enclosed stratum of fructifying cells, and forming a hymenium.— Cooke and Berkeley.

Prof. J. de Seyne states that the three elements which form the hymenium in the families Hymenomycetes and Gasteromycetes are (1) the normal basidium, that is, the fruitful club-shaped cell which supports the naked spores, (2) the cystidium or sterile cell, an aborted or atrophied basidium, and (3) the paraphyses, hypertrophied basidium, the one organ, the basidium, being the basis of it all, according as it experiences an arrest of development, as it grows and fructifies, or as it becomes hypertrophied.

In the family Ascomycetes a minute ascus or spore case envelops the sporidia, and takes the place of the basidium, and the hymenium consists of (1) the asci containing the sporidia, (2) the paraphyses, and (3) a colorless or yellowish mucilage which envelops the paraphyses and asci. The asci are present in all species. In some species, however, the paraphyses are rare, and the mucilaginous substance is entirely wanting. The asci differ in shape and size, according to the species. The paraphyses, when present, are at first very short, but they rapidly elongate, and are wholly developed before the appearance of the asci. They are linear, simple or branched according to the species of plant, usually containing oily granules. There is some difference of opinion among mycologists as to the special functions of the paraphyses, some considering them as abortive asci, and others, like Boudier, as excitatory organs for the dehiscence of the asci, by which the spores are liberated.

The family Ascomycetes is rich in genera and species.

It consists largely of microscopic fungi, however, and the only group which will be considered here is that which includes plants of the mushroom family which are edible and indigenous to this country, viz., the sub-family Discomycetes.

DISCOMYCETES.

The name Discomycetes, "disk-like fungi," does not give an accurate idea of the distinguishing characteristics of this sub-family, the discoid form only belonging to the plants of one of its groups. In the Discomyceteæ the hymenium is superior, that is, disposed upon the upper or exterior surface of the mushroom cap. The sporidia are produced in membraneous asci, usually four or eight, or some multiple of that number, in each ascus; Cooke says "rarely four, most commonly eight." The sporidia are usually hyaline, transparent; colored sporidia are rare.

The asci are so minute as to be imperceptible to the naked eye; but if a small portion of the upper surface of the cap is removed with a pen knife and placed under a microscope having a magnifying power of from 400 to 800 diameters, the asci, or spore sacks, can be separated and their structure studied.

Of the genera included in the Discomycetes the genus Peziza comprises by far the largest number of described species. The plants in this genus are generally small, thin, and tough. A few of them have been recorded as edible by European authors, but not specially commended; one form, Peziza *cochleata*, has been spoken of by Berkeley as being gathered in basketfuls in one county in England, where it is used as a substitute, though a very indifferent one, for the Morel.

Vittadini says the Verpa *digitaliformis* Persoon, a small brownish-colored mushroom, is sold in Italian markets for soups, but that, "although sold in the markets, it is only to be recommended when no other fungus offers, which is sometimes the case in the spring." P. *aurantia* Vahl., a small Peziza growing in clusters in the grass, is reported as edible by a member of the Boston Mycological Club, who speaks well of it.

The genera Morchella, Gyromitra, Helvella, and Mitrula contain, however, what may be considered the most desirable edible species. Types of these four groups are represented in Figs. 1, 3, 5, 7, and 10, Plate C.

The plants of these genera have a stem and cap. The cap, however, differs very much from that of the ordinary mushroom. In the genus Morchella the cap is deeply pitted and ridged so that it presents a honeycombed appearance. In Gyromitra the cap is convolutely lobed but not pitted. In Helvella the cap is very irregular and reflexed, and in Mitrula the cap is ovate or club shaped and smooth. In all four of these genera the hymenium is superior, *i. e.*, it is on the upper and outer surface of the cap, the interior surface being barren.

In Plates C and D are figured 9 types of edible fungi included in the family Ascomycetes, sub-family Discomycetes.

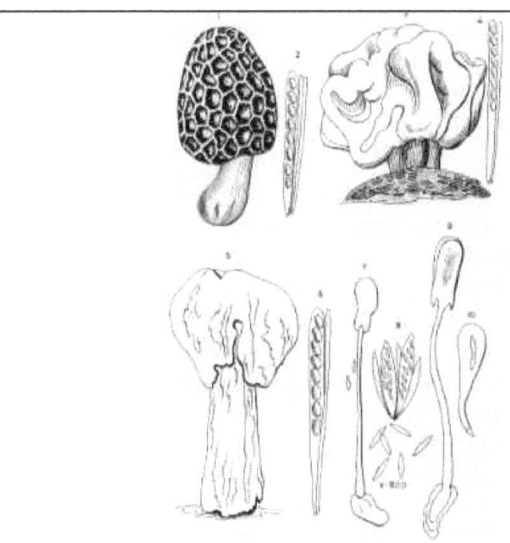

ASCOMYCETES

SUB-FAMILY DISCOMYCETES

TYPES OF FOUR OF THE LEADING GENERA OF
DISCOMYCETES, IN WHICH OCCUR EDIBLE SPECIES

T. TAYLOR, DEL.

THE NORRIS PETERS CO., PHOTO-LITHO., WASHINGTON, D. C.

PLATE C.

FIG. 1. **Morchella esculenta** Pers. *"Common Morel."*

EDIBLE.

Genus Morchella Dill. Receptacle pileate or clavate, impervious in the centre, stipitate, covered with hymenium, which is deeply folded and pitted.—Cooke.

In this genus the species have a general resemblance to each other in size, color, form, texture, and flavor. The cap is usually a dull yellow, sometimes slightly olive-tinted, darkening with age to a brownish leather tinge. The stems are stout and hollow, white or whitish. This genus has a very wide geographical distribution, but the species are not numerous. Cooke describes twenty-four, some of them found in India, Java, Great Britain, Central and Northern Europe, Australia, and North America. Peck describes six species found in New York State. The lines of demarcation between species are not very decided; but as none of the species are known to be poisonous, it may be considered a safe genus to experiment with.

In the Morchella esculenta the cap is ovate, in one variety rotund, the margin attaching itself to the stem; ribs firm and anastomosing, forming deep hollows or pits; color yellowish tan, olivaceous; spores hyaline, colorless; asci very long. The Morel, though rare in some localities, is found in large quantities in some of the midwestern States, sometimes in the woods along the borders of streams, often in peach orchards, at the roots of decaying trees.

I am informed by correspondents who have collected and eaten them that the Morels can be gathered in abundance in the springtime along the banks of the Missouri and tributary streams. A lieutenant in the United States Army informs me that he found fine specimens of this species in the mountains of California, five or six thousand feet above sea-level. A correspondent, Mr. H. W. Henshaw, writes that he has made many excellent meals of them, finding them on the banks of Chico Creek, Sacramento Valley, California, on Gen. Bidwell's ranch, in April. A correspondent in Minnesota writes: "The Morel grows abundantly in some places here, but so prejudiced are many of the natives against 'toad-stools' that I had to eat the Morel alone for a whole season before I could induce any one else to taste it." Mr. Hollis Webster, of the Boston Mycological Club, reports the Morchella *conica* as appearing in abundance in eastern Massachusetts in May of this year. A correspondent in West Virginia reports that quantities of a large-sized Morel are found in the mountain regions there.

I have reports also of the appearance of the Morel in Western New York, and on the coast of Maine and of Oregon. A miner writes to me from Montana that he and several other miners, having lost their way in the mountains of that State during the spring of the year, subsisted entirely for five days on Morels which they collected.

The specimen represented in Plate C, Fig. 1, is figured from a Morchella *esculenta* which grew in the vicinity of Falls Church, Va., less than ten miles from the District of Columbia. The reports which I have received from correspondents in twenty States show that the Morel is not so rare in this country as was formerly supposed. The advantages which this mushroom possesses over some others are (1) the readiness with which it can be distinguished, (2) its keeping qualities, and (3) its agreeable taste. It is easily dried, and in that condition can be kept a long time without losing its flavor. Though it has not the rich flavor of the common field mushroom, it is very palatable when cooked, and when dried it is often used in soups. It is very generally esteemed as an esculent among mycophagists.

Fig. 2 represents the sporidia enclosed in the ascus, or spore sack, with accompanying paraphyses.

FIG. 3. **Gyromitra** *esculenta* Fries. "*Esculent Gyromitra.*"

Genus Gyromitra Fries. This genus contains very few species, but all are considered edible, though differing somewhat in flavor and digestibility. Five or six species are figured by Cooke. Peck speaks of several species found in New York. One of these, G. curtipes Fries, is also figured by Cooke as found in North Carolina. This species Cooke regards as equal in flavor to G. esculenta. G. esculenta has a rounded, inflated cap, irregularly lobed and hollow, smooth and brittle in texture, reddish brown. It falls over the stem in heavy convolutions, touching it at various points. The stem is stout, stuffed, at length hollow, whitish or cinereous; spores elliptical with two nuclei, yellowish, translucent. The plant is usually from two to four inches in height, but larger specimens are found.

Fig. 4 represents the spore sack with enclosed sporidia.

Mr. Charles L. Fox, of Portland, Maine, records the Gyromitra *esculenta*, of which he sent me a very good specimen last spring, as quite abundant during May in the open woods near the city named. Speaking of this species, he says: "From the point of view of their edibility, we have classed them under two heads—the light and the dark varieties. These differ in the locality in which they are found, in their color and in the convolutions of their surface. Both grow large.

"The *Light Gyromitra* is the more easily digested of the two. Its height varies from three to five inches, cap three to five inches in diameter. Its cap is inflated, very irregular, and twisted in large convolutions. These convolutions are almost smooth on the surface, sometimes showing small depressions; margin generally attached to the stem in parts. It is a transparent yellow in color. This variety does not grow dark brown with age. Stem white or very light buff, smooth, and hollow. It grows best on slopes facing the south, in scant woods of birch, maple, and pine. We have found no specimens in open places or on the borders of woods.

"The *Dark Gyromitra* is more common than the light variety. Its color is generally of dark lake brown, even in the young plant, though it is sometimes of a light warm yellow, which grows darker with age. Stem flesh-colored or pallid, but not white, nor so light as in the first variety. Its cap is similar in its large convolutions to that of the light variety, but it is covered with many intricate vermiform ridges, sometimes in high relief or even strongly undercut. Grows in mossy places, in light sandy soil, on borders of pine woods. Its flesh is brittle, but not so tender as that of the first variety. Both varieties dry readily. We should advise eating the *Dark Gyromitra* only in moderate amounts, as, if eaten in quantity, or if old specimens are used, indigestion or nausea is liable to follow. In regard to both varieties, I would advise that only young specimens should be eaten at first, as they are more tender and less pronounced in flavor than the older plants. We have eaten, however, a considerable quantity of the *Light Gyromitra* with no unpleasant results. The flavor of the Gyromitras is quite strong, and some have found it too much so to be agreeable on the first eating. The general opinion here, however, is favorable to the Gyromitra as an excellent addition to the table."

Some German authorities speak well of the flavor of the G. esculenta, and it is sold in the German markets. Cordier records it as agreeable in taste when cooked. Peck says that he has repeatedly eaten it without experiencing any evil results, but does not consider its flavor equal to that of a first-class mushroom. He advises also that it should be eaten with moderation, and that only perfectly fresh specimens should be used, sickness having resulted from eating freely of specimens that had been kept twenty-four hours before being cooked.

I have not been fortunate in securing a sufficient quantity of fresh specimens to test its edible qualities personally, but the testimony received from those who have eaten it seems to point to the necessity for moderation in eating and care in securing fresh specimens to cook.

Fɪɢ. 5. **Helvella crispa**. *"Crisp Helvella."*

Genus Helvella Linn. The plants of this genus are usually small, though a few of the species are of good size. They are not plentiful, but they are very generally regarded as edible, the flavor bearing a resemblance to that of the Morel. The cap has a smooth, not polished, surface, and is very irregular, revolute, and deflexed, not honeycombed like the Morel, nor showing the brain-like convolutions of the Gyromitras. Color brownish pale tan, or whitish. The stem in the larger species is stout, and sometimes deeply furrowed in longitudinal grooves, usually white or whitish.

The species Helvella crispa is white or pallid throughout, cap very irregular, sometimes deeply concave in the centre, with margin at first erect, then drooping; again it is undulating, much divided and deflexed; in fact, so irregular is the shape that scarcely two specimens will show the cap the same in outline; stem stout and deeply channelled. Spores elliptical, transparent. Habitat woods, growing singly or in groups, but not cæspitose.

Fig. 6, the ascus or spore sack and paraphyses.

Genus Mitrula Fries. Soft and fleshy, simple capitate, stem distinct, hymenium surrounding the inflated cap; head ovate, obtuse, inflated.—M. C. Cooke.

Cooke says of this genus that it is scarcely so well characterized as many with which it is associated, and that some of the species are evidently so closely allied to some of the species of the genus Geoglossum that it is difficult to draw the line of demarcation between them, particularly so with the species Mitrula *pistillaris* B. from Louisiana.

The plants are very small, and though none are recorded as poisonous, only one or two have any value as esculents.

FIG. 7. Mitrula sclerotipes Boudier.

The cap in this species is small, and the stem long and slender. The spores are transparent, the asci club-shaped. The plants of this species are always found springing from an oblong sclerotium; hence the name sclerotipes.

Fig. 8 represents the sporidia enclosed in their asci with paraphyses and individual spores, the latter magnified 800 diameters. Fig. 9, sectional view of mature plant.

FIG. 10. Mitrula vitellina Sacc., var. irregularis Peck.

Saccardo, in his Sylloge Fungorum, includes in this genus those having a club-shaped cap, which brings into it, with others, the species Mitrula *vitellina* Sacc., formerly classed in the genus Geoglossum, and its variety *irregularis* Peck. The latter was first described in 1879, in Peck's Thirty- Second Report, under the name Geoglossum *irregulare*. Prof. Peck now gives preference to the name assigned to it by Saccardo, and it is so recorded in Peck's later reports.

Prof. Peck records this species as edible, and recommends it as having tender flesh and an agreeable flavor. It sometimes grows in profusion in wet mossy places, in woods, or swampy ground. It is bright yellow in color, clean and attractive. The cap is much longer than the stem, often deeply lobed, extremely irregular in outline, and tapers to a short yellowish or whitish stem. The spores are narrowly elliptical and transparent. The specimen illustrated is from a small one figured by Peck. The plants sometimes reach two inches in height. They are most abundant in temperate climates.

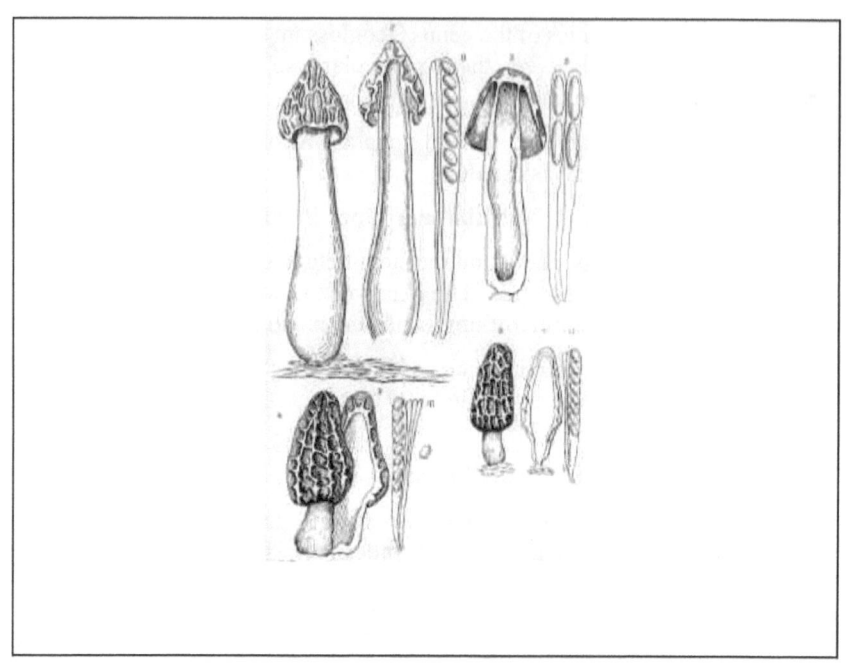

PLATE D.

In Plate D are represented four species of the genus Morchella, viz., M. *semilibera*, M. *bispora*, M. *conica*, and M. *deliciosa*. Morchella *esculenta* is figured in Plate C.

FIG. 1. **Morchella semilibera** De Candolle. *"Half Free Morel."*

EDIBLE.

Cap conical but half free from the stem as the name of the species indicates. The ribs are longitudinal, forming oblong pits; stem hollow, much longer than the cap, white; spores elliptical. Peck says that this species has been described by Persoon under the name Morchella *hybrida*, and this name is adopted in Saccardo's Sylloge Fungorum, but most English writers prefer the first.

Fig. 2. Sectional view of Morchella *semilibera*.

Fig. 8. Sporidia of same inclosed in ascus with accompanying paraphyses.

FIG. 3. Sectional view of **Morchella bispora** Sorokin. *"Two-Spored Morel."*

EDIBLE.

Cap free from the stem to the top, somewhat resembling that of M. *semilibera*, but blunt at its summit instead of conical, the outward surface

52

deeply pitted, inner surface smooth and barren. A characteristic of this species which distinguishes it from others of the same genus is found in the number of its sporidia, spores as seen in the ascus or spore sack. In the plants of the genus Morchella the spore sacks, with one or two exceptions, contain eight spores.

In the species M. *bispora* the spore sacks contain but two spores and these are much larger than the sporidia of those which contain eight. This characteristic, however, can only be determined by the aid of the microscope.

Cooke figures a specimen taken from those published by Sorokin in Thumen's Exsiccata, and calls it a variety of Morchella *Bohemica* Kromb. He says that it is not unusual to find M. *Bohemica* with two or four sporidia in some of the asci, mixed with others containing more, some specimens being entirely tetrasporous, and some, as the variety *bispora*, usually containing but two sporidia. Cooke contends that M. bispora is simply a bisporous form of Morchella *Bohemica*, and calls it M. *Bohemica* var. *bispora*. It is not as common as other species.

Fig. 9 represents asci of M. bispora showing the two spores in each ascus.

FIG. 4. **Morchella conica.** *"Conical Morel."*

EDIBLE.

Cap conical or oblong-conical, margin adhering to the stem, the prominent ridges longitudinal and irregularly bisected with shorter ones; the whole plant hollow throughout; color pale tan or ochraceous yellow, growing dingy and darker with age; stem white; spores elliptical.

This species is quite plentiful in some localities; the flavor is like that of M. *esculenta*.

Fig. 5. Sectional view of M. *conica*. Fig.

10. Ascus, sporidia and paraphyses.

FIG. 6. **Morchella deliciosa** Fries. *"Delicious Morel."*

Cap nearly cylindrical, blunt at the top, and usually much longer than the stem, adnate. Plant hollow throughout. Stem white. Spores elliptical.

Fig. 7. Sectional view of M. *deliciosa*.

Fig. 11. Ascus, sporidia, and paraphyses.

The Morchella *deliciosa* is highly esteemed as an esculent wherever eaten. Split open and stuffed with bread crumbs seasoned with pepper, salt, and butter and a pinch of thyme or onion, steamed in a hot oven, and served with butter sauce, this mushroom makes a very savory dish.

Note.—Small specimens have been selected for illustration in this plate in order to utilize as much as possible the plate space.

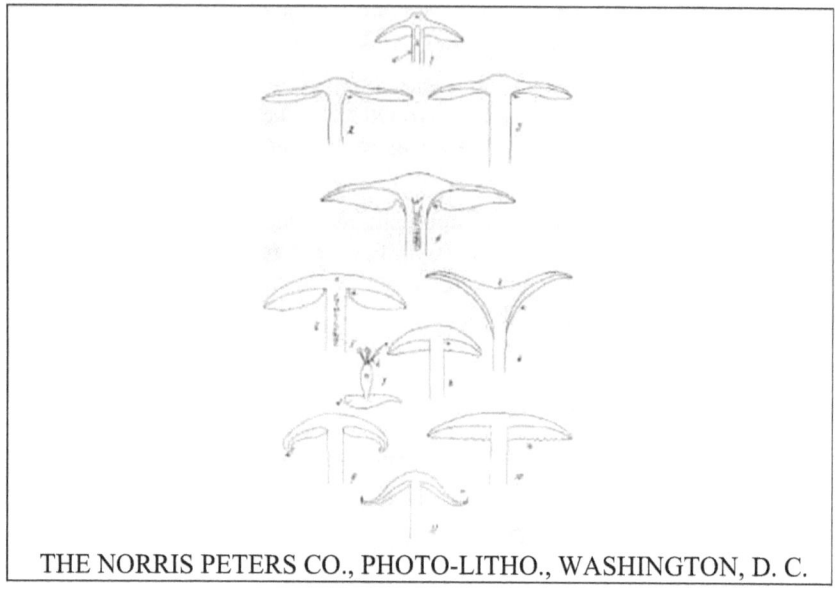

PLATE IV. STRUCTURE OF THE AGARICINI, GILL-BEARING MUSHROOMS.

Fig. 1. Cap or pileus umbonate, *a*; stem or stipe fistulose, tubular, *b*; gills or lamellæ adnate, and slightly emarginate.

Fig. 2. Gills remote, *i. e.*, distant from the stem. (See *a*.)

Fig. 3. Gills adnexed, partly attached to the stem at their inner extremity, *a*.

Fig. 4. Gills emarginate, with a tooth, as at *a*; stem stuffed.

Fig. 5. Cap obtuse, *e*; gills free, *i. e.*, reaching the stem but not attached thereto (see *a*); *b* stem stuffed.

Fig. 6. Cap umbilicate, slightly depressed in the centre, *b*; gills decurrent, *i. e.*, running down the stem. (See *a*.)

Fig. 7. Basidium, cell *a*, borne on the hymenium, or spore-bearing surface of the gills; *b*, stigmata; *c*, spores.

Fig. 8. Gills adnate, *i. e.*, firmly attached to the stem at their inner extremity, as at *a*.

Fig. 9. Cap, with border involute, *i. e.*, rolled inward. (See *a*.)

Fig. 10. Lamellæ or gills dentated or toothed. (See *a*.)

Fig. 11. Cap with border revolute, *i. e.*, rolled backward. (See *a*.)

AGARICINI. Fries.

Genus Lactarius Fries. The plants of this genus have neither veil nor volva. They somewhat resemble the *Russulæ*, but can be readily distinguished from them by the greater fleshiness of the stem and by the milky juice which exudes from the flesh. The latter is a characteristic feature of the *Lactars*, giving to the group its name.

The species were originally arranged by Fries into groups according to the color and quality of the milk, and of the naked or pruinose character of the gills. Prof. Peck, however, considering the latter character not sufficiently constant or obvious to be satisfactory, in his early reports makes the color of the milk alone the basis of the primary grouping of the American species.

Saccardo, in his Sylloge, follows Fries in his classification of the species of the genus Lactarius.

In some species the milk is at first bright colored and continues unchanged; in others it is always white or whitish, and in others again it is at first white, changing to different hues on exposure to the air, becoming pinkish, pale violet, or yellow. In one species (C. indigo) both plant and milk are of indigo blue. The taste of the milk varies, as does that of the flesh, according to species. Sometimes it is mild or very slightly acrid, and again it resembles Cayenne pepper in its hot, biting acridity. It is somewhat viscid or sticky in character, and permeates to some extent the whole flesh of the mushroom, but is most profuse in the gills, where in fresh young specimens it is seen exuding on the slightest pressure. In old or wilted specimens it does not flow so freely, but may be found by breaking off portions of the cap.

The plants usually present a fleshy cap, the flesh quite brittle, and breaking in clean, even fractures. In a number of the species the upper surface of the cap shows bands or zones of warm coloring, not found in any of the species of the allied genus Russula. The gills are sometimes even, more often forked, acute on the edge, color white or whitish, but changing to yellowish or reddish tints as the plants mature, or when cut or bruised. While they are at first adnate they become, with the expansion of the cap, somewhat decurrent, showing in this particular a resemblance to the plants of the genus Clitocybe. The stem is central, except in a few species, where it is eccentric or lateral, notably the latter in L. *obliquus*; spores white or yellowish, according to species; Cooke says, "rarely turning yellow." They are globose, or nearly so, and slightly rough.

This genus is a large one, and contains many acrid species. Out of fifty-three described and figured by Cooke, more than half are given as having the milk more or less acrid. More than forty species have been recorded as growing in this country, and many of these are extremely acrid in taste.

A number of the species are edible, while others have been recorded as deleterious, poisonous, etc. L. torminosus, L. piperatus, and L. insulsus are species about which there seems to be difference of opinion among authors as to their wholesomeness or edibility, some contending that, in spite of their extreme acridity, they are edible when cooked, and others that they are deleterious in their effects. L. *deliciosus* and L. *volemus* have a good reputation in this country as well as abroad, and are quite abundant in some localities. They are more frequent in temperate climates than in northern latitudes or in the tropics.

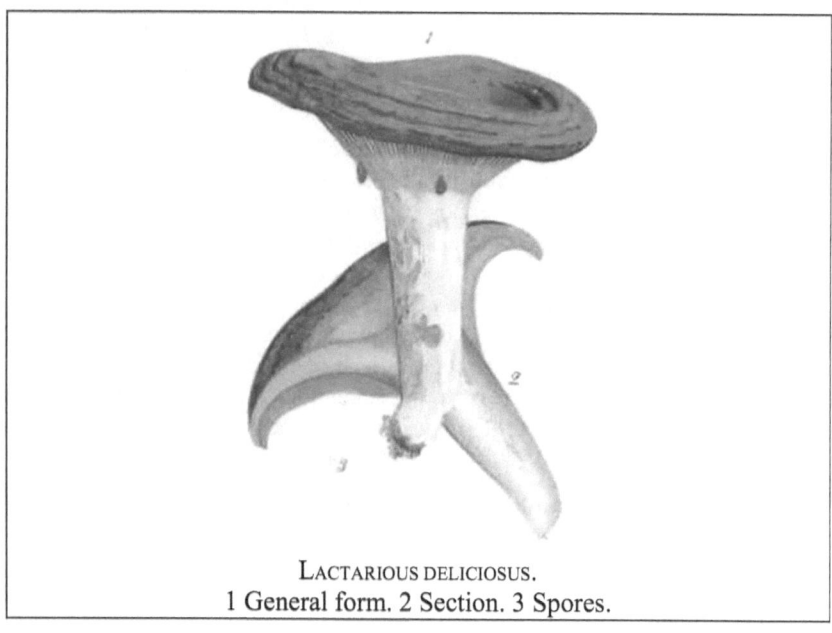

LACTARIOUS DELICIOSUS.
1 General form. 2 Section. 3 Spores.

PLATE V.

Lactarius deliciosus Fries. *"Delicious Lactarius" or "Orange Milk Mushroom."*

EDIBLE.

Cap fleshy, viscid, at first convex, then nearly plane, becoming much depressed in the centre, funnel-shaped, marked in the adult plant with rings or rust-colored zones. Color of the cap dull orange, turning paler, and grayish or greenish yellow when old or dried; margin at first turned inwards; flesh whitish or tinged with yellow; gills decurrent, crowded rather thick, sometimes slightly forked at the base, pale yellow, sometimes a saffron yellow, exuding when bruised a saffron-red or orange-colored liquid, hence the popular name of "Orange Milk Mushroom;" stem smooth, somewhat spotted, stout, stuffed with a yellowish pith, eventually becoming hollow; color about the same as that of the cap. Spores subglobose, yellowish. Taste mild or very slightly acrid when raw.

Mycophagists generally concur in the opinion that it is of very pleasant flavor when cooked, and some speak very enthusiastically of its esculent qualities.

Over-cooking is apt to make it tough. I find steaming in the oven with butter, pepper, and salt, and a very small quantity of water, as oysters are steamed, a very good method of preserving the juices and flavor.

It is found in Maryland, under the pines and sometimes in mossy and swampy places. Prof. Underwood, President of the New York Mycological Club, reports it as fairly abundant in Connecticut.

Lactarius *volemus* Fries, the "Orange-Brown Lactar," somewhat resembles the L. *deliciosus* in shape and size, but the cap is dry and glabrous and the skin is apt to crack in patches in somewhat the same manner as does that of the Russula *virescens*. It is a warm orange-brown in color, varying slightly with age, and is not zoned. The gills are white or yellowish and crowded, adnate in the young specimens, and decurrent in the mature, exuding a white milk when bruised. The spores are globose, and white. It is found in open woods. The flavor is much like that of L. *deliciosus*, although perhaps not so rich.

One author states it as his experience that the Lactars which have *bright*-colored milk, unchanging, are usually edible and have a mild taste. L. *indigo* Schwein has been recorded as less abundant than some other species, but edible. The plant is a deep blue throughout, the milk of the same color and unchanging. The taste of both flesh and milk is mild. Specimens of this species were sent to me from western New York several years ago by a correspondent who found it growing in quantities in a corn field. He had cooked several dishes of it, and reported its flavor as very agreeable.

L. *vellereus* and L. *piperatus* are very common in fir woods. The plants are large and stout, white throughout, the milk white and excessively acrid; gills decurrent, unequal and narrow. The milk in *vellereus* is apt to be scanty but copious in *piperatus*.

Of L. *piperatus*, Worthington Smith says: "So strongly acrid is the milk that if it be allowed to trickle over tender hands it will sting like the contact of nettles; and if a drop be placed on the lips or tongue the sensation will be like the scalding of boiling water." He records it as "poisonous." Fries and Curtis say that, "notwithstanding its intense acridity, it is edible when cooked."

Cordier, while recording it as edible, says that the milk, and butter made from the milk of cows fed with it, are bitter and nauseous, although cows eat it with avidity. Gibson, while quoting one or two authors as to its edibility when cooked, says: "Its decidedly ardent tang warns me not to dwell too enthusiastically upon its merits in a limited selection of desirable esculents." The Secretary of the Boston Mycological Club, writing in the Club bulletin, says "it has been eaten as a sort of duty after the acridity was cooked out," but does not commend it. It is spoken of as "an unattractive fungus which usurps in the woods the place that might well be occupied by something better." In this opinion I fully concur.

L. *torminosus*, *"Wooly Lactarius,"* sometimes called the *"Colic Lactarius,"* has been termed acrid and poisonous by Badham. Cordier and Letellier, on the other hand, say that it can be eaten with impunity when cooked. Gillet declares it deleterious and even dangerous in the raw state, constituting a very strong and drastic purgative. One author states that, although it does not constitute an agreeable article of food, it is eaten in some parts of France and in Russia. Considering the differences of opinion which exist with regard to this and other extremely acrid species, it would seem the part of prudence for persons with delicate stomachs to avoid the use of very acrid species, for, though the acridity may be expelled by cooking, there would seem to be no necessity for risking unpleasant or dangerous results while the range of unquestionably wholesome and agreeable species is sufficiently wide to satisfy the most enthusiastic mycophagist.

AGARICINI.

LEUCOSPORI (SPORES WHITE OR YELLOWISH).

Armillaria Fries. Cooke places Armillaria in the order Agaricini, *genus Agaricus*, making of it a *sub*-genus. Saccardo, in taking it out of Agaricus, elevates it to the position of a separate genus. The name Armillaria is derived from a Greek word, meaning a ring or bracelet, referring to its ringed stem.

In the plants of the Armillaria the veil is partial in infancy, attaching the edge of the cap to the upper part of the stem; the stem furnished with a ring. Below the ring the veil is concrete with the stem, forming scurfy scales upon it. The gills are broadly adnexed. In abnormal specimens the ring is sometimes absent, or appearing only in scales, running down the stem. Spores white. The species are few; eight are recorded as growing in the United States. Cooke describes twelve species found in Great Britain.

AGARICUS (ARMILLARIA) MELLEUS.
Group from Hynesboro Park, Md., U. S.
K. MAYO, del.

PLATE VI.

Ag. (Armillaria) melleus Vahl. *"Honey-Colored Armillaria."*

EDIBLE.

Cap fleshy, rather thin at the margin, at first subconical, then slightly rounded, or nearly plane, clothed with minute hairy tufts; margin sometimes striate, color varying, usually a pale-yellowish or honey color or light reddish brown; flesh whitish. Gills whitish or paler than the cap, growing mealy with the shedding of the profuse white spores, and often spotted with reddish-brown stains, adnate, ending with decurrent tooth. Stem fibrillose, elastic, stuffed or hollow, ringed, and adorned with floccose scales which often disappear with age; in some varieties distinctly bulbous at the base, in others showing tapering root. Specimens occur in which the ring is wanting or only traces of it appear in the form of scales encircling the stem. Veil usually firm, membraneous, and encircling the stem in a well-pronounced ring or collar, but sometimes filmy as a spider's web, in very young specimens hiding the gills, but breaking apart as the cap expands.

Manner of growth cæspitose, generally on decayed tree stumps, although the group figured in the plate was found growing on moist sand, mixed with clay, on a roadside in Hynesbury Park.

Authors differ widely as to the value of this species as an esculent. I have only eaten the very young and small specimens when cooked, and found them very palatable. A Boston mycophagist records it as "very good," fried after five minutes' boiling in salted water. Prof. Peck, having tried it, considers it "a perfectly safe species, but not of first-rate quality." It is very common in Maryland and Virginia, and in the mountain districts prolific. I have talked with Bohemians and with Germans who have gathered it in basketfuls in the vicinity of the District of Columbia, who speak well of it, considering it a valuable addition to the table. Its prolific growth makes it valuable to those who like it. There are no species recorded as dangerous in this group.

Ag. (Armillaria) robustus, a very stout species, with a fleshy, compact, smooth cap, bay color or tawny, occurs in the Maryland woods, and in the open woods of the Massachusetts coast.

AGARICINI. Fries.

Genus Cantharellus Adans. In the plants of this genus the hymenophore or fleshy substance of the cap is continuous with the stem. They are fleshy, membranaceous, and putrescent, having neither veil, ring, nor volva. The stem is central, except in a few species, where it is lateral. A characteristic of the genus which separates it from other genera of the Agaricini is the vein- like appearance of the gills. They are very shallow and so obtuse on the edges as to present the appearance of a network of swollen branching veins. They are usually decurrent and anastomosing. It is a small genus. Cooke figures nineteen species. Among the described species C. cibarius is the only one whose edible qualities have been highly recommended. C. umbonatus, a very small plant, found in eastern Massachusetts is commended by those who have eaten it. They are usually found in woods, and amongst moss. One species, *C. carbonatus*, is found upon charred ground.

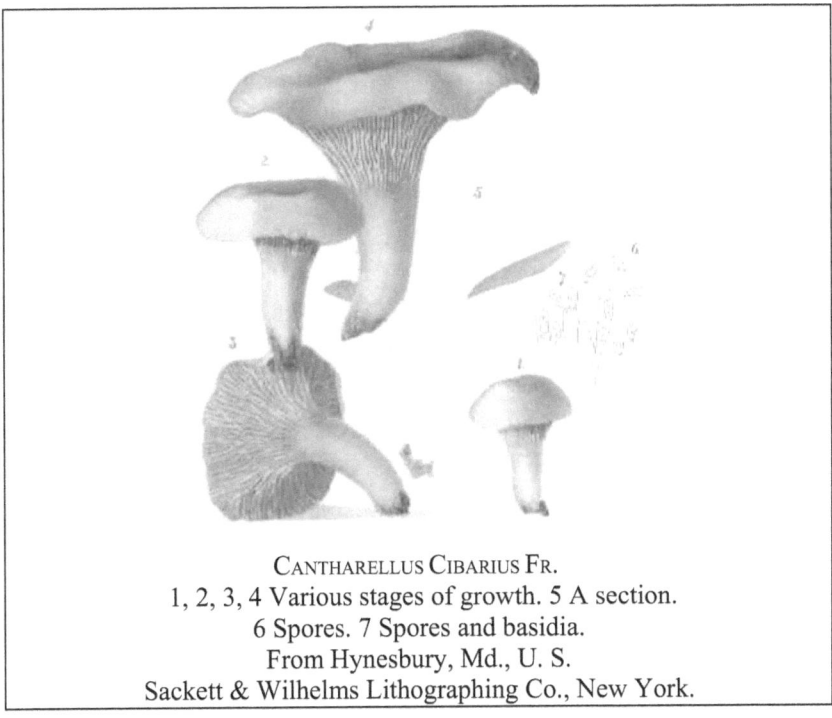

PLATE VII.

Cantharellus cibarius Fries. "*The Edible Chantarelle.*"

EDIBLE.

Cap a rich golden yellow, like the yolk of an egg; at first convex, later concave and turbinated; margin sinuous, undulate, smooth, shining, and more or less lobed; diameter from two to four inches; flesh pale yellow or whitish; veins or gills rather thick and wiry, remarkably decurrent, usually very much bifurcated and of the same golden yellow as the cap; stem solid or stuffed, slightly attenuated downwards, yellow; spores white or pale yellowish, elliptical.

European authors esteem it very highly, and some speak of the odor as like that of ripe apricots. The plant as found in Maryland and Virginia has a slightly pungent but agreeable taste when raw, and a pleasant odor when cooked. It is ranked as one of the best of the wood mushrooms by those who have eaten it in this locality (District of Columbia). It is found here in abundance, after light rains, in fir woods. Berkeley states that it is somewhat rare in England, where it is held as a delicacy, but quite common on the continent. We have had specimens from various localities throughout the States. Cooke says the spores are white. Peck and Gibson record them as yellow. I find them white, sometimes slightly tinted with yellow.

The *Chantarelle* takes its name from a Greek word signifying a cup or vase, referring to its shape and possibly also to its rich golden color; *cibarius* refers to its esculent qualities.

The variety *rufipes* Gillet closely resembles C. *cibarius*, but is darker, with the stem *rufous*, reddish, at the base.

C. *aurantiacus* Fries bears a sufficient resemblance to C. *cibarius* to be sometimes taken for it, although the cap is tomentose and of a much deeper orange in tint, the gills more crowded, darker than the cap, and the stem less stout. In the variety *pallidus* the whole plant is very light or buff yellow, and the gills nearly white. C. aurantiacus has been recorded as poisonous or unwholesome by some of the earlier authors, others say that they have eaten it, but do not commend it.

RECEIPTS FOR COOKING.

Stuffed Morels.—Choose the freshest and lightest colored Morels, open the stalk at the base, fill with minced veal and bread-crumbs, secure the ends of the stalk and place between thin slices of bacon.

The Morel should not be gathered immediately after heavy rains, as it becomes insipid with much moisture. The flavor is said to grow stronger in drying.

Escalloped Mushrooms.—(From Mr. Frank Caywood, Fredericktown, Ohio, November 14, 1893.) Season as directed in the usual methods for mushrooms and add a small quantity of vinegar to hasten the cooking. Cook slowly until tender; rapid boiling evaporates the flavor. When done, put in from a pint to a quart of sweet milk and heat. Take a pudding dish and put in a layer of broken crackers; light milk crackers are the best. Put lumps of butter and pepper and salt over the crackers. Next a layer of the tender mushrooms with some of the hot gravy and milk. Continue these layers until the dish is full, having a layer of crackers on top. Place the dish in the oven and bake slowly until the crackers are browned.

Mushroom Fritters.—Take nice large tops, season, and dip into batter and fry in hot butter as other fritters.

Mushrooms en ragout.—Put into a stewpan a little "stock," a small quantity of vinegar, parsley, and green onions chopped up, salt and spices. When this is about to boil, the cleaned mushrooms are put in. When done remove them from the fire and thicken with yolks of eggs.

The Lactarius *deliciosus* may be served with a white sauce or fried. Badham says the best way to cook them is to season first with pepper, salt, and small pieces of butter, and bake in a closely covered pie dish for about three quarters of an hour.

The Cantharellus, being somewhat dry, requires more fluid sauce in cooking than the juicier mushrooms, and is best minced and slowly stewed until quite tender. Some advise soaking it in milk a few hours before cooking. The Italians dry or pickle it or keep it in oil for winter use.

Persoon gives the following recipes for cooking the Morel: 1st. Wash and cleanse thoroughly, as the earth is apt to collect between the ridges; dry and put them in a saucepan with pepper, salt, and parsley, adding or not a piece of bacon; stew for an hour, pouring in occasionally a little broth to prevent burning; when sufficiently done, bind with the yolks of two or three eggs, and serve on buttered toast.

2. *Morelles à l'Italienne.*—Having washed and dried, divide them across, put them on the fire with some parsley, scallion, chives, tarragon, a little salt, and two spoonfuls of fine oil. Stew till the juice runs out, then thicken with a little flour; serve with bread crumbs and a squeeze of lemon.

MUSHROOM GROWING. [A]

[A] A part of the matter presented under this caption was contributed by the author to the Health Magazine and appeared in the March number (1897) of that periodical.

To France is due the credit of being the first country to cultivate mushrooms on a large scale, and France still supplies the markets of the world with canned mushrooms. The mushroom which is cultivated in the caves and quarries of France, to the exclusion of all others, is the Agaricus arvensis (the "Snowball"), a species of field mushroom.

Of late years France has found a formidable competitor in the culture of mushrooms in Great Britain. The English market gardeners find their moist, equable climate favorable to outdoor culture, and abundant crops are grown by them in the open air, chiefly, however, for the home market.

That mushroom growing can be made a lucrative business is shown by the experience of a well-known English grower, Mr. J. F. Barter, who on one acre of ground has produced in the open air, without the aid of glass, an average of from ten to twelve thousand pounds of mushrooms annually; the price obtained for them varying according to the season, but averaging ten pence, or twenty cents, per pound for the whole year. The value of twelve thousand pounds of mushrooms at ten pence per pound would be £500 sterling or $2,500.

For the purposes of comparison the following are quoted from the Pall Mall Gazette, as exceptional prices realized in England for other fruits and vegetables in recent years:

Pounds sterling per statute acre:

Very early gooseberries, 100; onions, 192; early lettuces, 100; plums, 100; potatoes, 100; strawberries, 150; black currants, 168; filberts, 200.

It will be seen that onions and filberts head the list, but the product of an acre of mushrooms has been shown to be worth more than double that of either filberts or onions.

In the localities specially favorable to hop growing 30 cwt. of hops to the acre is considered exceptional, while the average price has been quoted at 3 pounds sterling, or about one-fifth of the sum obtained from Mr. Barter's acre of mushrooms. Three months in the year the weather does not favor outdoor culture, and these months Mr. Barter spends in manufacturing brick spawn, which he exports to this and other countries. Among those who have been very successful in indoor culture are Mr. William Robinson, editor of the "London Garden," and Mr. Horace Cox, manager of the "Field."

In America, where mushroom culture is still comparatively in its infancy, there have already been obtained very encouraging results by painstaking growers. Most of the cultivation has been in the northern and midwestern States, where the climatic conditions seemed most favorable to indoor culture. A few figures as to the revenue obtained in this way may be interesting to readers.

An experienced Pennsylvania grower states that from a total area of 5,500 square feet of beds, made up in two mushroom houses, he obtained a crop of 5,000 pounds of mushrooms in one season, or about one pound to the square foot. These sold at an average of a little over 50 cents per pound. A third house, with 19,000 square feet of beds, produced 2,800 pounds, or one and one-half pounds to the square foot. This house yielded a net profit of one thousand dollars. This, however, can be quoted only as showing the possibilities of careful culture by experienced growers under very favorable circumstances. Amateurs could scarcely expect such good results. Three- fourths of a pound to the square foot would probably come nearer the average. A Philadelphia grower gives the average price secured from fifty shipments of mushrooms in one season at 54 cents per pound. New York dealers report higher rates than this. A Washington florist who utilizes the lower shelves of his propagating houses for the purpose of mushroom growing informed me that during two seasons he received 60 cents per pound wholesale, shipping to New York, and that he sold one thousand dollars worth in one season. Mr. Denton, a market gardener of Long Island, who cultivates in houses built for the purpose, markets from 1,700 to 2,500 pounds per year.

Thus far the market is in the hands of a comparatively few dealers in the neighborhood of large cities, but there is certainly no good reason why the growing of mushrooms should not be more generally undertaken by the farming community. Certainly no one has better facilities than are at the command of the enterprising American farmer. On most farms the conditions are favorable or could easily be made so for mushroom culture, on a moderate scale, at least. Generally there are disused sheds, old barns, etc., which with a small outlay could be transformed into mushroom houses, and where timber is plentiful the cost of building a small mushroom house would be repaid by the profits accruing from the business.

In the culture of mushrooms there are open, to the enterprising with small capital, four sources of profit: first, the sale of the fresh mushrooms; second, the manufacture of mushroom catsup; third, the canning of the small button mushroom for exportation; and, fourth, the manufacture of spawn.

It is well in this, as in all new industries, to begin in a small way, and if success is attained it is easy to extend operations on a larger scale. My advice to amateurs is to begin with one or two beds in a well-drained cellar or shed where good ventilation and even temperature can be secured at moderate cost. In the underground cellar economy is secured by the saving in fuel. The beds can be made on the floor, flat, ridged or banked against the wall, ten or twelve inches deep in a warm cellar, and from fifteen to twenty inches in a cool cellar. The boxing for the sides and ends may be built six or eight inches higher than the beds to give the mushrooms plenty of head room.

DIRECTIONS FOR PREPARING THE COMPOST FOR THE BEDS.

Procure not less than a cartload of clean, fresh stable manure. Place it under cover, to protect it from rain and drain water, mix well and heap up the whole mass into a mound three feet high then beat the mound firmly down to prevent undue heating. Repeat this operation every other day until its rank smell is gone, taking care that on each turning the outside dry manure is placed in the centre of the mound. By this means the stable odor is dissipated while its heating properties are equally distributed. Add to this from one- fourth to one-fifth of clean, rich garden mould. Mix well. After this careful handling, the mass may be considered fit for bedding purposes. When placed in the beds the mass should be compacted again by beating with the back of a spade or trowel. The bed surface should appear moist but not wet, smooth and of firm consistence. From day to day it will be necessary to test its general temperature by means of a thermometer. To this end make at various places at different depths openings sufficiently large to admit the use of a thermometer. It will be found that the temperature is highest nearest the bottom. Test at various points. At first the temperature will run high; 105° to 120° Fahrenheit is probably as high as it will reach, but in a few days it will fall to 85° or 80° Fahrenheit. At this point spawn the bed. For this purpose make holes in the top of the bed about six inches apart and two inches deep with a blunt dibble or broom handle. Place in these holes or openings a piece of brick spawn about the size of a hen's egg, and cover the holes with manure; finish by packing the same, keeping the surface of the bed smooth and moist. The spawn should be slightly moistened before using. Should the surface of the bed become dry, use water from a fine sprinkling pan. The temperature of the cellar or house in which the bed may be placed should range between 55° and 75°, and should not be lower than 50°. If the spawn is good and all conditions attended to, the white filaments should appear spreading through the bed within eight or ten days after spawning. When the white spawn is observed on or near the surface, cover the whole surface with from one to two inches of garden loam well pulverized. A good general rule for spawning the bed is to wait until the heat of the bed is on the decline and has fallen to at least 90° Fahrenheit. If the heat in the middle of the bed runs too high the spawn is killed. The experience of a number of growers has shown that a bed spawned at 60° to 80° and kept at 55° after the mushrooms appear gives better results than one spawned at 90°.

The quality of the manure makes some difference in its temperature. That obtained from stables where horses are grass fed will be of lower normal temperature and will chill quicker than that obtained from corn or oat fed stock.

A solution of saltpeter in proportion of about fifteen grains to a quart of water, occasionally spread over the bed with a fine hose, helps to accelerate the growth of the mushrooms.

The proper condition of the manure as regards dryness or moistness can be readily ascertained by squeezing it in the hand; it should be unctuous enough to hold together in a lump, and so dry that you cannot squeeze a drop of water out of it. Excessive moisture in the manure has been often a cause of failure. It should be remembered also that when the heat of the manure is on the decline it falls rapidly, five, often ten degrees a day, till it reaches about 75°, and between that and 65° it may rest for weeks.

One of the principal causes of the failure of mushroom culture in this country is the use of old or poor spawn. Good spawn should have a fresh, mushroomy odor, and a bluish-white appearance on the surface. In buying spawn one should always go to reliable seedsmen.

Compost for Mushroom Beds.

Sawdust has been used in England for mushroom beds, after having been used for stable bedding, with very good results. It has also been used successfully in the District of Columbia. In fact, the very large models of cultivated mushrooms exhibited by the Division of Microscopy of the Department of Agriculture at the World's Fair in Chicago were moulded from mushrooms which were grown on the writer's premises, in a composition of sawdust stable bedding, combined with about one-fourth garden mould, but I am confident, at the same time, that much depends on the kind of timber the sawdust is made from. In this case the sawdust came from spruce.

MUSHROOM CULTURE IN CANADA.

A Canadian correspondent informs me that he, with others, has been very successful in growing mushrooms in the open air during the summer months in Canada, and gives the following directions for preparing the beds in the colder latitudes:

Place under a shed such amount of clean stable manure as may be required for the beds, turning it over and over until all free ammonia has escaped and the tendency of undue fermentation and evolution of high temperature has greatly modified. To effect this, it is necessary to heap up the manure each time in a mound, say three feet high after turning, and beat it firmly down (the exclusion of free air prevents overheating). To put the manure in proper condition for use in the beds, from two to four weeks' treatment may be required, but much depends on the quality of the manure and temperature of the atmosphere. Before making the beds, and several days after the last turning, test the internal temperature of the mound in the following manner: Make a hole with a broomstick through the mound from top to bottom, and suspend a thermometer half way down in the hole for, say, an hour. The temperature may be as high as 150° F. After the lapse of the time stated, beat the mound more firmly down to prevent rise of temperature. Test again two days after in the same manner. If the temperature has risen several degrees the mound must be again taken down, turned over, and remade. If, on the other hand, the temperature has fallen to 100° F., the permanent bed may be made. If indoor growth is desired, such as a cellar, outbuilding, or cave, the atmosphere must not fall below 50° F., nor be over 80° F. Air drafts cannot be permitted. The floor must be dry and the atmosphere moist. The cellar may be dark, or moderately light. Growers differ in opinion in this respect. Growers generally add to the manure about one-fourth or one-fifth garden soil, but success has been attained without the use of garden soil, except as surface dressing after spawning the bed; an excessive use of loam, in any case, tends to lower the temperature too rapidly. Having prepared a box or frame-work for the bed twelve inches deep, fill it up to within two inches of the top; beat gently down with a board, or a brick, until it is even and compact. On the following day make holes in the bed, with a dibble, ten inches deep, in which suspend a thermometer half way down for an hour. Should the temperature have fallen to 90° F., cover lightly with straw and test on the following day. Should the temperature prove to be going down, say to 80° F., or 85° F., it is safe to plant the spawn; but should the temperature be on the rise, wait until it is falling. One grower has stated that his greatest success has been when the spawn was planted at the temperature of 75° F. Should the temperature fall too quickly and the surface be too dry, sprinkle with water at blood heat, using a very fine hose, and cover the bed with straw.

The spawn brick should be cut into pieces, about the size of an egg, and planted in holes made in the bed, about two inches deep and about six inches apart. The holes are then filled up and about two inches of garden soil sifted over the surface of the bed. Tamp the bed surface gently with the back of a spade. Mushrooms may be expected for table use in about six or seven weeks, provided the spawn is good and the temperature has not fallen below 50° F. In outdoor culture the beds must be well covered with straw or canvas, and had better be under a shed roof with southern exposure.

The spawn used by this grower is the "brick" spawn, imported from Carter & Holborn, London, England.

CULTIVATION OF MUSHROOMS IN JAPAN.

The Japanese are very successful in cultivating a mushroom which they call "Shiitake" or "Lepiota shiitake." China also produces the same mushroom, but of an inferior quality. The Chinese therefore prefer the mushroom cultivated by the Japanese, which they import from Japan in large quantities. It is cultivated on a variety of trees, but is said to grow best on the "Shiinoki," a species of oak (Quercus cuspidata).

There are three varieties of "Shiitake," the spring, summer, and autumn crops differing somewhat in quality. The method of growing the "Shiitake" is given by the Japanese Commissioner of Agriculture as follows:

"Trees of from twenty to fifty years' growth are cut down at the approach of winter when the sap has ceased to run, and after the lapse of twenty or thirty days, according to the condition of the drying of the wood, are sawed into logs of 4 or 5 feet in length. Into each of these logs incisions are made with a hatchet, at intervals of about 6 inches, and they are piled regularly upon a frame-work erected at a height of about 1 foot above the ground, under the trees. The location of the ground selected for piling the logs should be the slopes of a forest, facing southeast or southwest. After keeping the logs as above described for from two to three years, they are immersed in water for twenty-four hours in the middle of November, and again laid one upon another for about four days; if it is in a cold district, the pile is covered with straw or mats. At the expiration of the fourth day the logs are obliquely tilted against poles fixed horizontally to the trees at a height of about 4 feet in a well-ventilated and sunny situation. The mushrooms soon appear in quantity, and, after twenty or thirty days' growth, are ready for harvesting."

Recent reports of the Japanese Agricultural Department show the total value of the annual export of "Shiitake" to be nearly five hundred thousand "yen" (silver).

MANUFACTURE OF SPAWN.

As many tons of artificial spawn are yearly imported into this country, it would seem that the manufacture of spawn in the United States might prove a profitable form of investment.

"BRICK SPAWN."

For commercial purposes the English method of making the spawn into bricks has some advantages over the French "flake" process. Its compact and uniform shape makes the brick more convenient for storage and general handling, and greatly facilitates its transportation to long distances. Brick spawn is made in the following manner: Clean horse droppings, cow manure, loam, and road sweepings are beaten up in a mortar-like consistency and then formed into bricks, moulds being used, slightly differing in shape with different makers, but usually thinner and wider than common building bricks. The following proportions are given: (1) Horse droppings the chief part; one-fourth cow dung; remainder loam. (2) Fresh horse droppings mixed with short litter for the greater part; cow dung, one third; and the rest mould or loam. (3) Horse dung, cow dung, and loam, in equal parts. When about half dry, depressions are made in the bricks, sometimes in the centre, and sometimes in each corner, and small pieces of good spawn are placed in these depressions, and plastered over with the material of the brick. The cakes are then laid out to dry, standing on their edges, and when nearly dry are piled in pairs with the spawn-larded surfaces face to face. The bricks are then stacked away, and covered with sweet fermenting litter, sufficiently to cause a heat of 60° F. It should not be over 70° F. One spawn manufacturer says that the most rapid and successful growth of the mycelium is attained when the temperature is from 63° F. to 67° F. The bricks are examined frequently during the process, and when the mycelium of the old spawn has permeated the whole mass like a fine white mould, the bricks are taken out and dried in a well-ventilated dark place. They are then placed in a cool, dark storehouse, where they are not subject to dampness and where the temperature is about 50° F., not over 65° or below 35° F. Slight ventilation is necessary, but not enough to make the bricks dust-dry. Keeping the spawn dry merely suspends its growth; as soon as it is again submitted to favorable conditions of moisture and heat, its pristine activity returns. Dampness, combined with heat, stimulates the growth of mycelium; frost also destroys the vitality of the spawn. It is evident, therefore, that these conditions should not exist in the store-room.

One manufacturer advocates piling the bricks, after spawning, on a clay floor, packing closely four bricks deep, and covering them with sifted loam. By this method it is claimed that danger of "fire fang" will be avoided, as the bricks will be kept at a perfectly uniform temperature of about 60° or 66°, which causes the spawn to run quickly and uniformly. In from four to six weeks they are ready to take out and dry for use or storage.

The French or "Flake" spawn comes in light masses of loose, dry litter. It is obtained in the following way: A bed is made up as if for mushrooms in the ordinary way, and spawned with "virgin" spawn, and when the bed is thoroughly impregnated with spawn, it is broken up and set aside to dry. This spawn is usually sold in small boxes, containing from two to five pounds, but it also can be obtained in bulk when it is purchased by weight. The French or "flake" spawn is much more expensive than the English or "brick" spawn. It is claimed by some very successful growers, who have tried both, that the brick spawn produces heavier and fleshier mushrooms than the French "flake."

"MILL TRACK" SPAWN.

"Mill track" spawn was formerly considered the best in England, but since horse power has given place to steam power in the mills there is now no further supply of mill track, and it is practically superseded by the "brick" spawn. The real "mill track" is the natural spawn that has spread through the thoroughly amalgamated horse droppings in mill tracks, or the sweepings from mill tracks.

SPAWN PRODUCED IN A MANURE HEAP.

During the past year I have made some experiments in the pine and oak woods of Hynesboro' Park, Maryland, with relation to spawn culture, an account of which may prove of interest to students in this line of investigation. Several loads of stable manure and oak-leaf bedding were well mixed and formed into a mound about three feet in height, having a diameter of six feet, and tapering to about four inches in depth at the outer edge. The mass was quite moist and slightly tamped to give it general consistency. It was exposed to the open air, without protection, during the months of September, October, and November. In the meantime, frequent rains occurred. On examination it was found that the rains did not penetrate to a depth of more than four inches. On opening up the centre of the mound, it was observed that the portion thus exposed consisted of highly decomposed leaves, and presented a white mass of matted, "burned" mycelium. It was evident that the temperature at that point had risen considerably above 100° Fahr. The mycelium was, doubtless, produced in abundance before the temperature reached 100 Fahr. and became scorched as the temperature increased. On examining the outer edges, where the depth was only twelve inches, I found an abundance of mycelium which did not show any appearance of having been scorched by undue temperature. Since no mycelium had been added to the mound, it is evident that the spores which produced it must have been present, although unobserved, and awaiting only the proper conditions for development, *i. e.*, for budding and the production of mycelium. At the end of the third month, groups of the common meadow mushroom, Agaricus campestris, together with some fine examples of Tricholoma terreum, an edible mushroom, common to these woods, appeared on the edges of the mound.

APPENDIX A.

CONTINUATION OF GLOSSARY OF TERMS USED IN DESCRIBING MUSHROOMS.

Maculate, spotted.

Marginate, having a distinct border.

Matrix, the substance upon which a mushroom grows.

Medial, at the middle; of the ring of a mushroom which is between superior or near the apex of the stem, and distant or far removed from the apex.

Merismoid, having a branched or laciniate pileus.

Moniliform, contracted at intervals in the length, like a string of beads.

Multifid, having many divisions.

Multipartite, divided into many parts.

Mycelium, the delicate threads proceeding from the germinating spores, usually white and popularly termed spawn.

Narrow, of very slight vertical width.

Netted, covered with projecting reticulated lines.

Nucleus, the reproductive germ in the spore.

Obconic, inversely conical.

Obcordate, like an invertedheart.

Oblique, slanting.

Oblong, longer than broad.

Obovate, inversely egg-shaped, broadest at the apex.

Obtuse, blunt or rounded.

Ochrospore, ochre-colored spore.

Orbicular, having the form of an orb.

Order, group of a classification intermediate between tribe and family.

Ostiole, ostiolum, mouth of the perithecium; orifice through which the spores are discharged.

Ovate, egg-shaped.

Pallid, pale, undecided color.

Papillate, papillose, covered with soft tubercles.

Paraphyses, sterile cells found with the reproductive cells of some plants.

Parasitic, growing on and deriving support from another plant.

Partial, of a veil clothing the stem and reaching to the edge of the cap but not extending beyond it.

Patent, spreading.
Pectinate, toothed like a comb.
Pedicel, foot-stock.
Pedicillate, having a pedicel.
Pelliculose, furnished with a pellicle or distinct skin.
Penciled, with pencil-like hairs either on the tip or border.
Peridium, general covering of a puff-ball, simple or double, dehiscent or
        indehiscent at maturity.
Perithecia, bottle-like receptacles containing asci.
Peronate, used when the stem has a distinct stocking-like coat.
Persistent, inclined to hold firm, tenacious.
Pervious, forming an open tube-like passage.
Pileate, having a cap.
Pileoli, secondary pilei; arising from a division of the primary pileus.
Pileus, the cap, receptacle, or one part of a mushroom; other parts are the
        stem and gills.
Pilose, covered with hairs.
Pits, depressions in cells or tubes resembling pores, applied also to
        hollow depressions in the surface of the cap of the morel.
Plumose, feathery.
Pore, orifice of the tubes of polypores.
Poriform, in the form of pores.
Porous, having pores.
Powdery, covered with bloom or powder.
Projecting, the anterior end jutting out beyond the margin.
Proliferous, applied to an organ which gives rise to secondary ones of
        the same kind.
Pruinose, covered with frost-like bloom.
Pruniform, plum-shaped.
Pubescent, downy.
Pulverulent, covered with dust.
Pulvinate, cushion-shaped.
Punctate, dotted with points.
Pyriform, pear-shaped.

Quaternate, arranged in groups of four.

Receptacle, a part of the mushroom extremely varied in form,
        consistency, and size, inclosing the organs of reproduction.
Remote, when the margin of the gill comes to an end before reaching the
        stem.
Reniform, kidney-shaped.

Repand, bent backwards.

Resupinate, of mushrooms spread over the matrix without any stem and with the hymenium upwards; inverted by twisting of the stalk.

Reticulate, marked with cross lines like the meshes of a net.

Revolute, rolled backwards; of the margin of a cap, the opposite of involute.

Rhodospore, rose or pink spore.

Rimose, cracked.

Ring, a part of the veil adhering to the stem of a mushroom in the shape of a ring.

Rivulose, marked with lines like rivulets.

Rubiginous, rust colored.

Rufescent, reddish in color.

Rugose, wrinkled.

APPENDIX B.

Through the courtesy of Mr. Hollis Webster, Secretary of the Boston Mycological Club, the following list of mushrooms, which have been collected and eaten by members of that club during the past year, has been supplied to me:

AMANITA.
>A. *Cæsarea* Scop., "True Orange."
>A. *rubescens* Persoon.
>A. *vaginata* Bull.

LEPIOTA.
>L. *procera* Scop., "Parasol Mushroom."
>L. *rachodes* Vilt.
>L. *Americana* Pk.
>L. *naucinoides*.

ARMILLARIA.
>A. *mellea* Vahl, "Honey Mushroom."

TRICHOLOMA.
>T. *equestre* L.
>T. *sejunctum* Low, "Yellow Blusher."
>T. *portentosum* Fr.

T. *coryphacum* Fr.
T. *russula* Schaeff.
T. *columbetta* Fr.
T. *gambosum* Fr., "St. George's Mushroom."
T. *personatum.*
T. *nudum.*
HYGROPHORUS.
H. *virgineus* Fr.
H. *fuligineus* Frost.
H. *flavo discus* Frost, "Yellow Sweet-Bread."
H. *hypothejus* Fr.
H. *puniceus* Fr.
LACTARIUS.
L. *piperatus* Fr.
L. *deliciosus* Fr.
L. *volemus* Fr.
RUSSULA.
R. *virescens* Fr.
R. *lepida* Fr.
R. *punctata* Gt.
R. *aurata* Fr.
R. *ochracea* Fr.
R. *alutacea* Fr.
CANTHARELLUS.
C. *cibarius* Fr.
C. *umbonatus* Fr.
MARASMIUS.
M. *oreades* Fr., "Fairy Ring."
M. *scorodonius* Fr.
M. *alliaceus* Fr.
HYPHOLOMA.
H. *sublateritium* Schaeff.
H. *candolleanum* Fr.
H. *perplexum.*
H. *appendiculatum* Bull.
COPRINUS.
C. *comatus* Fr., "Shaggy Mane."
C. *ovatus* Fr.
C. *atramentarius.*
C. *micaceus* Fr.
C. *fimetarius* Fr.
CORTINARIUS.

C. *turmalis* Fr.

C. *sebaceus* Fr.

C. *cærulescens* Fr.

C. *collinitus* Fr.

C. *violaceus* Fr.

C. *albo violaceus* Pers.

C. *cinnamomeus* Fr.

C. *cinnamomeus* var. *semi-sanguineus* Fr.

CLITOCYBE.

C. *clavipes* Fr.

C. *odora* Fr.

C. *dealbata* Low.

C. *laccata* Scop.

C. *multiceps* Pk.

C. *infundibuliformis* Schaeff.

COLLYBIA.

C. *dryophila* Bull.

C. *velutipes* Curt.

PLEUROTUS.

P. *ostreatus* Fr.

P. *sapidus* Kalch.

P. *ulmarius* Fr., Elm-tree Mushroom.

P. *pluteus cervinus* Schaeff.

CLITOPILUS.

C. *prunulus* Scop.

C. *orcella* Bull.

C. *unitinctus* Pk.

C. *Seymourianus* Pk.

PHOLIOTA.

P. *caperata* Pers., "The Gypsy."

P. *præcox* (when too old is bitter).

P. *adiposa.*

AGARICUS (Psalliota).

A. *arvensis.*

A. *cretaceus* Fr.

A. *campester* L.

A. *silvicola* Vilt.

SPARASSIS.

S. *crispa* Fr.

CLAVARIA.

(Any and all Clavarias found are generally eaten by us without identification).

C. *botrytes* Pers.
C. *amethystina* Bull.
C. *coralloides* L.
C. *cinerea* Bull.
C. *aurea* Schaeff.
C. *rugosa* Bull.
C. *pistillaris* L.
LYCOPERDON.
L. *cyathiforme* Bose.
L. *giganteum* Batsch.
L. *pyriforme* Schaeff.
L. *saccatum* Fr.
MORCHELLA.
M. *esculenta* Bull.
M. *conica* Pers.
PEZIZA.
P. *aurantia* Vahl.
STROBILOMYCES.
S. *strobilaceus* Berk.
FISTULINA.
F. *hepatica* Fr., "Beef Steak Mushroom."
POLYPORUS.
P. *betulinus* Fr. (coriaceous when old).
P. *sulphureus* Fr.
HYDNUM.
H. *imbricatum* L.
H. *repandum* L.
H. *caput-medusæ* Bull.
Also thirteen of the Boleti.

STUDENT'S HAND-BOOK

OF

MUSHROOMS OF AMERICA

EDIBLE AND POISONOUS.
BY
THOMAS TAYLOR, M. D.
AUTHOR OF FOOD PRODUCTS, ETC.

Published in Serial Form—**No. 3**—Price, 50c. per number.

WASHINGTON, D. C.:
A. R. Taylor, Publisher, 238 Mass. Ave. N.E.
1897.

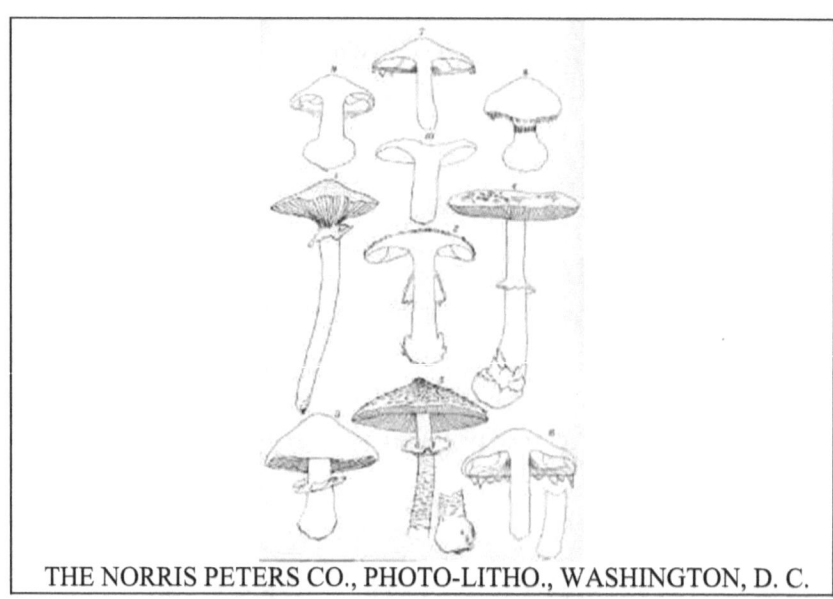

THE NORRIS PETERS CO., PHOTO-LITHO., WASHINGTON, D. C.

Plate E.

Plate E illustrates various forms and positions of the annulus or ring characteristic of certain species of mushrooms, together with the cortina or veil of which the ring, if present, is the remnant, in some species, either as it appears entire or as a fringe on the margin of the cap, contrasting these forms with a sectional view of a species in which the veil or ring is always wanting.

Fig. 1. Ring broad, reflexed or deflexed, or both; situated high up on the stem, as in *Armillaria mellea*.

Fig. 2. Ring situated about midway of the stem, deflexed and pendulous as in *Amanita muscaria*.

Fig. 3. Ring about half midway of the stem, split, and radiating outwards, as in *Agaricus arvensis*.

Fig. 4. Ring drooping.

Fig. 5. Ring persistent, movable, wholly detached, in age, from the tall and slender stem, upon which it easily slips up and down. A species of great beauty, *Lepiota procera*.

Fig. 6. Ring narrow, scarcely perceptible above the middle of the stem; remnants of the veil adhering to the margin of the cap as a fugacious web.

Fig. 7. Ring generally wanting—*Tricholoma nudum*. Remnants of the veil seen on the margin of the cap.

Fig. 8. Remnants of the veil appearing on the margin of the cap as a fringe, and particularly on the stem as a mere fibrillose zone of a darker color as in the *Cortinarii*.

Fig. 9. Plant exhibiting the cortina unbroken, the extremities of its delicate arachnoid threads attached to cap and stem, respectively.

Fig. 10. Section of a Russula, in which genus the ring is always wanting; veil none.

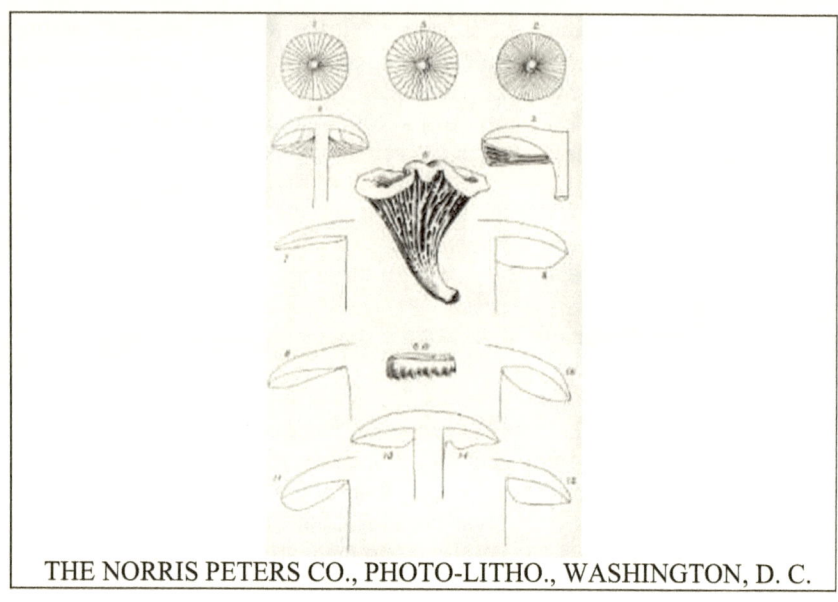

PLATE F.

Plate F illustrates by section or otherwise various forms of these gill-like processes characteristic of species, considered either with regard to marginal outline or position of their posterior extremity:

Fig. 1. Gills distant.
Fig. 2. Gills crowded.
Fig. 3. Gills flexuose.
Fig. 4. Gills unequal.
Fig. 5. Bifurcated.
Fig. 6. Anastomosing veins.
Fig. 6a. Sectional view.
Fig. 7. Gills narrow.
Fig. 8. Gills broad.
Fig. 9. Lanceolate.
Fig. 10. Ventricose.
Fig. 11. Anteriorly rounded.
Fig. 12. Posteriorly rounded.
Fig. 13. Emarginate.
Fig. 14. Emarginate and denticulate.

AGARICINI.

Subgenus Hypholoma. Hymenophore continuous with the stem, veil woven into a fugacious web, which adheres to the margin of the pileus. Gills adnate or sinuate; spores brownish purple, sometimes intense purple, almost black.— M. C. Cooke.

This subgenus has been divided into the following five groups:

1. Fasciculares.—Pileus smooth, tough, bright colored when dry, not hygrophanous. Examples, Ag. (Hypholoma) *sublateritius* and Ag. (Hypholoma) *fascicularis.*
2. Viscidi.—Pileus naked, viscid. Example, Ag. (Hypholoma) *œdipus.*
3. Velutini.—Pileus silky, with innate fibrils. Example, Ag. (Hypholoma) *velutinus.*
4. Flocculosi.—Pileus clad with floccose superficial evanescent scales. Example, Ag. (Hypholoma) *cascus.*
5. Appendiculati.—Pileus smooth and hygrophanous. Example, Ag. (Hypholoma) *Candollianus.*

The species are not numerous. They are generally either gregarious or cæspitose, and are often found in clusters upon tree stumps, or springing from the buried roots of stumps. A few species are found in short grass in open places; but few are recorded as edible, and one, H. *fascicularis*, has been classed as deleterious by Berkeley, Cooke, and some of the earlier authors. I find, however, no authenticated case of poisoning by this species, and, indeed, have as yet found no species of Hypholoma which could be satisfactorily identified as H. fascicularis.

The few species of Hypholoma which I have tested have been palatable, and one or two are of very delicate flavor.

Plate VIII.

PLATE VIII.

Ag. (Hypholoma) sublateritius Schaeff. *"Red Tuft."* (**Hypholoma sublateritium**) *"The Brick Top."*

EDIBLE.

The cap of this species is fleshy and obtuse, convexo-plane, sometimes showing a superficial whitish cloudiness upon the margin coming from the veil, which soon disappears, leaving it smooth and dry; color tawny brick red, with pale straw margin; flesh compact and whitish, turning yellow when wilted. Stem stuffed and fibrillose, tapering downward. Near its attachment to the cap the color is very light yellow; lower down and towards the root it is covered with patches and lines of burnt sienna color. It bears no distinct ring. In very young plants the filmy veil is sometimes perceived, reaching from the margin of the cap to the stem. This disappears as the cap expands, sometimes leaving the stem obscurely annulate. Gills adnate in full-grown specimens, slightly decurrent, somewhat crowded, dingy white or cinereous, turning to dark olive, never yellow; in old or wilted specimens changing to a dark brown. In old specimens the cap is a reddish brown and the gills are sometimes stained with the purplish brown of the spores.

This is a very common species and very abundant in pine and oak woods. I have seen an oak stump in Prince George's County, Md., measuring from 3 to 4 feet in height, literally covered with mushrooms of this species. This mushroom has been recorded as suspicious by some writers, probably owing to its slightly bitter taste, but I have thoroughly tested its edible qualities, both uncooked and prepared in various ways for the table, using the caps only. It keeps well when dried, and when ground into powder, with the addition of boiling water and a little pepper and salt, makes a very pleasant and nutritious beverage. It is most abundant in the early autumn, and is gathered in this latitude well into the winter, even when the snow is on the ground.

Our American plant is less heavy and more graceful in aspect than the same species in England, as figured in English works, but the general characteristics are the same.

Ag. (Hypholoma) *fascicularis* Hudson, recorded as deleterious, is figured in "Cooke's Illustrations."

Dr. Berkeley thus distinguishes these two species from each other. Cap of *sublateritius* is obtuse, discoid; that of *fascicularis*, subumbonate. Flesh of the former, compact, dingy-white; that of the latter, yellow. Stem in *sublateritius* is "stuffed," attenuated downwards, ferruginous; stem of *fascicularis* hollow, thin, flexuose. The gills in both species are adnate, crowded; but in *fascicularis* they are also linear and deliquescent, and are *yellow* in color.

NOTE.—In the Friesian arrangement of the genera of the order Agaricini, which is adopted by M. C. Cooke, Hypholoma finds place as a subgenus of the genus Agaricus, spore series Pratelli. Saccardo in his Sylloge elevates Hypholoma to the rank of a separate genus and places it in his spore series Melanosporæ.

EDIBLE

Agaricus (Hypholoma) *Candollianus*, Fries., variety *incertus* Peck
Figured from specimens collected in the District of Columbia
T. Taylor, del.

PLATE IX.

Agaricus (Hypholoma) incertus Peck. (*Hypholoma incertum.*)

EDIBLE.

Cap fleshy but fragile, smooth and hygrophanous, moist; at first convex, then expanding; color creamy white. Gills adnate, narrow, crowded, whitish in young specimens, turning to a pinkish dun color, later to a rosy cinnamon, sometimes showing when mature a slightly purplish tint. Stem smooth, slender, long and hollow, with slight striations near the apex, white. Specimens occur in which the stem is obscurely annulate arising from the attachment to it of fragments of the veil, but usually it is ringless.

The typical species of Hypholoma have the fleshy part of the cap confluent with the stem, but in H. *incertum* the stem is not confluent and is easily separated from the cap as in the Lepiotas. This mushroom was first recorded by Peck in his early reports as the variety "*incertus*" of the species Agaricus (Hypholoma) Candollianus, but has since been recorded by Saccardo as a distinct species, Hypholoma incertum.

Two species of Hypholoma have the same habit and sufficiently resemble *incertum* to be taken for it, if not carefully examined as to points of difference. These are H. *Candollianum,* named in honor of A. De Candolle, and H. *appendiculatum.* In the first named of these two species the cap is whitish, the gills at first violet in color, changing to dark cinnamon brown. In H. appendiculatum the pileus is rugose when dry, and sprinkled with atoms. It is darker in color than that of H. incertum; Cooke says tawny or pale ochre; Massee says bay, then tawny. The gills are sub-adnate, in color resembling those of H. incertum; stem slender, smooth, and white.

From the foregoing it will be seen that H. *incertum* agrees more nearly with H. *Candollianum* in the color of the cap, but more nearly with H. *appendiculatum* in the color of the gills. Saccardo recognizes the three as "distinct species of the *genus Hypholoma.*" As all are edible, the slight differences observed are interesting chiefly to the mycologist. The mycophagist will find them equally valuable from a gastronomic point of view. In taste they resemble the common mushroom. They are more fragile, however, and require less cooking than the cultivated mushroom. Broiled on toast or cooked for ten minutes in a chafing dish, they make a very acceptable addition to the lunch menu.

The specimens figured in Plate IX were selected from a crop of thirty or more growing in the author's garden, in very rich soil at the base of a plum-tree stump. For several seasons past small crops have been gathered from the same spot, as well as around the base of a flourishing peach tree. Quantities of all three species have been gathered in the short grass of the Capitol grounds for a number of seasons, and in the various parks of the District of Columbia. Specimens have been received from western New York and Massachusetts. Those growing upon soil very heavily fertilized are apt to be somewhat stouter and shorter stemmed than those coming up through the short grass in the parks.

ANALYTICAL TABLE.

The following compendious analytical table showing prominent characteristics of the leading genera and subgenera of the order Agaricini, according to Fries, Worthington Smith, and other botanists, which appears in Cooke's Hand Book, revised edition, will be found helpful to the collector in determining the genus to which a specimen may belong.

ORDER AGARICINI

I. Spores white or very slightly tinted—Leucospori
  1. Plant fleshy, more or less firm, putrescent (neither deliquescent nor coriaceous)
    2. Hymenophore free
      3. Pileus bearing warts or patches free from the cuticle (volvate) *Amanita*
      3. Pileus scaly, scales concrete with the cuticle (not volvate) *Lepiota*
    2. Hymenophore confluent
      4. Without cartilaginous bark
        5. Stem central
          6. With a ring *Armillaria*
          6. Ringless
            7. Gills sinuate *Tricholoma*
            7. Gills decurrent
              8. Edge acute *Clitocybe*
              8. Edge swollen obtuse CANTHARELLUS
            7. Gills adnate
              9. Parasitic on other Agarics NYCTALIS
              9. Not parasitic
                10. Milky LACTARIUS
                10. Not milky
                  11. Rigid and brittle RUSSULA
                  11. Waxy HYGROPHORUS
        5. Stem lateral or absent *Pleurotus*
      4. With cartilaginous bark
        12. Gills adnate *Collybia*

12. Gills sinuate *Mycena*
12. Gills decurrent *Omphalia*
1. Plant tough, coriaceous or woody
13. Stem central.
14. Gills simple MARASMIUS
14. Gills branched XEROTUS
13. Stem lateral or wanting
15. Gills toothed LENTINUS
15. Gills not toothed PANUS
15. Gills channelled longitudinally or crisped TROGIA
15. Gills splitting longitudinally SCHIZOPHYLLUM
15. Gills anastomosing LENZITES
I. Spores rosy or salmon color—Hyporhodii
16. Without cartilaginous bark
17. Hymenophore free
18. With a volva *Volvaria*
18. Without a volva
19. With a ring *Annularia*
19. Ringless *Pluteus*
17. Hymenophore confluent, not free
20. Stem central
21. Gills adnate or sinuate *Entoloma*
21. Gills decurrent *Clitopilus*
20. Stem lateral or absent *Claudopus*
16. With cartilaginous bark
22. Gills decurrent *Eccilia*
22. Gills not decurrent
23. Pileus torn into scales *Leptonia*
23. Pileus papillose, sub-campanulate.
24. Gills membranaceous, persistent *Nolanea*
24. Gills sub-deliquescent BOLBITIUS
I. Spores brownish, sometimes rusty, reddish or yellowish brown.—Dermini.
25. Without cartilaginous bark.
26. Stem central.
27. With a ring.
28. Ring continuous *Pholiota*
28. Ring arachnoid, like a spider's web filamentous or evanescent.

29. Gills adnate terrestrial
CORTINARIUS
29. Gills decurrent, or acutely adnate,
mostly epiphytal, *Flammula*
27. Without a ring.
30. With rudimentary volva
Acetabularia
30. Without a volva.
31. Gills adhering to the
hymenophore, and sinuate.
32. Cuticle fibrillose or silky
Inocybe
32. Cuticle smooth viscid
Hebeloma
31. Gills separating from the
hymenophore, and decurrent,
PAXILLUS
26. Stem lateral or absent *Crepidotus*
25. With cartilaginous bark.
33. Gills decurrent *Tubaria*
33. Gills not decurrent.
34. Margin of pileus at first incurved
Naucoria
34. Margin of pileus always straight.
35. Hymenophore free *Pluteolus*
35. Hymenophore confluent *Galera*
. Spores purple, sometimes brownish purple, dark
purple, or dark brown.—Pratellæ.
36. Without cartilaginous bark.
37. Hymenophore free.
38. With a volva *Chitonia*
38. Without a volva *Psalliota*
37. Hymenophore confluent.
39. Veil normally ring shaped on the stem
Stropharia
39. Veil normally adhering to the margin
of the pileus *Hypholoma*
36. With cartilaginous bark.
40. Gills decurrent *Deconica*
40. Gills not decurrent.
41. Margin of pileus at first incurved
Psilocybe

41. Margin of pileus at first straight
Psathyra
. Spores black or nearly so.—Coprinarii.
42. Gills deliquescent COPRINUS
42. Gills not deliquescent.
43. Gills decurrent GOMPHIDIUS
43. Gills not decurrent.
44. Pileus striate *Psathyrella*
44. Pileus not striate *Panæolus*

In the Friesian classification which, with modifications, has prevailed for many years among mycologists, the *genus Agaricus* included in its *subgenera* the greater part of the species of the order *Agaricini*. The subgenera, printed in the above table in italics, were included in this genus. The genera are printed in capitals. In the Saccardian system, all the *subgenera* of *Agaricus* having been elevated to *generic* rank, the term Agaricus is limited to a very small group which includes the *subgenus Psalliota* of Fries, the species being characterized by fleshy caps, free gills, ringed stem, and dark brown or purplish brown spores. As restricted, it naturally falls into the spore series *Melanosporeæ*.

In the white-spored section, Leucospori, the recorded edible species occur in the following genera: Marasmius, Cantharellus, Lactarius, Russula, Hygrophorus, Collybia, Pleurotus, Clitocybe, Tricholoma, Armillaria, Lepiota, and Amanita. The plants of Marasmius are usually thin and dry, reviving with moisture. Cantharellus is characterized by the obtuseness of the edges of the lamellæ, Lactarius by the copious milky or sticky fluid which exudes from the plants when cut or bruised. Russula is closely allied to Lactarius, and the plants bear some resemblance in external appearance to those of that genus, but they are never milky, and the gills are usually rigid and brittle. In Hygrophorus the plants are moist, not very large, often bright colored, and the gills have a waxy appearance. The Collybias are usually cæspitose, the stems exteriorly cartilaginous, in some species swelling and splitting open in the centre.

In Pleurotus the stem is lateral or absent. The plants are epiphytal, usually springing from the decaying bark of trees and old stumps.

In Clitocybe the plants are characterized by a deeply depressed, often narrow cap, with the gills acutely adnate, or running far down the stem, which is elastic, with a fibrous outer coat covered with minute fibers. Many of the species have a fragrant odor. The Tricholomas are stout and fleshy, somewhat resembling the Russulas, but distinguished from them by the sinuate character of the gills, which show a slight notched or toothed depression just before reaching the stem (represented in Fig. 4, Plate IV). Typical species of Armillaria show a well-defined ring and scales upon the stem, the remains of the partial veil, and the plants are usually large, and cæspitose. The Lepiotas are recognized by the soft, thready character of the fleshy portion of the cap, and the fringed scales formed by the breaking of the cuticle. The ease with which the ringed stem is removed from its socket in the cap is another characteristic which distinguishes the plants from those of other genera.

The Amanitas are distinguished by the volva, which sheathes the somewhat bulbous stem at its base and the ring and veil which in the young plant are very distinct features, the whole plant in embryo being enveloped in the volva.

The Amanita group, besides containing some very good edible species, is also credited with containing the most dangerous species of all the mushroom family, and some which are undoubtedly fatal in their effects.[A]

[A] A more detailed description of this group will appear in No. 5 of this series.

The Nyctali are minute mushrooms parasitic on other mushrooms.

In Omphalia, the plants are quite small, with membranaceous caps, gills truly decurrent, and cartilaginous stems.

The Myceneæ are generally very small, slender, and fragile, usually cæspitose, with bell-shaped caps, sinuate gills, not decurrent, and cartilaginous stems. In some species the plants exude a milky juice.

In the genera Panus, Lentinus, Lenzites, Schizophyllum, Xerotus, and Trogia, the plants are leathery or coriaceous, dry and tough, and though none are recorded as poisonous, they are too tough to be edible.

The mushrooms having pink or salmon colored spores, section Rhodosporii, form the smallest of the four primary groups of Agaricini, the number of known species not exceeding 400, and most of these are tasteless, or of disagreeable odor, while some are recorded as unwholesome.

The species are pink-gilled when mature, though often white or whitish when very young.

The recorded edible species are found in Volvaria, Clitopilus, and Pluteus. The Volvariæ are characterized by the very large and perfect volva which wraps the base of the stem in loose folds, the ringless stem, and the pink, soft, liquescent gills, which are free and rounded behind. The cap is not warted; in some species it is viscid, and in *bombycinus*, recorded by several authors as edible, and by some as doubtful, it is covered with a silky down.

In Clitopilus the odor of the edible species is more or less mealy. The cap is fleshy, and the margin at first involute. Two edible species which closely resemble each other—viz., Clitopilus *prunulus*, "Plum mushroom," and Clitopilus *orcella*, "Sweetbread mushroom,"—are highly recommended for their delicacy of flavor.

In Leptonia most of the species are small, thin, and brittle, corresponding with Mycena in the white-spored series, and with Psathyra and Psathyrella in the dark-spored series.

Eccilia corresponds with Omphalia. Claudopus corresponds with Pleurotus in its habit of growth and lateral stem, differing in the color of the spores.

Annularia includes only a few small species having a ringed stem, no volva, and free pink gills. Cooke says of this subgenus that no British species are known.

The recorded species of Pluteus have their habitat on tree stumps, sawdust, or upon fallen timber. One species, Pluteus *cervinus*, is recorded as edible, but not specially commended. Of Entoloma, Worthington Smith says, "It is allied to Tricholoma, though most of the species are thinner and often brittle. It agrees also in structure with Hebeloma and Hypholoma." None of the species are recorded as having value as esculents.

The genus Bolbitius is described by Cooke as a small genus intermediate between Agaricus and Coprinus on the one side, and Coprinus and Cortinarius on the other. The species are small and ephemeral. Saccardo places Bolbitius in his division Melanosporæ, although the spores are ochraceous.

In the section Pratelli Psalliota and Hypholoma contain mushrooms which are of exceptionally fine flavor. In the first of these is found the common field mushroom Agaricus campester and its allies.

The black-spored section Coprinarii contains two genera which include a few recorded edible species, viz., Coprinus and Gomphidius. The Psathyrellas correspond in size to the Mycenas in the white-spored series and to the Psathyras in the purple-spored section; the gills are free or adnate and turn black when mature. None of the species are edible.

In Paneolus the plants are somewhat viscid when moist, the gills are described as "clouded, never becoming purple or brown." They are usually found on manure heaps near cities. None are edible.

Saccardo in his Sylloge combines the Pratellæ and Coprinarii, making of them one section which he calls *Melanosporeæ*.

G. Massee, the British mycologist, makes of the black-spored and the purple and purplish-brown spored series two divisions, calling them, respectively, *Porphyrosporeæ* and *Melanosporeæ*.

The recorded edible species of the spore section Dermini are found in Pholiota, Cortinarius, and Paxillus. The larger proportion of the Pholiotas grow upon tree stumps. They have a fugacious, persistent friable ring, and are liable to be confused with the Cortinarii, unless attention is paid to the spidery veil and the iron-rust tint of the spores of the latter. Only a few of the species are recorded as edible, but none are known to be poisonous. Cortinarius is a large genus. It contains a larger proportion of edible species than Pholiota, and none are recorded as poisonous. The cobweb-like veil which extends from stem to margin of cap in the young species, and the rust-colored spores which dust the gills as the species mature, distinguish the genus from all others.

A characteristic feature of Paxillus, and one which makes it easily distinguishable from others of the same group, is the ease with which the gills as a whole can be separated from the substance or fleshy portion of the cap. There is an exception to this in the species Paxillus involutus, recorded by Peck as edible.

POLYPOREI.

Hymenium lining the cavity of tubes or pores which are sometimes broken up into teeth or concentric plates.—Berkeley's Outlines.

The plants of this second primary group or order of the family Hymenomycetes exhibit a greater dissimilarity of form and texture than do those of the Agaricini. Some of its genera consist almost wholly of coriaceous or woody plants. A few contain fleshy ones. Some of the species have a distinct stem, while others are stemless. With regard to the receptacle in the plants of the genera *Boletus*, *Strobilomyces*, etc., it forms a perfect cap, like that of the common Agaric, a cushion of tubes taking the place of gills on the under surface of the cap, the hymenium in this case lining the inner surface of the tubes from which the spores drop when mature.

In some species, such as those of the genus Poria, the receptacle is reduced to a single thin fibrous stratum, adhering closely to the matrix and exposing a surface of crowded pores, and in others it consists of fibrous strata formed in concentric layers.

A number of groups, each of which was treated in the original Friesian classification as a single genus, have more recently been recognized as comprising several distinct genera. In the Saccardian system the genera Trametes, Dædalea, Merulius, Porothelium, and Fistulina still retain the generic rank assigned to them by Fries, but the old genus Boletus is subdivided into four genera, Boletus, Strobilomyces, Boletinus, and Gyrodon, while Polyporus, originally a very large genus, is subdivided into the genera Polyporus, Fomes, Polystictus, and Poria. This arrangement was in part suggested by Fries in his later works, and is accepted by M. C. Cooke, as indicated in his latest work on fungi.

Quoting M. C. Cooke, "*Strobilomyces* is *Boletus* with a rough warty and scaly pileus; *Boletinus* is *Boletus* with short, large radiating pores; and *Gyrodon* is *Boletus* with elongated sinuate irregular pores, all fleshy, firm fungi of robust habit, possessing stem and cap." The species of the genus Polyporus as now restricted are somewhat fleshy in the young stage, shrinking as they mature and dry, and becoming indurated with age. In Fomes the species, of woody consistency from the first, have no room for shrinkage, and are quite rigid; the tubes being in strata, and the strata growing yearly, the species are virtually perennial. The pileus of the plant shows a rigid polished crust resulting from resinous exudations.

In Polystictus the plants are usually small, thin, tough, and irregular in outline, the tubes exceedingly short, with thin walls, which easily split up, giving the pores at times a toothed or fringed appearance. The surface is velvety, or hairy, and zoned in varying colors. They are very common upon decaying tree stumps, often covering the surface of the stump in gaily colored layers. Not esculent.

Poria is composed of resupinate species with the pores normally in a single series, the whole stratum spread over, and adhering to the matrix. The species are coriaceous or woody. Not esculent.

The plants of the genus Trametes allied to Fomes are epiphytal, with the trama the same in substance and color as the hymenophore. The tubes do not form in regular strata, but are sunk into the substance of the pileus. The plants are coriaceous, and none are edible.

Dædalea closely resembles *Trametes* with the tubes forming deep labyrinthiform depressions. Whole plant woody, sessile.

Hexagonia, allied by its characteristics to Polystictus, has large hexagonal pores, with firm, entire dissepiments.

In Favolus the plants are slightly fleshy and substipitate with the pores angular, and radiating from the stem. Not edible.

The species of the genus Laschia are recognized by the shallow irregular pores and the vein like character of their dissepiments (or pore walls). Substance slightly gelatinous.

In the plants of Porothelium, irregular papillæ take the place of tubes, and the plants are sub-membranaceous and resupinate, having the habit of those of Poria.

The genus Merulius has been termed the lowest and most imperfect of the genera of Polyporei. It presents a soft, waxy spore-bearing surface, reticulated with obtuse folds. Solenia, by early authors placed in Discomycetes, thence transferred to Auricularini, and by some authors associated with Cyphella in Theleporei, now finds place as one of the genera of Polyporei as given by Saccardo.

The above-mentioned genera, together with Myriadoporus, Ceriomyces, Bresadolia, Theleporus, Glœporus, and Cyclomyces, constitute the Polyporeæ of the Saccardian system.

Myriadoporus is a North American genus. It is a form of the genus Polyporus, but with pores in the *interior* as well as on the *exterior* surface. *Ceriomyces* is generally regarded as a spurious genus. It is similar to *Myriadoporus*, but with internal pores and only spurious pores externally. Of *Bresadolia* Cooke says "there is only one described species, and of this only one specimen has been found." *Theleporus* is an African genus of which only one species is known. *Glœporus* is a form of resupinate Polyporus, except that the hymenium or pore-bearing surface is gelatinous instead of being firm. *Cyclomyces* is a genus with some features of Lenzites; it is leathery. All of these are more or less coriaceous. None are edible. *Campbellia* is a new genus. It is *Merulius* with a pileus and central stem.

The edible Polyporeæ are found in the genera Boletus, Strobilomyces, Gyrodon, Boletinus, Polyporus, and Fistulina. Of these, the first four genera contain most of the edible species as well as a few which have been regarded as unwholesome or poisonous.

In the genus Polyporus as now restricted, the species Polyporus *sulphureus* Fries is perhaps the one most likely to be selected for table use, the others becoming very quickly indurated or tough, and this should be gathered when very young, as in maturity it loses its fleshy consistency and becomes dry and tough. It is common on old tree stumps and is often found on the dead wood of living trees, the bright yellow and vivid orange red tints which characterize the young plant making it very conspicuous.

It is easily recognized by its irregular, closely overlapping frond-like caps, white flesh, and the very small sulphur-yellow tubes. The spores are white, elliptical. The flesh of young specimens is somewhat juicy.

The geographical distribution is wide, and in places where a moist, warm temperature prevails plants of this species often attain very large proportions, sometimes completely encircling the trunk of a tree at its base. The bright colors fade as the plant matures, and the plant becomes indurated and friable, when very old crumbling readily in the hands.

To prepare for the table, very thin slices of young specimens should be cut and either allowed to slowly simmer on the back of the range, or soaked in milk and then fried in butter.

Of the genus Fistulina but one species, Fistulina hepatica, figured in Plate X, is recorded as edible and indigenous to this country.

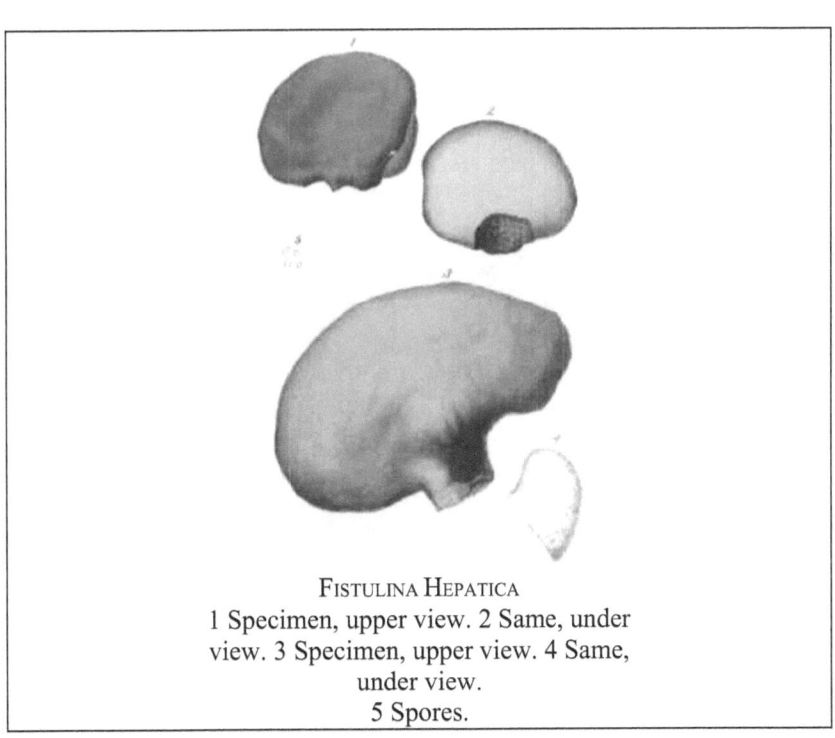

FISTULINA HEPATICA
1 Specimen, upper view. 2 Same, under
view. 3 Specimen, upper view. 4 Same,
under view.
5 Spores.

PLATE X.

Fistulina hepatica Bull. *"Beefsteak Mushroom,"* *"Liver Fungus."*

Genus Fistulina Bull. Hymenophore fleshy, hymenium inferior, that is, on the under surface of the cap, at first papillose; the papillæ at length elongated, and forming distinct tubes.

Besides Fistulina *hepatica*, five species of this genus are recorded in Saccardo's Sylloge, viz., F. *radicata* Schw., F. *spathulata* B. & C., F. *pallida* B. & R., F. *rosea* Mont., and F. *antarctica* Speg.; the last indigenous to Patagonia.

F. *hepatica* is the only species with which I am familiar. The plants of this species are very irregular in form, rootless, epiphytal, often stemless, and sometimes attached to the matrix by a very short stem. This fungus is frequently found upon old oak, chestnut, and ash trees, developing in the rotting bark. It appears first as a rosy pimple, or in a series of red granules. In a very short time it becomes tongue-shaped, sometimes kidney shaped, assuming the color of a beet root. As it increases in size it changes form again, becoming broad in proportion to its length, and changing in color to a deep blood red, and finally to a dull liver tint. Its lower surface is often paler than its upper, it being tinged with yellow and pinkish hues.

One author states that it requires about two weeks to attain its highest development, after which it gradually decays.

It varies in size from a few inches to several feet in circumference. Rev. M. J. Berkeley mentions one which weighed thirty pounds. It has been styled, the *"poor man's fungus,"* and in flavor resembles meat more than any other.

The substance is fleshy and juicy in the early stage. The pileus is papillose, the papillæ elongated, and forming distinct tubes as the pileus expands. These tubes are separable from each other, and with age become approximate and jagged at their orifices. The tubes are at first yellowish, with a pink tinge, becoming dingy with age. The fleshy substance, or hymenophore, is often veined in light and dark red streaks. The juice is pellucid, red, and slightly acid. Spores at first nearly round, becoming elliptical, salmon color.

This fungus is esteemed in Europe, where it is eaten prepared in a variety of ways.

When young and tender it can be sliced and broiled or minced and stewed, making a delicious dish. When too old the stock is rather tough for good eating, but the gravy taken from it forms a rich flavoring for a vegetable stew or a meat ragout. The following recipe for cooking this mushroom has been recommended:

Slice and macerate it, add pepper and salt, a little lemon, and chopped onions or garlic; then strain and boil the liquid, which makes most excellent gravy, resembling that of good beefsteak.

The Fistulina hepatica is well known in Europe, and is found in different parts of the United States, in some places growing abundantly. I have gathered some fine specimens in Maryland and Virginia, but none as large as that described by Dr. Berkeley.

RECIPES FOR COOKING MUSHROOMS.

To Pot Mushrooms.—The small open mushrooms suit best for potting. Trim and rub them; put into a stewpan a quart of mushrooms, 3 ounces of butter, 2 teaspoonfuls of salt, and half a teaspoonful of cayenne and mace, mixed, and stew for ten or fifteen minutes, or till the mushrooms are tender; take them carefully out and drain them perfectly on a sloping dish, and when cold press them into small pots and pour clarified butter over them, in which state they will keep for a week or two. Writing-paper placed over the butter, and over that melted suet, will effectually preserve them for weeks in a dry, cool place.

To Pickle Mushrooms.—Select a number of sound, small pasture mushrooms, as nearly alike as possible in size. Throw them for a few minutes into cold water, then drain them, cut off the stalks, and gently rub off the outer skin with a moist flannel dipped in salt; then boil the vinegar, adding to each quart two ounces of salt, half a nutmeg grated, a dram of mace, and an ounce of white pepper corns. Put the mushrooms into the vinegar for ten minutes over the fire; then pour the whole into small jars, taking care that the spices are equally divided; let them stand a day, then cover them.

Baked Mushrooms.—Peel the tops of twenty mushrooms; cut off a portion of the stalks and wipe them carefully with a piece of flannel dipped in salt. Lay the mushrooms in a tin dish, put a small piece of butter on the top of each, and season with pepper and salt. Set the dish in the oven and bake them from twenty minutes to half an hour. When done, arrange them high in the centre of a very hot dish, pour the sauce around them, and serve quickly and as hot as you possibly can.

Mushrooms with Bacon.—Take some full-grown mushrooms, and, having cleaned them, procure a few rashers of nice streaky bacon and fry them in the usual manner. When nearly done add a dozen or so of mushrooms and fry them slowly until they are cooked. In this process they will absorb all the fat of the bacon, and with the addition of a little salt and pepper will form a most appetizing breakfast relish.

Mushroom Pie.—A very good mushroom pie is made in the following manner: Chop a quart of mushrooms into small pieces, season to taste, and add one pound of round steak chopped fine and seasoned with a small piece of onion. If the steak is lean, add a small piece of suet, unless butter is preferred to give flavor. Put the chopped steak and mushrooms in deep saucepan with cover, and stew slowly until tender. Make a crust as for beefsteak pie and put in a deep earthern dish, lightly browning the under crust before adding the stew, and cover with a crust lightly punctured.

In some parts of Russia mushrooms form an important part of the diet of the people, especially during the Lenten season, when the fast of the Greek church is very strictly kept, and meat, fish, eggs, and butter are forbidden.

Provision is made for this season in the securing of quantities of dried and salted mushrooms, which are cut up in strips and made into salads with a dressing of olive oil and vinegar. The poorer classes to whom the olive oil is unattainable use the rape seed and other vegetable oils in the cooking of their mushrooms.

The following recipes are translated from a recently published Russian work on the subject of mushrooms, cultivated and wild:

Select fresh, sound Boleti, cut off the caps, and, after wiping clean with a napkin, place them in a sieve, pouring over them scalding water; when thoroughly drained, leave them where there is a free current of air until perfectly dry. Next string them upon stout twine, leaving spaces between to allow of free circulation of air. If convenient, they can be dried artificially by placing in a not too hot oven with the door open. Dried by either method, they can be kept all winter. Before using, they should be soaked in water or milk until soft. In this condition they make very good flavoring for soup or gravy, and can also be used as filling for pies.

Mushrooms Cooked in Butter.—Wipe the mushrooms clean and dip in dry flour. Heat a quantity of butter to boiling temperature in a saucepan, seasoning with a small piece of onion. Drop the flour-covered mushrooms into the boiling butter, shaking the pan constantly over the fire. When the mushrooms are cooked add sour cream to taste. Before serving, sprinkle with grated muscat nut.

Mushroom Pickle.—Select only young button mushrooms. Put them for a few moments in boiling water lightly salted and vinegared. Boil vinegar (only the best should be used), spicing it according to taste. Allow the vinegar to cool. Put the mushrooms in layers in a jar and pour over them enough spiced vinegar to cover. Seal tightly.

Salted Piperites.—Only the caps are taken of the Lactarius piperites. They are placed first in salted scalding water for several minutes. The water is then gently pressed out with a napkin, the mushrooms are placed on sieves and cold water poured over them. They are then placed in layers in a jar, each layer sprinkled with salt, and whole pepper and minced onion scattered over the layer. When the jar is full a thin round board is placed upon the top layer and pressed down with weights, and as the mass gives way mushrooms are added until the jar is compactly filled. The jar is then covered with parchment or otherwise tightly sealed. Eight gallons of mushrooms require from one to one and a half glasses of salt. This makes a good salad when treated with oil.

NOTE.—L. piperites is an extremely acrid mushroom when in the raw state, and the Russians do not stew it, but prepare it in the above way, taking the precaution to scald thoroughly with salted water before putting away. The precaution of scalding through several waters is a wise one to use in the preparation of all mushrooms inasmuch as the poisonous principle of most mushrooms is soluble in scalding water. Dilute vinegar is frequently used in the same manner. Vinegar should not be used in metal vessels unless porcelain-lined.

LIST OF THE GENERA OF HYMENOMYCETES.

The following list of the genera of Hymenomycetes, summarized from Kellerman's Synopsis of Saccardo's Sylloge Fungorum, will be found useful for reference:

I. AGARICACEÆ.
  Leucosporeæ. (Spores white or slightly tinted yellowish.)
  GENERA.
    Amanita Pers.
    Amanitopsis Roze.
    Lepiota Fries.

Schulzeria Bres.
Armillaria Fries.
Tricholoma Fries.
Clitocybe Fries.
Collybia Fries.
Mycena Fries.
Hiatula Fries.
Omphalia Fries.
Pleurotus Fries.
Hygrophorus Fries.
Lactarius Fries.
Russula Pers.
Cantharellus Adans.
Arrhenia Fries.
Nyctalis Fries.
Stylobates Fries.
Marasmius Fries.
Heliomyces Lev.
Lentinus Fries.
Panus Fries.
Xerotus Fries.
Trogia Fries.
Lenzites Fries.
Tilotus Kalch.
Hymenogramme B. & Mont.
Oudemansiella Speg.
Pterophyllus Lev.
Rachophyllus Berk.
Schizophyllum Fries.

Rhodosporæ (spores pink or salmon color), corresponding to the Hyporhodii of Fries.
GENERA.
Volvaria Fr.
Annularia Schulz.
Pluteus Fries.
Entoloma Fries.
Clitopilus Fries.
Leptonia Fries.
Nolanea Fries.
Eccilia Fries.
Claudopus Worth. Smith.

Ochrosporæ (spores tawny ochraceous, or light rusty tint of brown),

corresponding to the Dermini of Fries.
GENERA.

> Pholiota Fries.
> Locillina Gill.
> Inocybe Fries.
> Hebeloma Fries.
> Flammula Fries.
> Naucoria Fries.
> Pluteolus Fries.
> Galera Fries.
> Tubaria Worth. Smith.
> Crepidotus Fries.
> Cortinarius Fries.
> Paxillus Fries.

Melanosporæ (spores black, dark-brown or purplish-brown), combining the attributes of both the Coprinarii and the Pratelli of Fries.
GENERA.

> Chitonia Fries.
> Agaricus Linn.
> Pilosace Fries.
> Stropharia Fries.
> Hypholoma Fries.
> Psilocybe Fries.
> Deconica Worth. Smith.
> Psathyra Fries.
> Bolbitius Fries.
> Coprinus Pers.
> Panæolus Fries.
> Annellaria Karsh.
> Psathyrella Fries.
> Gomphidius Fries.
> Anthracophyllum Ces.
> Montagnites Fries.

II. POLYPORACEÆ (Polyporei).
GENERA.

> Boletus Dill.
> Strobilomyces Berkeley.
> Boletinus Kalchbr.
> Gyrodon Opatowski.
> Fistulina Bull.
> Polyporus Mich.

Fomes Fries.
Polystictus Fries.
Poria Pers.
Trametes Fries.
Hexagonia Fries.
Dædalea Pers.
Myriadoporus Peck.
Ceriomyces Corda.
Bresadolia Speg.
Cyclomyces Kunz.
Favolus Fries.
Glœoporus Mont.
Laschia Fries.
Merulius Hall.
Theleporus Fries.
Porothelium Fries.
Solenia Hoffm.

III. HYDNACEÆ (Hydnei).
GENERA.
Hydnum Linn.
Caldesiella Lace.
Hericium Pers.
Tremellodon Pers.
Sistotrema Pers.
Irpex Fries.
Radulum Fries.
Plebia Fries.
Lopharia K. & M. Ow.
Grandinia Fries.
Grammothele B. & C.
Odontia Pers.
Kneiffia Fries.
Mucronella Fries.

IV. THELEPHORACEÆ (Thelephorei).
GENERA.
Craterellus Fries.
Hypolyssus Pers.
Thelephora Ehrh.
Cladoderris Pers.
Beccariella Ces.
Stereum Pers.
Hymenochæte Lev.

Skepperia Berk.
Corticium Fries.
Peniophora Cooke.
Coniophora D. C.
Michenera B. & C.
Matula Mass.
Hypochnus Fries.
Exobasidium Weron.
Helicobasidium Pat.
Cyphella Fries.
Friesula Speg.
Cora Fries.
Rhipidonema Matt.

V. CLAVARIACEÆ (Clavariei).
GENERA.
Sparassis Fries.
Acartis Fries.
Clavaria Vaill.
Calocera Fries.
Lachnocladium Lev.
Pterula Fries.
Ptifula Pers.
Pistallaria Fries.
Physalacria Peck.

VI. TREMELLACEÆ (Tremellini)
GENERA.
Auricularia Bull.
Hirneola Fries.
Platyglœa Schroet.
Exidia Fries.
Ulocolla Bref.
Craterocolla Bref.
Femsjonia Fries.
Tremella Dill.
Næmatelia Fries.
Gyrocephalus Pers.
Delortia Pat. & Gail.
Arrhytidia Berk.
Ceracea Cragin.
Guepinia Fries.
Dacryomitra Pul.
Collyria Fries.

GENERA MINUS CERTA.
Hormonyces Bon.
Ditiola Fries.
Apyrenium Fries.

BREFIELD'S CLASSIFICATION OF FUNGI.

A system of classification of fungi which is receiving attention from mycologists is that recently presented by the distinguished German author Dr. Oscar Brefield. Dr. Brefield's exhaustive investigations into the life-history of fungi in general have been such as to entitle his views to consideration, although the system presents some inconsistencies which may prevent its adoption in its entirety.

According to the Brefield system, as summarized by his colleague Dr. Von Tavel, Fungi are divided into two primary classes: (1) the *Phycomycetes,* or lower fungi nearest like the algæ, *consisting of a one-celled thallus with sexual as well as non-sexual modes of reproduction*, and (2) the Mesomycetes and the Mycomycetes, *having a divided or many celled thallus, propagated by non-sexually formed spores*. The Phycomycetes are further divided into two large sections, based on their methods of reproduction, termed, respectively, Zygomycetes and Oomycetes. These include the old typical Mucors, the Peronosporeæ or "rotting moulds," once classed with the Hyphomycetes, the Saprolegniaceæ, "Fish Moulds," of aquatic habit, the Entomophthoraceæ, "Insect Moulds," together with some minor groups. The Mesomycetes connect the Phycomycetes with the Mycomycetes. The class Mycomycetes is primarily divided into two sections, viz., Ascomycetes and Basidiomycetes, with the Ustilagineæ, "Smut Fungi," in Mesomycetes, forming a transitional group between Phycomycetes and the Basidiomycetal group of the higher fungi.

The Ascomycetes are primarily subdivided into *Exoasci* and *Carpoasci,* groups based on the character of the asci. In the first, *Exoasci,* the asci are naked and borne directly on the mycelium; in the second, *Carpoasci,* they are enclosed in a wrapper composed of fertile hyphæ and sterile threads, having also accessory fruit forms. The first includes Endomycetes and Taphrineæ. In the second are included the groups Gymnoasci, Perisporaceæ, Pyrenomycetes,

Hysteriaceæ, Discomycetes, and Helvellaceæ.

The Basidiomycetes characterized by the possession of basidia are arranged in two groups, based on the character of the basidia: (1) the Protobasidiomycetes, in which the basidia are septate, divided, and (2) the Autobasidiomycetes, in which the basidia are not divided, and bear a definite number of spores.

The first of these (Protobasidiomycetes) includes the following distinct groups: (1) the Uredineæ, "Rust Fungi," which have horizontally divided basidia, always free, never enclosed; (2) the Auricularieæ, having basidia somewhat resembling those of the Uredineæ, but which are borne in fruit bodies with open hymenia; (3) Pileacreæ, having horizontal septate basidia in closed receptacles; and (4) Tremellineæ, having vertically divided basidia borne in gymnocarpous receptacles—that is, those in which the hymenium is exposed while the spores are growing.

The Autobasidiomycetes are characterized by undivided basidia, bearing spores only at the apex. This group is subdivided into three sections: (1) Dacryomycetes, which includes the lowest of the Tremelloid forms, with club-shaped basidia, nearly approaching the true Hymenomycetal type, together with several groups of minor import; (2) Gasteromycetes; and (3) Hymenomycetes, with Phalloideæ placed in the group as a subsection of Gasteromycetes.

The above can only be considered as a very brief abstract of the system of classification proposed by Dr. Brefield, but it will serve to give some idea of the principle on which the system is based, which is sufficient for our present purpose. Those who wish to study the system in detail will find it treated in a comprehensive manner in Dr. Von Tavel's summary as it appears in the *Vergleichende Morphologie der Pilze*, Jena, 1892.

CONIOMYCETES AND HYPHOMYCETES.

In the original classification of Fries two of the primary divisions of the sporiferous Fungi were termed, respectively, *Coniomycetes* and *Hyphomycetes*. This arrangement was accepted by Berkeley, the term *Coniomycetes* being applied to all fungi in which the naked spores, appearing like an impalpable dust, were the principal feature of the plant, and the term *Hyphomycetes* to fungi in which the threads or hyphæ bearing the spores were the most conspicuous feature.

Coniomycetes, as broadly interpreted by Berkeley and other mycologists of his day, included the Uredineæ or "rust fungi," the Ustilagines or "smut fungi," the Sphæropsideæ, and the Melanconieæ. This arrangement was very unsatisfactory on account of the distinctively different character of the methods of reproduction of the respective groups, and they have since been disassociated and by some authors ranked as distinct orders or families. Others combine Uredinei and Ustilaginei in one group under the name Hypodermei.

Familiar examples of Uredinei are seen in the rust of the Barberry leaf, etc., and of the Ustilaginei in the "smut" of corn and the "bunt" of wheat.

Some authors combine the Sphæropsideæ with the closely allied Melanconieæ. M. C. Cooke contends that the *Sphæropsideæ* should be considered apart from the *Melanconieæ,* on the fundamental basis that the former possess a distinct perithecium, while the latter do not.

The *Sphæropsideæ* as recently defined by Cooke are "Fungi *possessed of a perithecium, but without asci,* ... sporules or stylospores being produced internally at the apex of more or less distinct supporting hyphæ or pedicels, termed sporophores."

The Sphæropsideæ somewhat resemble the Pyrenomyceteæ in external characteristics, but differ from them in the absence of asci and paraphyses. Saccardo retains all the species in his Sylloge, but relegates them to an inferior position as imperfect fungi.

The group *Pyrenomycetes*, or *Sphæriacei*, as at first recognized by *Fries*, included not only the *Sphæriacei* and the *Perisporacei*, but also the *Sphæropsidei* and *Melanconiaceæ*. Later, when ascigerous fungi were separated from stylosporous fungi, this group was revised, the ascigerous species only being retained. As at present limited, the Pyrenomycetes are "*ascigerous* fungi having the fructification enclosed within a perithecium."

They constitute a very large group, the described species, according to Cooke's Census of Fungi, numbering not less than 10,500, or at least 1,000 more than all the recorded species of Hymenomycetes. The plants are microscopic in size, and grow upon vegetable or animal substances.

HYPHOMYCETES.

With regard to the Hyphomycetes, Cooke takes the ground that in their internal relations to each other, and their external relations to the remaining orders, the Hyphomycetes are undoubtedly a well-defined and natural group, and should have place as such in a systematic work. It is a large order, containing nearly 5,000 species, mostly parasitic on dead animals and vegetable matter. The spores, termed conidia, are free, as in Hymenomycetes. The species are microscopic in size, and the hyphæ are strongly developed. They have no hymenium and no true basidia, and are non-sexual in their reproduction.

The four primary sections are the Mucedineæ, or "white moulds;" the Dematieæ, or "black moulds;" the Stilbea, with the hyphæ or thread-like filaments pallid or brown, and densely cohering, and the Tubercul!arieæ, with the hyphæ densely compacted in wart-like pustules of somewhat gelatinous consistency.

The divisions called Melanconieæ, Sphæropsideæ, and Hyphomyceteæ are not recognized in the Brefield system of classification as distinct groups. Massee and Cooke, with other mycologists, take exception to this omission and its implication, in their discussion of the subject, giving consistent reasons for the retention of these groups in systematic works.

PHYCOMYCETES OR PHYSOMYCETES.

As originally defined by Berkeley, this group was composed chiefly of the old typical Mucors and their allies, and was then termed Physomycetes. In the newer system of classification its original definition has been extended so as to include a number of groups somewhat dissimilar in their habits and characteristics, but "united under the conserving bond of a dimorphic reproduction," and the name has been changed to Phycomycetes. As at present recognized "the Phycomycetes are characterized by a unicellular mycelium, often parasitic on plants or animals, sometimes saprophytic, developed in the air or in water. Reproduction sexual or asexual." As thus interpreted, Phycomycetes includes the Mucoracei; the Peronosporaceæ, or "rotting moulds;" the Cystopi, or "white rusts;" the Saprolegniaceæ, or "fish moulds;" the Entomophthoraceæ, or "insect moulds," together with a few minor groups of doubtful natural affinity.

BIBLIOGRAPHY.

Saccardo, P. A. "Sylloge Sphæropsidearum et Melanconiearum," in Sylloge Fungorum. Vol. iii. Imp. 8vo. Padua, 1884.

L. A. Crie. *Recherches sur les Pyrenomycetes inferieurs du group de Depazées.* 8vo. Paris, 1878.

J. C. Corda. *Icones Fungorum.* Fol. 6 vol. Prague, 1837-'54.

Bonorden. *Zur Kenntniss der Coniomyceten u. Cryptomyceten.* 4to. Halle, 1860.

M. C. Cooke. *The Hyphomycetous Fungi of the United States.* 8vo. 1877.

P. A. Saccardo. *Sylloge Fungorum.* Vol. iv.—"Hyphomyceteæ." Padua, 1886.

De Toni, J. B. "Sylloge Ustilaginearum et Uredinearum," in Saccardo, *Sylloge Fungorum.* Imp. 8vo. Vol. vii, pt. ii. Padua, 1888.

Geo. Winter in Rabenhorst's *Kryptogamen Florader Pilze.* 8vo. Cuts. 1884.

Geo. Massee. *British Fungi—Phycomycetes and Ustilagineæ.* 8vo. Cuts. London, 1891.

O. Brefield. *Bot. Untersuch. ü. Hefenpilze.* Leipzig, 1883.

Tulasne. "Memoire sur les Ustilaginées comparées aux Uredinées." Ann. des Sci. Nat., 3d series, vol. vii. Paris, 1847.

M. Woronin. Beitrag zur Kenntniss der Ustilagineen. 1882.

M. C. Cooke. Rust, Smut, Mildew, and Mould. 12mo. Col. plates. London, 1870.

C. B. Plowright. *A Monograph of the British Uredineæ and Ustilagineæ.* 8vo. London, 1889.

W. C. Smith. *Diseases of Field and Garden Crops.* 12mo. Cuts. London, 1884.

D. D. Cunningham. *Conidial Fructification in the Mucorini.*

R. Thaxter. "The Entomophthoreæ of the United States." Memoirs of Boston Society of Natural History. Vol. iv, 4to. Plates. 1888.

L. Mangin. *Sur le Structure des Peronosporées.* Paris, 1890.

K. Lindstedt. *Synopsis d. Saprolegniaceen.* 8vo. Four plates. Berlin, 1872.

M. Cornu. "Monographie des Saprolegniées." Ann. des Sci. Nat., 5th series. Vol. xv. Paris, 1872.

M. C. Cooke. *Synopsis Pyrenomycetum.* 2 parts. 8vo. London, 1884-'86.

A. de Zaczewski. "Classification naturelle des Pyrenomycetes." Bull. Soc. Myc. de France, vol. x. 1894.

J. B. Ellis and B. M. Everhart. *The North American Pyrenomycetes.*

M. C. Cooke. *Mycographia,* vol. i. "Discomycetes." Col. plates. Imp. 8vo. London, 1879.

W. Phillips. *A Manual of British Discomycetes.* Im. 8vo. Plates. London, 1887.

P. A. Saccardo. "Sylloge Discomycetum," in *Sylloge Fungorum.* Vol. viii. Padua, 1889.

R. Hartig. *Text Book of Diseases of Trees.* Roy. 8vo. London, 1894.

Geo. Massee. The Evolution of Plant Life, Lower Forms. 12mo. London, 1891.

Marshall Ward. Diseases of Plants. 12mo. Cuts. London, 1884.

A. De Bary. *Recherches sur le Developpement de quelques champignons parasites.* 8vo. Plates. Berlin, 1878-'94.

APPENDIX.

Superior, the upper surface; applied to the ring when near the apex of the stem.

Tetraspore, tetra Gr. four; spores.
Theca, cell-mother, the protoplasm of which originates by segmentation; a certain number of spores, usually eight, held in suspension in the protoplasm of the theca without being attached to

each other or to the cell walls.

Thecaspore, the spore thus encased.

Tomentose, downy, with short hairs.

Torsive, spirally twisted.

Torulose, a cylindrical body swollen and restricted alternately.

Toxic, poisonous.

Trama, the substance proceeding from the hymenophore, intermediate between the plates (central in) of the gills of agarics.

Transverse, crosswise.

Tremelloid, jelly-like.

Truncate, ending abruptly, as if cut short; cut squarely off.

Tubæform, trumpet-shaped.

Tubercle, a small wart-like excrescence.

Tubular, hollow and cylindrical.

Turbinate, top-shaped.

Typical, agreeing closely with the characters assigned to a group or species.

Umbilicate, having a central depression.

Umbo, the boss of a shield; applied to the central elevation of the cap of some mushrooms.

Umbonate, having a central boss-like elevation.

Uncinate, hooked.

Unequal, short imperfect gills interspersed among the others.

Universal, used in relation to the veil or volva which entirely envelops the mushroom when young.

Variety, an individual of a species differing from the rest in external form, size, color, and other secondary features, without perpetuating these differences only under exceptional circumstances.

Veil, in mushrooms a partial covering of the stem or margin of the pileus.

Veliform, a thin veil-like covering.

Venate, Veined, intersected by swollen wrinkles below and on the sides.

Ventricose, swollen in the middle.

Vernicose, shining as if varnished.

Verrucæ, warts or glandular elevations.

Verrucose, covered with warts.

Villose, villous, covered with long, weak hairs.

Virescent, greenish.

Virgate, streaked.

Viscid, covered with a shiny liquid which adheres to the fingers when touched.

Viscous, gluey.

Volute, rolled up in any direction.

Volva, a substance covering the mushroom, sometimes membranous, sometimes gelatinous; the universal veil.

Walnut brown, a deep brown like that of some varieties of wood. (Raw umber, and burnt sienna and white.)

Wart, an excrescence found on the cap of some mushrooms; the remains of the volva in form of irregular or polygonal excrescences, more or less adherent, numerous, and persistent.

Zone, a broad band encircling a mushroom.

Zoned, furnished with one or more concentric circles.

Although some writers apply the terms spore, sporidia, sporophore, sporules, and conidia somewhat indiscriminately to all spore bodies, in order to avoid confusion, it is now recommended by the best authorities that certain distinctive limitations should be adhered to in the use of these terms. Saccardo, in defining the terms which he employs, accepts the term spores as applicable exclusively to the naked spores supported on basidia, as found in the Basidiomyceteæ. The term sporidia he limits to spores produced or enclosed in an ascus, as in the Ascomyceteæ. The term sporules he applies to the spores of imperfect fungi, where they are enclosed in perithecia (microscopic cups or cells), such as the Sphæropsidea. The term conidia he uses to designate the spores of imperfect fungi without perithecia or asci, such as the Hyphomyceteæ and the Melanconieæ. This arrangement is in accordance with M. C. Cooke's published views on the subject, except in the case of the spore bodies of the Melanconieæ, which he prefers, for well- defined reasons, to call sporules.

In accordance with these limitations, the terms *spermatia*, *stylospores*, and *clinospores* are merged in *sporule*.

Other terms appropriate to their development are employed to designate the spores of Uredineæ, Phycomyceteæ, etc.

STUDENT'S HAND-BOOK

OF

Mushrooms of America

EDIBLE AND POISONOUS.

BY

THOMAS TAYLOR, M. D.

AUTHOR OF FOOD PRODUCTS, ETC.

Published in Serial Form—**No. 4**—Price, 50c. per number.

WASHINGTON, D. C.:
A. R. Taylor, Publisher, 238 Mass. Ave. N.E.
1897.

GASTEROMYCETES.

Hymenium more or less permanently concealed, consisting in most cases of closely packed cells of which the fertile ones (the basidia) bear naked spores on distinct spicules, exposed only by the rupture or decay of the investing coat or peridium. Berkeley's Outlines.

This family has been subjected to numerous revisions since the days of Fries, when its structural characteristics were not so well understood as at present. Montagne and Berkeley are credited with being the first to show the true structure of the hymenium in the puff-balls, as well as to demonstrate the presence of basidia. This important discovery led to the correlating of the Gasteromycetes with the Hymenomycetes under the common title Basidiomycetes, both having the spores borne upon basidia. The two families still remained distinct, however, not only because of the dissimilarity in their external features but principally on account of the difference in the disposition and character of the hymenium.

In the Hymenomycetes the hymenium is exposed to the light from the first, and the spores drop from the basidia as they mature; whereas in the Gasteromycetes the hymenial pulp, or gleba, consisting of the spores with the supporting basidia and the hyphæ, is enclosed within the substance of the fungus, and the spores are exposed only on the decay of the investing coat.

The basidia of the Gasteromycetes, though resembling those of the Hymenomycetes, are more variable in form and the number of the spores not so constant. They perform the same functions and bear spicules, sometimes in pairs, sometimes quaternate, each spicule being surmounted by a spore. They dissolve away as the spores mature and can, therefore, only be observed in the very young stage of the plant. The spores of the Gasteromycetes are usually colored and, except in the subterranean species, globose. As seen through the microscope they have often a rough warty appearance, sometimes spinulose. Paraphyses may be present as aborted basidia, but cystidia are rarely distinguished. A characteristic of a large proportion of the plants is the drying up of the hymenial substance, so that the cavity of the receptacle becomes at length filled with a dusty mass composed of spores and delicate threads, the remains of the shriveled hyphæ.

The following table will serve to show the distinctive features of the four primary divisions of the GASTEROMYCETES:

Lycoperdaceæ.—Hymenium fugitive, drying in a dusty mass of threads and spores, dispersed by an opening or by fissures of the peridium. Terrestrial.

Phalloideæ.—Hymenium deliquescent and slimy; receptacle pileate; volva universal. Fœtid fleshy fungi.

Hypogæi, or *Hymenogastreæ.*—Hymenium permanent, not becoming dusty or deliquescent except when decayed. Capillitium wanting. Subterranean.

Nidulariaceæ.—Receptacle cup-shaped or globose; spores produced on sporophores or short basidia enclosed in globose or disciform bodies (sporangia) contained within a distinct peridium. Terrestrial.

The section Lycoperdaceæ contains upwards of 500 species or more than two-thirds of the whole number of recorded species of the Gasteromycetes. Lycoperdon, Bovista, and Geaster, its most conspicuous genera, are said to contain the largest number of well-known species. A few are edible.

The Phalloideæ include about 90 species. The plants are usually ill-smelling and unwholesome. Some are stipitate, others are latticed, etc. Some are conspicuous for their bright coloring. In the young stage they are enclosed in an egg-shaped volva having a gelatinous inner stratum.

The plants of the Nidulariaceæ are very minute, tough, and widely distributed. The species Cyathus, the "bird's-nest fungus," is quite common in some localities, and is interesting because of its peculiar form. The individual plant is very small, not more than two centimeters high. It resembles an inverted bell, or a miniature wine-glass. A delicate white membrane covers the top at first. This disappears as the plant matures, revealing lentil-shaped bodies packed closely together like eggs in a nest. These oval bodies are the peridiola containing the spores. They are usually found upon rotten wood or sticks on the ground. Sixty-five species are recorded, but none are edible.

The plants of the division Hypogæi or Hymenogastreæ are subterranean in habit, preferring a sandy soil. They are usually somewhat globose in form, having a thick outer coat or peridium, though in some of the genera the outer coat is very thin or obsolete. They are dingy in color. In the young plants the interior substance somewhat resembles that of the truffle, but is streaked and mottled. When old the gleba consists of a dusty mass of threads and spores. They are known under various appellations, such as "underground puff-balls," "false truffles," etc.

The Hypogæi are analogous to the Tuberacei, except that the spores are not contained in asci as in the latter. Cooke says they appear to be the link which unites the Basidiomycetes to the Ascomycetes by means of the Tuberacei or genuine Truffles. In the young stage the basidia in the Hypogæi are easily distinguished by the aid of the microscope.

In external features and habit of growth the species of Elaphomyces, a genus of Tuberacei, closely resemble the Hypogæi, and in old age, when the *asci* have disappeared, it is difficult to distinguish the plants of this genus from the Hypogæi.

The genus *Melanogaster* contains an edible species, *M. variegatus*, Tulasne, commonly known in Europe as the "Red Truffle" or "False Truffle." *M. variegatus* is usually gregarious and subterranean in habit. The exterior is minutely granular, tawny yellow or reddish rust color; the interior soft, bluish-black, streaked with yellow, the spore mass in maturity becoming pubescent. The odor is pleasantly aromatic, and the taste sweet. Under trees in woods. The variety *Broomeianus* Berk. is paler in the marbling, which shows reddish instead of yellow streaks. The pulpy mass is at first white, changing to a yellowish, smoky hue.

LYCOPERDACEÆ AND PHALLOIDEÆ.

The plants figured in Plates G and H belong to the Lycoperdaceæ and Phalloideæ.

LYCOPERDACEÆ.

Massee, who has given the Puff-Ball group very close study, says that in the gleba of the Lycoperdaceæ, "at a very early period two sets of hyphæ are present. One, thin-walled, colorless, septate and rich in protoplasm, gives origin to the trama, and elements of the hymenium, and usually disappears entirely after the formation of the spores; the second type consists of long thick-walled aseptate or sparsely septate, often colored hyphæ, which are persistent and form the capillitium. The latter are branches of the hyphæ forming the hymenium."

GENERA LYCOPERDON AND BOVISTA.

To the genera Lycoperdon and Bovista belong most of the "Puff-balls" and all of the species figured in Plate G. In the plants of these two genera the peridium is more or less distinctly double, and the hyphæ, or delicate threads which are seen mixed with the dusty mass of spores in the mature plant, forming what is called the capillitium, are an important element in classification.

Genus Lycoperdon Tourn. In this genus the investing coat or peridium is membranaceous, vanishing above or becoming flaccid; bark or outer shell adnate, sub-persistent, breaking up into scales or warts; capillitium soft, dense, and attached to the peridium, base spongy and sterile.

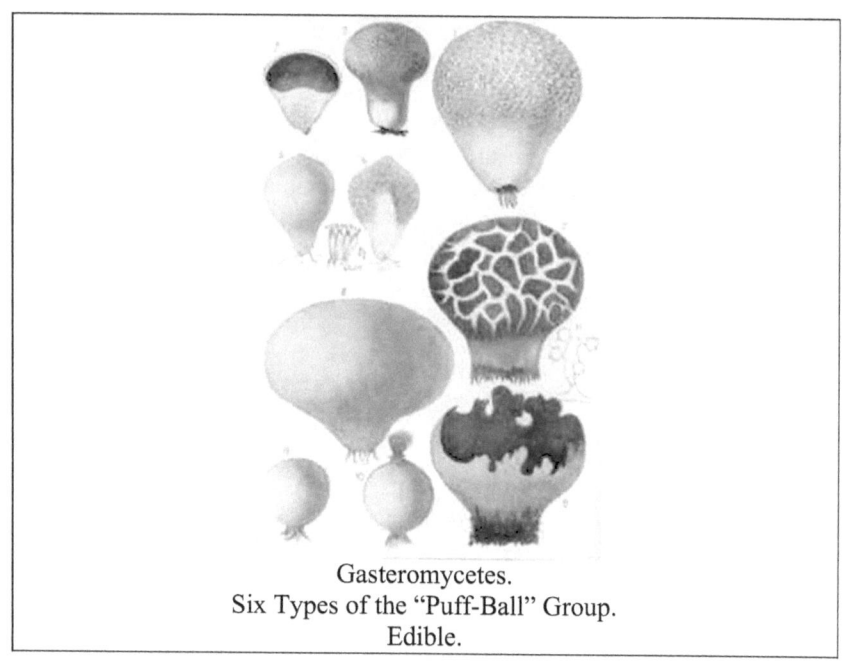

Gasteromycetes.
Six Types of the "Puff-Ball" Group.
Edible.

PLATE G.

EDIBLE PUFF-BALLS.

FIG. 1.—**Lycoperdon cælatum** Fries. *"Collapsing Puff-Ball."*

Peridium flaccid above, with mealy coating, obtuse, at length collapsing, the sterile stratum cellulose. Inner peridium distinct from the outer all round; capillitium nearly free, collapsing when mature, threads long and brittle; spores dingy olive, turning brown; base stem-like, broad and blunt, with root, obconical, somewhat spongy. Common in pastures and open woods. Edible when young, but not much commended. Plant pale cream color.

FIGS. 2 and 3.—**Lycoperdon gemmatum** Batsch. *"Warted Puff-Ball,"*
"Studded Puff-Ball."

Plant sub-globular, with a stem-like base; white or cinereous, turning to light greyish-brown, the surface warty, the warts unequal, the larger ones somewhat pointed, the smaller granular. As the warts fall off they leave the surface of the denuded peridium somewhat dotted or slightly reticulated. Flesh, when young, firm and whitish. The plants of this species are small, variable in form, sometimes turbinated, sometimes nearly globose, or depressed globose, but usually the basal portion is narrower than the upper portion. The stem varies in thickness and length; sometimes it is quite elongated, in some instances absent. Capillitium and spores yellowish-green, turning dark olive or brown. Columella present. When the spores are fully ripe the peridium opens by a small apical aperture for their dispersion. The plants are sometimes densely cæspitose, and crowd together on the ground or on decaying wood in large patches after warm rains. They are found both in fields and open woods during summer and autumn. They are edible when young, but not specially well flavored. There are several varieties. Plants sometimes oval or lens-shaped.

In Var. *hirtum* the plant is turbinate, subsessile, and hairy, with slender, spinous warts. The variety *papulatum* is subrotund, sessile, papillose and pulverulent, the warts being nearly uniform in size. Plants from one to two inches in height.

F<small>IGS</small>. 4 and 5.—**Lycoperdon pyriforme** Schaeffer. *"Pear-Shaped Puff-Ball."*

Plant dingy white or brownish yellow; pear-shaped, or obovate pyriforme, sometimes approaching L. gemmatum in size and shape, but easily distinguished from that species by the surface features of the peridium and the internal hyphæ. The persistent warts which cover the surface of the peridium are so minute as to appear to the naked eye like scales. In some instances the peridium is almost smooth, and sometimes cracks in areas, inner peridium thin and tough. The hyphæ are thicker than the spores and branched, continuous with the slightly cellular base, and forming a columella inside the peridium. Spores greenish-yellow, then brownish-olive, smooth and globose.

The short stem-like base of the plant terminates in fiber-like rootlets, creeping under the soil and branching, thus attaching large clusters of the young plants together. They are often found in quantity on the mossy trunks of fallen trees.

F<small>IG</small>. 6.—**Lycoperdon giganteum** Batsch. *"Giant Puff-Ball."*

The Giant Puff-Ball, so generally neglected, is one of the most valuable of the edible mushrooms. It is readily distinguished from other puff-balls and allied fungi by its large size. It is subglobose in form, often flattened at the top and usually wider than deep. The peridium or rind is membranaceous, smooth, or very slightly floccose, and creamy white at first, turning to pale yellowish-brown when the plant is old. When young it is filled with a white, seemingly homogeneous fleshy substance of pleasant flavor. This substance changes, when mature, to an elastic, yellowish or olivaceous brown, cottony but dusty mass of filaments and spores. The peridium is very fragile above, cracking into areæ in the mature plant and breaking up and falling away in fragments, thus allowing the dispersion of the spores. The capillitium and spores are at first greenish-yellow, turning to dingy olive. The plants vary in size, but average from ten to twenty inches in diameter. In the columns of the *Country*

Gentleman some years ago there appeared a description of a puff-ball of this species which weighed forty seven pounds and measured a little over eight feet in circumference. It was found in a low, moist corner of a public park. Specimens weighing from twenty to thirty pounds are recorded as being found in different parts of the country; but specimens of such large dimensions are unusual. This species is found in many parts of the United States. It is the L. *bovista* of Linn. Sacc.

A correspondent writes that he has found the giant puff-ball in great abundance growing on the Genessee Flats, Livingstone Co., New York. Another writes from Nebraska that it is quite abundant on the prairies there in summer. A third writes from Missouri, "Since the late rains we have had puff- balls in abundance, and find them delicious made into fritters."

The puff-balls should be gathered young. If the substance within is white and pulpy, it is in good condition for cooking, but if marked with yellow stains it should be rejected.

Vittadini says:

"When the giant puff-ball is conveniently situated you should only take one slice at a time, cutting it horizontally and using great care not to disturb its growth, to prevent decay, and thus one may have a fritter every day for a week."

Different authors write with enthusiasm of the merits of the giant puff-ball as an esculent.

Mrs. Hussey, an English botanist, gives the following receipt for "puff-ball omelet:"

First, remove the outer skin; cut in slices half an inch thick; have ready some chopped herbs, pepper, and salt; dip the slices in the yolk of an egg, and sprinkle the herbs upon them; fry in fresh butter, and eat immediately.

I have tested fine specimens of the giant puff-ball gathered in the public parks of Washington, D. C., finding it delicious eating when fried in batter.

Figs. 7 and 8.—**Lycoperdon cyathiforme** Bose. "*Cup-shaped Puff-Ball.*"

Synonyms—L. fragile Vitt. L. albopurpureum Frost.

Plant nearly globose, with a short, thick, stem-like base, color varying, cinereous, brown, tinged with violet.

Rind or peridium smooth, or minutely floccose, scaly in the mature plant, cracking into somewhat angular areas, the upper portion finally falling away in fragments, leaving a wide cup-shaped base, with irregular margin, which remains long after the dispersion of the spores and capillitium. This basal portion is often tinged with the purplish hue of the spores. Spores rough, purplish-brown. Capillitium same color as the spores.

Lycoperdon *cyathiforme* is a more common species than L. *giganteum*, and is deemed quite equal to the latter in flavor. The plants are of good size, being from 4 to 10 inches in diameter.

They are frequently found in open fields and grassy places after electric storms. When sliced and fried in egg batter, they taste much like the *giganteum* or *giant puff-ball.*

A puff-ball which is not inferior to either of the two last-named species, though not as large, and perhaps not as abundant as either, is the Lycoperdon *saccatum* of Fries, sometimes called the "Long-stemmed puff-ball," because of its elongated stem.

The plants of this species are attractive in appearance, usually hemispherical, or lentiform in shape, with cylindrical stem-like base. The peridium is thin and delicate, breaking into fragments; creamy white in the young stage, and clothed with delicate warts, so minute as to give the surface a soft mealy appearance, the under surface somewhat plicate. Capillitium sub-persistent and dense. Both spores and capillitium brown.

LYCOPERDACEÆ.

Genus Bovista Dill. Peridium papery (or sometimes corky), persistent; the outer rind, sometimes called the bark, quite distinct from the inner, at length shelling off. Capillitium sub-compact, equal, adnate to the peridium on all sides; spores pedicillate, brownish.

F$_{\text{IGS}}$. 9 and 10.—**Bovista plumbea** Pers. *Lead-Colored Bovista.*

Plant small, spherical, having a double shell or peridium, the inner one white and the outer one smooth and greyish lead-color or bluish-grey, and shelling off at maturity. When young the interior is filled with a creamy white substance. This soon begins to disintegrate, and, as the spores mature, changes to a mass of dusty brown spores and threads. When the spores are ready for dissemination a small aperture appears in the top of the peridium, through which they push their way outwards like a little puff of smoke.

When young, and while the flesh is white throughout, the plant is edible, although so small that it would take a quantity to make a good dish. It is found chiefly in pastures in the autumn. Sometimes found growing in company with Agaricus campestris. Of pleasant flavor when young.

Fig. 11. Basidium and spores of a Lycoperdon highly magnified.

An English author states that inflammation of the throat and swelling of the tongue have been known to ensue from eating some of the small species of Lycoperdon in the raw state. It would be a wise precaution, therefore, to cook all of the smaller species well before eating.

The genus Scleroderma is allied to Lycoperdon, but differs from it in the absence of a capillitium, and in the thick indehiscent outer skin, or peridium, which bursts irregularly on the maturity of the spore-mass, the flocci adhering on all sides to the peridium and forming distinct veins in the central mass.

The species Scleroderma *vulgare* is very common in woods, and has sometimes been mistaken for a form of Truffle. The plants are not very attractive, and the odor is rank. They are subsessile and irregular in shape, with a hard outer skin, the larger form of a yellowish or greenish brown hue, and covered with large warts or scales, the smaller very minutely warty, and of a darker brown hue. The internal mass is of a bluish-black hue, threaded through with white or greyish flocci. Spores dingy. The interior becomes pulverulent when the plant matures. This species has been eaten in its young state when cooked, but the flavor is by no means equal to that of the large puff-balls. It is sometimes attacked by a fungus larger than itself, called Boletus *parasiticus*, and this parasite is again attacked by a species of Hypomyces, one of the genera of the Pyrenomycetes, which grows in patches upon dead fungi.

PHALLOIDEÆ OR PHALLACEÆ.

The Phalloideæ, sometimes called the "Stink-horn" fungi on account of their fœtid odor, are not numerous, the whole number of described species being about eighty. The plants are watery, quick in growth, and decay very rapidly. They are varied in form and are quite unlike the ordinary mushroom types. In some of the genera the plants are columnar and phalloid, in other clathrate or latticed, in others again the disk is stellate, and in one genus it is coralloid, but they are all enclosed, in the early stage, in a volva which is at first hidden or partially hidden beneath the surface of the ground. A gelatinous stratum is contained within the firmer outside membrane.

Genus Ithyphallus. In this genus the cap is perforated at the top, free from the stem and reticulate. No veil. The mature plants are columnar in form with the remains of the volva enclosing the column-like stem at the base; the cap in its deeply pitted reticulations somewhat resembling that of the *Morel*, although of different texture.

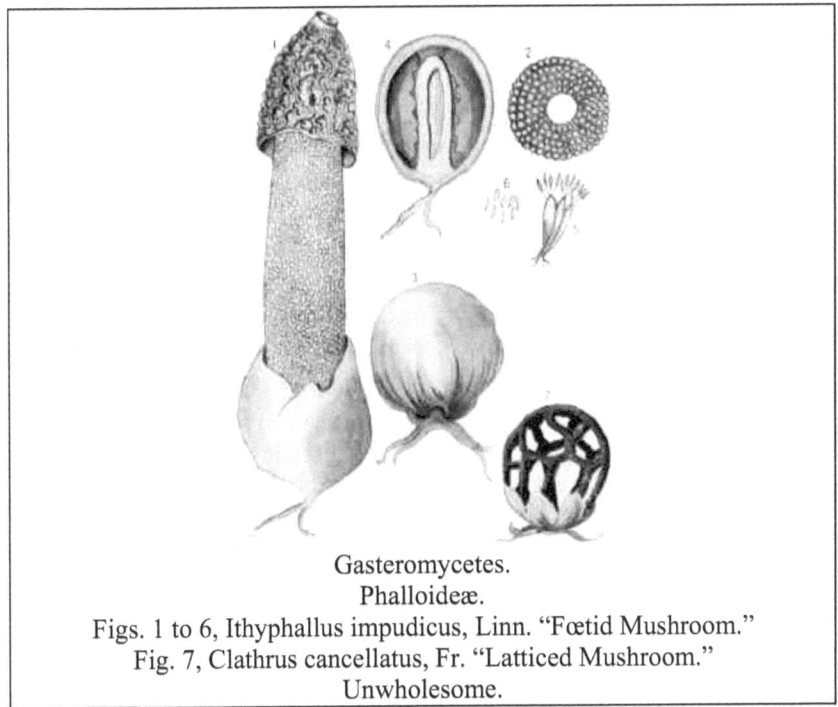

Gasteromycetes.
Phalloideæ.
Figs. 1 to 6, Ithyphallus impudicus, Linn. "Fœtid Mushroom."
Fig. 7, Clathrus cancellatus, Fr. "Latticed Mushroom."
Unwholesome.

PLATE H.

FIGS. 1 to 6.—**Ithyphallus** *impudicus* Linn. *"Fœtid Wood Witch."*

In the embryonic stage the plant is enclosed in a volva which is composed of three layers, the outer one firm, the intermediate one gelatinous, and the inner one consisting of a thin membrane. The gleba, or spore-bearing portion, in the early stage forms a conical honeycombed cap within the inner shell or membrane, concealing the stem to which it is attached. The stem at this stage is very short, cylindrical, and composed of small cells filled with a gelatinous substance. The volva is about the size of a hen's egg. On maturity it ruptures at the apex. The stem rapidly expands and, elongating, elevates the cap into the air. The stem becomes open and spongy, owing to the drying of the gelatinous matter and its quick expansion.

The whole plant attains a height of from four to ten inches in a few hours. The hymenial surface is on the outside of the cap, the spores being embedded in its glutinous coated ridges and depressions. The hymenium is at first firm but rapidly deliquesces, holding the spores in the liquid mass. The cap is greenish or greenish-gray in color, changing to a dark bottle-green. In its deliquescent state the odor is very repulsive. While enclosed in the volva the unpleasant odor is not so perceptible, and it has been eaten in that condition without unpleasant effects, but in its mature stage it is considered unwholesome, and certainly its offensive odor would be quite sufficient to deter most persons from attempting to test its edible qualities. Flies, however, are very fond of the fluid, and consume it greedily and with impunity. It is found in gardens and woods, its presence being detected several rods away by the offensive odor. Specimens occur in which the color of the cap is white or reddish.

In the allied genus *Mutinus* the pileus is adnate and is not perforated at the apex. Mutinus *caninus* resembles *impudicus* in form, but the cap is continuous with, not free from the stem, and is crimson in color, covered with a greenish-brown, odorless mucus. The stem is hollow, whitish, tinted with a pale yellow or orange color. Not common.

Genus Clathrus Mich. In this genus the receptacle is sessile, and formed of an obovate globular net-work. At first wholly enclosed in a volva which becomes torn at the apex and falls away, leaving a calyx-like base at its point of contact with the stem.

F<small>IG</small>. 7.—**Clathrus cancellatus** Tourn.

U<small>NWHOLESOME</small>.

Receptacle bright vermillion or orange red, covered at first with a greenish mucus which holds the colorless spores. Volva white or pale fawn color. Odor strongly fœtid.

MYXOMYCETES OR MYXOGASTERS.—*"Slime Fungi."*

In their early history the Myxomycetes, or "slime moulds," were classed with the gasteromycetal fungi, and by Fries grouped as a sub-order of the Gasteromycetes, under the name Myxogasters. From this connection they were severed in 1833 by Link, who, recognizing certain distinctive features which entitled them to consideration as an entirely separate group, ranked the Myxogasters, as a separate order, under the title *Myxomycetes, Slime moulds.* De Bary, in a monograph on the subject written some years later, questioned the right of this group to the place assigned it in the vegetable world, claiming that the Myxogasters were as nearly related to the animal as to the vegetable kingdom, and changing the name to Mycetozoa. Massee assailed this position in his "Monograph of the Myxogasters," pointing out that De Bary derived his reasons and deductions from the early or vegetative stage of the fungi, without taking sufficiently into account the characteristics of the later or reproductive stage in which the great disparity between these organisms and those of the lower animals becomes apparent.

Dr. Rostafinski, the Polish botanist, and pupil of De Bary, adopts the name given the group by De Bary, but applies it in a more restricted sense, classifying on a botanical basis. Both De Bary and Massee have their earnest disciples. M. C. Cooke takes the ground that the Myxomycetes are entitled to mention as "*fungi*" which produce their fructification enclosed within a peridium," although considering them as an aberrant group which, on account of certain peculiarities of their early or vegetative stage, should no longer be classed as having affinity with Gasteromycetes. Without further discussion of the subject, it is sufficient, for our present purpose, to state that mycologists now very generally agree in regarding this group as quite distinct from the Gasteromycetes.

The species are minute, rarely exceeding a millimeter in diameter, at first pulpy, then dry. In the early or vegetative stage the "slime mould" is plasmoidal, consisting of a mass of protoplasm without cell wall, and prefers damp surfaces, such as rotting leaves, moist logs, etc. The whole substance is slippery or slimy and presents different hues, red, orange, violet, brown, etc., according to species, but never green. It is in the reproductive or fruiting stage that their resemblance to microscopic puff-balls appears, the sporangium in many species exhibiting a distinct peridium or outer coat which encloses the spores together with the hair-like threads called the capillitium. On the ripening of the spores this peridium ruptures, allowing their escape, the capillitium lending valuable aid in their dissemination.

GENERA OF GASTEROMYCETES, ACCORDING TO SACCARDO.

I. PHALLACEÆ, OR PHALLOIDEÆ.
   Dictyophora, Desvaugh.
   Ithyphallus, Fr.

Mutinus, Fr.
Kalchbrennera, Berk.
Simblum, Klotzsch.
Clathrus, Mich.
Colus, Cav. & Sech.
Lysurus, Fr.
Anthurus, Kalchbr.
Calathiscus, Mont.
Aseroë, La Bill.
Staurophallus. (?)

II. NIDULARIACEÆ.

Nidularia, Fr. & Nordh.
Cyathus, Hall.
Crucibulum, Tul.
Thelebolus, Tode.
Dacryobolus, Fr.
Sphærobolus, Tode.

Polyangium, Link. } Genera delenda.
Atractobolus, Tode.

III. LYCOPERDACEÆ.

Gyrophragmium, Mont.
Secotium, Kunze.
Polyplocium, Berk.
Cycloderma, Klotzsch.
Mesophellia, Berk.
Cauloglossum, Grev.
Podaxon (Desv.) Fr.
Sphæriceps, Welw. & Curr.
Tylostoma, Pers.
Queletia, Fr.
Battarrea, Pers.
Husseya, Berk.
Mitremyces, Nees.
Geaster, Mich.
Diplocystis, B. & C.
Diploderma, Link.
Trichaster, Czern.
Broomeja, Berk.
Coilomyces, B. & C.
Lanophila, Fr.
Eriosphæra, Reich.

Bovista, Dill.
Calvatia, Fr.
Lycoperdon, Tourn.
Hippoperdon, Mont.
Scleroderma, Pers.
Castoreum, C. & M.
Xylopodium, Mont.
Areolaria, Forquigu.
Phellorina, Berk.
Favillea, Fr.
Polygaster, Fr.
Polysaccum, D. C.
Testicularia, Klotzsch.
Arachnion, Schw.
Scoleciocarpus, Berk.
Paurocotylis, Berk.

IV. HYMENOGASTRACEÆ (HYPOGÆI).
Hysterangium, Vitt.
Octaviania, Vitt.
Rhizopagon, Fr.
Melanogaster, Corda.
Hymenogaster, Vitt.
Hydnangium, Walk.
Gautieria, Vitt.
Macowanites, Kalchbr.

BIBLIOGRAPHY.

E. Fischer, etc. "Gasteromycetæ," Saccardo, *Sylloge Fungorum*. Vol. vii, part i. Padua, 1888.

Chas. H. Peck. "United States species of Lycoperdon."

Geo. Massee. "Monograph of the British Gasteromycetes." *Annals of Botany,* Nov., 1889. "Monograph of the Genus Lycoperdon" in *Journal Royal Micro. Soc.* London, 1887.

C. Bambeke. *Morphologie du Phallus impudicus.* Gand, 1889.

A. P. Morgan. "North American Geasters" in *American Naturalist.* Roy. 8vo.

1887.

L. and C. Tulasne. "Essai d'une Monographie des Nidulariees." Ann. des Sci. Nat. 8vo. Paris, 1844.

M. C. Cooke. *The Myxomycetes of Great Britain.* Plates. 8vo. London, 1877. *The Myxomycetes of the United States,* by the same author. New York, 1877.

Geo. Massee. *A Monograph of the Myxogasters.* Col. plates. Roy. 8vo. London, 1892.

A. De Bary. "Die Mycetozoon" (*Schleimpilz*). Plates. 8vo. Leipzig, 1864.

J. Rostafinski. *Sluzowce, Mycetozoa Monografia.* Plates. 4to. Paris, 1875.

Geo. A. Rex. New American Myxomycetes. Proc. Acad. Nat. Sci. Phila., part iii, Dec. 16, 1890, pp. 436-438.

Balliet Letson. "Slime Molds." The Ornithologist and Botanist. Vol. i. Binghamton, N. Y., Nov., 1891, p. 85. 1 col.

Thos. H. McBride. "The Myxomycetes of Eastern Iowa." Bulletin from the Laboratories of Natural History of the State University of Iowa. Iowa City, Iowa, 1892.

AGARICINI.

Subgenus Lepiota Fries. Veil universal and concrete, with the cuticle of the pileus breaking up in the form of scales. Gills typically free, often remote, not sinuate or decurrent. Stem generally distinct from the hymenophore. Volva absent. Habitat terrestrial, mostly found on rich soil or in grassy places. (In Saccardo's *Sylloge*, Lepiota is given generic rank.)

The Lepiotas have a wide geographical distribution. No less than 225 species have been recorded as found in different parts of the world. These are pretty evenly divided between the torrid and temperate zones. They are generally smaller than the Amanitas, less fleshy and somewhat dry and tough. The flesh is soft and thready, not brittle. In the plants of most of the species the cap is rough, the cuticle being broken up into tufts or scales. These tufts are readily distinguished from the warts which characterize certain species of Amanita, being formed from the breaking up of the cuticle with the concrete veil, while the wart-like excrescences seen upon Amanita *muscaria*, for example, are composed of fragments of the volva, which is always found enclosing the very young plants of the genus Amanita.

A few of the species are characterized by a smooth cap; in some instances it is granulose or mealy. Usually the cuticle is dry, but in a few of the species it is viscid. The stem is generally long and hollow, and, being of different texture from the flesh of the cap, is easily separated from it, often leaving a distinct socket at the junction of stem and cap. It is sometimes smooth, sometimes floccose. In some species it is bulbous at the base, in others not. The ring which encircles the stem is at first continuous with the cuticle of the cap, breaking apart with its expansion. It is sometimes movable, sometimes evanescent.

The species generally are considered edible, or innoxious. None are recorded as dangerous. A mycophagist from Augusta, Ga., reports, however, that the members of a family in that vicinity were made quite ill from eating the Lepiota *Morgani*, a greenish-spored species of Lepiota, while he himself ate of the same dish, experiencing no unpleasant effects. I have had no personal experience with this species.

Two edible species of Lepiota, which are widely commended as of good quality, and which are sufficiently abundant to have value as esculents, are figured in Plate XI. A third, Ag. (Lepiota) cepæstipes, var. cretaceus—Lepiota *cretacea*, figured in Plate XI½, is an exotic species found in greenhouses. It is of very delicate flavor.

Figs. 1 to 4 Agaricus (Lepiota) procerus, Fries (Lepiota procera)
"Parasol Mushroom."
Figs. 5 to 9 Lepiota naucinoides Peck. (Agaricus naucinus Fries)
"Smooth White Lepiota."
T. Taylor, del.

PLATE XI.

FIGS. 1 to 4.—**Ag. (Lepiota) procerus** Scop. (**Lepiota procera**). *"Parasol Mushroom."*

EDIBLE.

Cap at first ovate, then expanded, showing distinct umbo, cuticle thick, torn into evanescent scales; gills remote from the stem, free, white, or yellowish-white; stem long, slender, variegated with brownish scales, hollow or slightly stuffed, bulbous at the base, and bearing a well-defined thickish ring, which in the mature plant is movable. Spores white, elliptical. The color of the cap varies from a light tan or ochraceous yellow to a dark reddish-brown. The surface showing beneath the lacerated cuticle is of a lighter hue than the cuticle, and is silky and fibrillose, giving the cap a somewhat shaded or spotted appearance. The flesh is dry, soft and thready, white. Taste and odor pleasant.

Cap from 3 to 5 inches broad; stem from 5 to 10 inches high.

This species is commonly found in pastures and in open grassy places;

sometimes in open woods near cultivated fields, usually solitary or in very small clusters. It is a favorite among mycophagists. Lepiota *racodes* closely resembles Lepiota *procera*, and by some botanists the two are regarded as forms of the same species. In L. *racodes* the pileus is at first globose, expanded, and finally depressed in the centre; the cuticle is thin and broken into persistent scales; the whole plant smaller than L. procera. Flesh slightly reddish when bruised. Edible. There is also a white variety (*puellaris*) with a floccose squamose cap.

PLATE XI.

FIGS. 5 to 9.—Ag. (Lepiota) naucinus Fries (Lepiota naucinoides Peck).
"*Smooth White Lepiota.*"

EDIBLE.

Cap at first sub-globose, then curved, the surface smooth and satiny when dry, creamy white; gills close and slightly rounded at the inner extremity towards the stem, free from the stem, white; stem white, smooth, hollow, and bulbous at the base; ring thick, distinct, movable, white. The gills, soon after gathering, become suffused with a faint pinkish or fleshy tint. The spores are white, sub-elliptical. Specimens occur in which there is a slight granulation in the centre of the cap, but they are rare. The variety *squamosa* shows the surface of the cap, somewhat broken into thick scales.

L. *naucinoides* is a very clean and attractive looking mushroom, usually symmetrical in shape. It is a fleshier mushroom than L. *procera*, and is found in grassy places, in lawns, sometimes in gardens, or by roadsides, especially where the soil is rich. The specimens figured in Plate XI were gathered in a rose garden, growing in loamy soil. Specimens have been received from different States, some of them much larger than those here illustrated.

This mushroom is recorded by some authors as equal in flavor to the Parasol mushroom. When stewed with butter it makes a very appetizing dish.

There is a fatally poisonous mushroom to which it bears some resemblance, and which might be taken for it, viz., Amanita *verna*, or "Spring mushroom." It is therefore necessary, in order to guard against such a mistake, to give particular attention to the characteristics of these two mushrooms. They are both white throughout, and both have white spores and ringed stem. Amanita *verna*, however, carries a white volva or cup-shaped sheath at the base of the stem, and the gills do not show a pinkish or flesh colored tinge at any stage. In Lepiota *naucinoides*, as in all the Lepiotas, the volva is wanting. Amanita *verna* is apt to be moist and clammy to the touch, and is tasteless. L. *naucinoides* is dry, and has a pleasant flavor. The first is found *wholly* in *woods*; the second prefers pastures, open grassy places, and gardens, though sometimes found in light woods. I have never found an Amanita in a lawn, pasture, or garden.

An edible mushroom, Agaricus (Psalliota) *cretaceus*, found in pastures, bears a slight resemblance to L. *naucinoides*, when the color of the spores and gills are not taken into consideration. In the former the gills very quickly change from their early stage of rosy pink to a dark purplish-brown color, like that of the common mushroom. The spores are purplish-brown, while in L. *naucinoides* the pinkish hue which tinges the fading plant is very faint, and changes to a very light tan color with age. The spores being white, the gills retain their white color for a long time, never changing to dark brown.

L. *Americana* Pk. A. & S., L. *excoriata* Schaeff., and L. *rubrotincta* Pk. have been tested and are of good flavor.

L. *Americana* has a reddish or reddish-brown cap, umbonate, with close adpressed scales and white flesh. The gills are broad and free from the stem, sometimes anastomosing near it, white; stem white, hollow, tapering towards the cap, annulate. When dried the whole plant has a brownish-red hue. When cut or bruised it sometimes exudes a reddish juice. Miss Banning reports specimens found in Druid Hill Park, Baltimore. I have gathered very beautiful specimens in Montgomery county, Md. This mushroom sometimes grows to a very large size.

L. *excoriata* has a pale fawn-colored cap, slightly umbonate, with thin cuticle, breaking into scales; gills remote, white; stem white, hollow, and short, nearly cylindrical. Odor faint, pleasant.

L. *rubrotincta* Pk. "*Red-tinted Agaric.*" Cap reddish or pinkish, broadly umbonate and clothed with adpressed scales; gills whitish, free, and close; stem nearly equal or slightly thickened at the base, with a well-developed persistent white or pinkish ring. Spores white, sub-elliptical.

L. *holosericeus* Fries has a fleshy white cap, soft, silky, and fibrillose, a solid bulbous stem, with persistent broad, reflexed ring, and free ventricose, white gills. Edible. It is found in gardens and cultivated places.

L. *acutesquamosa* Wein, found in greenhouses and soil in gardens, is a heavy but not very tall species. The cap is obtuse, and fleshy, at first floccose. As the cap expands it bristles with erect pointed tufts or scales. The gills are white or yellowish, lanceolate and simple, free from the stem. Stem bulbous, somewhat stuffed, rough or silky below the ring, and downy above. Ring persistent. Color of cap whitish or light brown, with darker scales.

L. *granulosus* Batsch. Cap thin, wrinkled or corrugated, granulose, mealy; gills white, *reaching the stem*, sometimes free. Plants very small and varying in color—pink, yellow, and white, according to variety.

L. *amiantha*. Plants very small, ochraceous in color, with yellow flesh and white gills *adnate* and crowded.

L. *cepæstipes* Sow. Cap thin, broad, sub-membranaceous, broadly umbonate, adorned with mealy evanescent scales, margin irregular; gills white, at length remote. Stem hollow and floccose, narrow at top, ventricose; ring evanescent. Generally found in hothouses. Cap 1 to 3 inches broad. Stem 3 to 6 inches high. Spores white.

L. *cristata* is a common species found on lawns and in fields where the grass is short. The plants are small, the cap from ½ to 1½ inches in width. Not very fleshy. The cuticle of the cap is at first continuous and smooth but soon breaks into reddish scales. The stem is fistulose, slender and equal; gills free. Odor and taste somewhat strong and unpleasant.

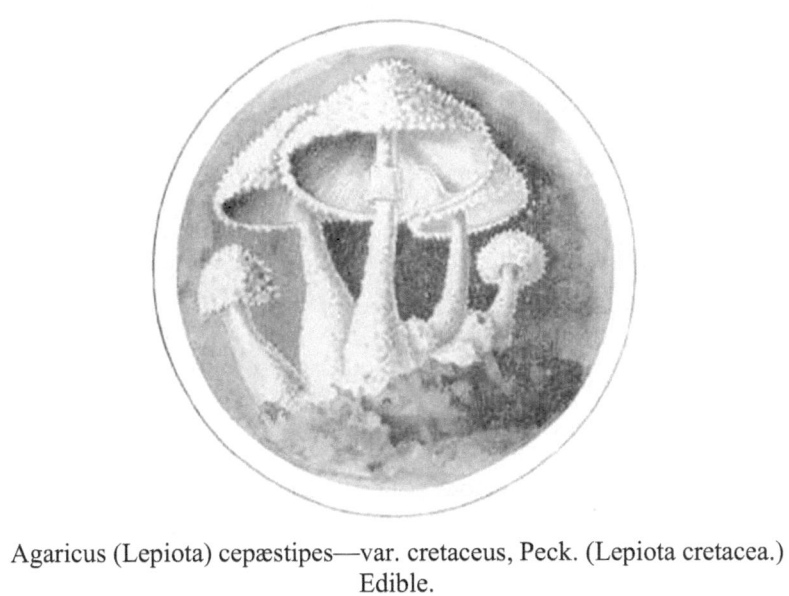

Agaricus (Lepiota) cepæstipes—var. cretaceus, Peck. (Lepiota cretacea.)
Edible.
From Nature.

PLATE XI½.

Ag. (Lepiota) cepæstipes, variety **cretaceus** Peck (**Lepiota cretacea**).

EDIBLE.

This very delicate and beautiful agaric is found on tan and leaves in hothouses.

The specimens here delineated were gathered in one of the hothouses of the Agricultural Department and first described and figured in *Food Products*, No. 2, of the report of the Division of Microscopy. The plants are a pure white throughout, and both stem and pileus are covered with small chalk-white mealy tufts. Berkeley says, "this species is probably of exotic origin, as it never grows in the open air." It is also met with in the hothouses of Europe. Specimens have been received from contributors who gathered them in greenhouses in different localities. This species should not be confounded with the purplish-brown spored mushroom Agaricus (Psalliota) cretaceus, which has pink gills turning to dark brown and is allied to the common meadow mushroom.

Lepiota *cretacea* is a delicious mushroom when broiled, or cooked in a chafing dish, and served on hot buttered toast. It has a pleasant taste when raw.

Lepiota *Morgani* Peck, the "*Green-Spored Lepiota*," is an exception to the general type of Lepiotas in the color of its gills and spores. It is western and southern in its range. This species is described by Peck in the Botanical Gazette of March, 1897, p. 137, as follows: "Pileus fleshy, soft, at first sub- globose, then expanded, or depressed, white, the brownish or alutaceous cuticle breaking up into scales except on the disk; lamellæ close, lanceolate, remote, white, then green; stem firm, equal, or tapering upwards, sub- bulbous, smooth, webby-stuffed, whitish, tinged with brown, annulus rather large, movable; flesh both of the pileus and stem white, changing to reddish, and then to yellowish hue when cut or bruised; spores ovate, sub-elliptical, mostly uninucleate, .0004 to .0005 inches long, .0003 to .00032 broad, sordid green.

"Plant 6 to 8 inches high, pileus 5 to 9 inches broad, stem 6 to 12 lines thick. Open dry grassy places. Dayton, Ohio. A. P. Morgan."

AGARICINI.

Genus Cortinarius Fries. This genus is distinguished by a cob-web-like veil, dry persistent gills, which in the mature plants become discolored, and pulverulent with the rusty or ochraceous colored spores. The veil is very delicate, resembling a spider's web. It is not concrete with the cuticle of the cap, but extends from its margin to the stem, in the young plants sometimes concealing the gills, but disappearing as the cap expands. Sometimes a few filaments are seen depending from the margin of the cap or encircling the stem.

In the young plants of this genus the gills vary very much in color. They are whitish, clay-color, violet, dark purple, blood-red, etc., according to species, but, as the plants mature, the gills become dusted with the rust-colored falling spores, and with age usually become a rusty ochraceous, or cinnamon color. The stem in some of the species is distinctly bulbous and in others equal, cylindrical, or tapering. In identifying the species it is necessary, in order to ascertain the true color of the gills, to examine the plants at different periods of growth.

The genus Cortinarius is a large one, and contains many beautiful species. It is mainly confined to temperate regions. Not a single species has been recorded as found in Ceylon, the West Indies, or Africa, but one tropical species is found in Brazil. Nearly four hundred species have been described, and over three hundred and seventy of these belong to the United States and Europe. A few are found in the extreme southern or temperate portion of South America, and several are reported from a temperate elevation among the Himalayas. Sweden and Great Britain, with their temperate climates, claim a large proportion of the European species. Not many of the Cortinarii have been recorded as edible, and none as dangerous. The Rev. M. J. Berkeley records, however, a case of poisoning by one of the species, C. (Inoloma) *bolaris* Pers., which though not fatal was somewhat alarming, the symptoms being great oppression of the chest, profuse perspiration, and the enlargement for two days of the salivary glands of the patient. I have seen no other statements relating to the poisonous properties of this species, and the results alluded to may have been owing to some individual idiosyncrasy.

Berkeley, in his "Outlines," gives the following description of this mushroom: "Pileus fleshy, obsoletely umbonate, growing pale, variegated with *saffron-red, adpressed, innate* scales; stem stuffed, then hollow, nearly equal, squamose, of the same color as the cap; gills subdecurrent, crowded, watery, cinnamon color. Cap 1 to 2 inches broad. Stem 2 to 3 inches long." In beech woods in September and October.

The genus Cortinarius has been divided by some authors into the following six groups: (1) *Phlegmacium*, in which the cap is fleshy and viscid, the veil partial, and the stem firm and dry; (2) *Myxacium*, in which the veil is universal and glutinous, hence the cap and stem both viscid; cap thin and the gills adnate or decurrent; (3) *Inoloma*, in which the cap is fleshy, dry, and at first silky with innate fibrils; veil simple and stem slightly bulbous; (4) Dermocybe, in which the pileus is thinly fleshy, dry, and at first downy, becoming smooth; the veil single and fibrillose; flesh watery, colored when moist, stem equal or attenuated downwards; (5) Telamonia, in which the cap is moist, at first smooth or dotted with the superficial fragments of the veil, the stem ringed below, or peronately scaly from the remains of the universal veil; (6) Hydrocybe, in which the cap is thin and moist, not viscid, smooth, or covered with superficial white fibrils; stem rigid, not scaly, veil thin, occasionally collapsed in an irregular ring. These subdivisions have been designated as *tribes* by some botanists and *subgenera* by others, etc. To the divisions Inoloma and Phlegmacium, respectively, belong the two species illustrated in Plate XII.

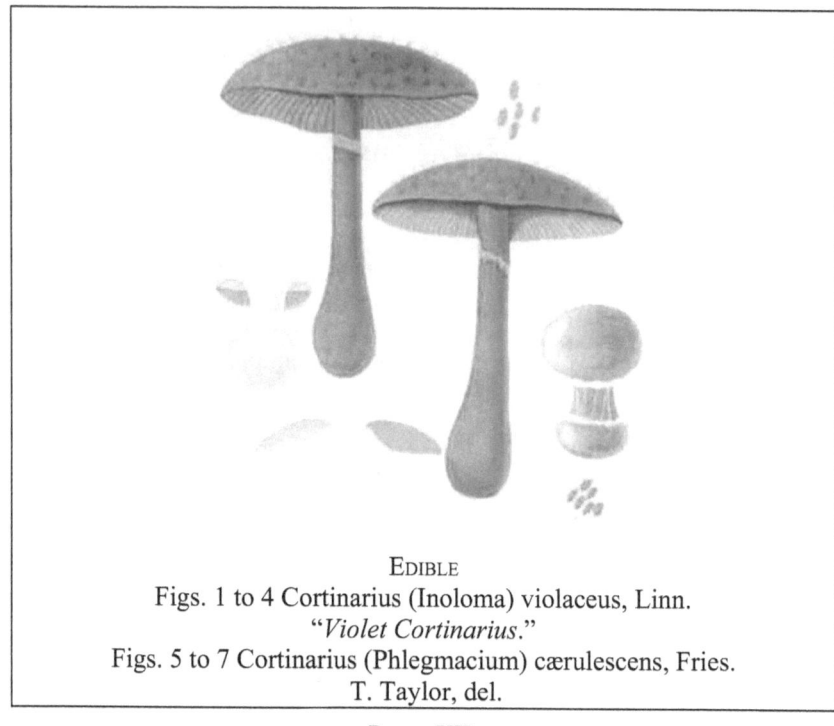

EDIBLE

Figs. 1 to 4 Cortinarius (Inoloma) violaceus, Linn.
"Violet Cortinarius."
Figs. 5 to 7 Cortinarius (Phlegmacium) cærulescens, Fries.
T. Taylor, del.

PLATE XII.

FIGS. 1 to 4.—**Cortinarius (Inoloma) violaceus** Fr. *"Violet Cortinarius."*

EDIBLE.

Cap fleshy, at first convex, then nearly plane, dotted with hairy tufts or scales, margin at first involute, color purple or dark violet, flesh soft, purplish; gills distant, broad, adnate, somewhat rounded near the stem, at first purplish violet, changing to an ochraceous or brownish cinnamon color as the plant matures; stem solid, somewhat bulbous at the base, purple; cortina or veil white or tinged with violet, sometimes bluish.

This is a handsome species, and though it is somewhat rare in many localities, its pretty and unusual coloring does not allow it to be easily overlooked. It is edible, and has a mushroomy taste when raw. Agaricus *nudus* Bull, a purple species with white spores, is sometimes confounded with it. There are other purple species of Cortinarius not so pleasant to the taste, which bear some resemblance to C. *violaceus*. The specimens figured in Plate XII were gathered near Dedham, Mass., on open ground on the border of a stretch of pine woods.

FIGS. 5 to 7.—**Cortinarius (Phlegmacium) cærulescens.**

EDIBLE.

Cap fleshy, at first convex, then plane, surface even, viscid; color bluish or violet; gills adnexed and crowded, at first bluish, changing to violet or purplish hues; stem solid, short, and thick, with a broadly bulbous base, same color as the cap; veil filmy, single. In woods and on the borders of woods. This mushroom varies in color, the bluish or purplish tints being quite susceptible to atmospheric changes. When growing in the shade or well- sheltered places, it is much darker in hue than when exposed unsheltered to the bright sunlight. The specimen figured in Plate XII was gathered on low ground near a pine grove in Essex County, Mass.

Cortinarius (Phlegmacium) *purpurascens* Fr. bears a slight resemblance to *cærulescens*, but can be distinguished from it by the spotted or zoned character of the cap and the broadly emarginate gills.

Cortinarius *turmalis*, an edible autumnal species, having an ochraceous or brownish-yellow cap with emarginate or decurrent gills, the latter at first whitish, then reddish clay color, is found in abundance in some parts of Maryland. The gills are never tinged with purple or blue. The flesh is white. The plants are easily discovered by those familiar with their habitat, as they grow under pine needles in groups, forming small mounds extending over large spaces, and in these hiding places, in the autumnal months, they are free from insects and dust. I have collected a bushel of them in less than an hour in fresh condition in October. Some of the French authors do not class this species as edible. Gillet, in his Hymenomycetes of France, enumerates fifty- three edible species of Cortinarius, but places *turmalis* among the suspects. I find this mushroom not only edible, but very valuable, because of its abundance in the localities where found. It is often densely cæspitose. The plant, when mature, is from 3 to 5 inches high.

C. *sebæceus*, found also in pine woods, is recorded as edible. The plant is tall, white-stemmed, with broad tan-colored, somewhat viscid cap; emarginate gills, clay color at first, at last cinnamon color; stem solid, stout, fibrillose, and equal.

Cortinarius *collinitus*, Smeared Cortinarius, and Cortinarius *cinnamomeus*, with its variety semi-sanguinea, have also been tested, and found edible. The first of these is somewhat common. The plants when fresh are covered with a glutinous substance, and this should be removed before cooking. Cap smooth under the glutinous coat, light brown or tawny yellow in color, flesh white; gills whitish or light gray when young, cinnamon-hued in the matured plant. Stem solid, nearly equal, cylindrical, yellowish, and somewhat scaly. C. *cinnamomeus* belongs to the division Dermocybe. The cap is thin at first, silky with innate fibrids, becoming smooth, and varies from light brown to a dark cinnamon color. The gills are yellowish, then cinnamon; stem downy or silky, yellow. The variety *semi-sanguinea* has the lamellæ red, almost as in the preceding species.

C. (Phlegmacium) *varius*, "Variable Cortinarius," edible, has a compact fleshy viscid, even cap, brownish in color, gills at first violet, changing to cinnamon, stout solid stem, white or whitish, adorned with adpressed flocci, flesh white.

Cortinarius (Telamonia) *armillatus* Fries is given in M. C. Cooke's list of edible Cortinarii. Cap fleshy but not thick, fibrillose and slightly scaly, bright bay color, thin uneven margin; stem solid, dingy, rufescent, showing irregular red zones or bands elongated and slightly bulbous at the base; gills distant, broad, pallid in color at first, changing to dark cinnamon. C. (Telamonia) *hæmatochelis* Bull. (edible), somewhat resembles the former in color and size, though not so bright a brown. Cap thin, silky-fibrillose; gills adnate, narrow and crowded, light cinnamon; stem long, solid, dingy, with a reddish zone.

C. (Hydrocybe) *castaneus* Bull., *Chestnut Cortinarius* (edible), is found in woods and gardens. The plants of this species are usually small. Cap at first campanulate, expanding, sometimes slightly umbonate in the centre, chestnut color; gills ventricose, crowded, purplish, changing to rust color; stem short, hollow or stuffed, cartilaginous, equal, pallid, reddish brown, or tinged with violet; veil white.

Subgenus Collybia Fries. Cap at first convex, then expanded, not depressed, with an involute margin; gills reaching the stem, but not decurrent, sometimes emarginate; stem hollow, with cartilaginous bark of a different substance from the hymenophore, but confluent with it; often swollen and splitting in the middle; spores white. The plants are usually found growing upon dead tree stumps; some grow upon the ground; a few are parasitic on other fungi or springing from *sclerotia*, small impacted masses of mycelium. The species are generally small and firm and of slow growth. A few are edible, some few have an unpleasant odor. On account of the cartilaginous stem and the dryness of their substance, some of the smaller species are apt to be taken for Marasmii. Note: Saccardo in his Sylloge gives Collybia generic rank.

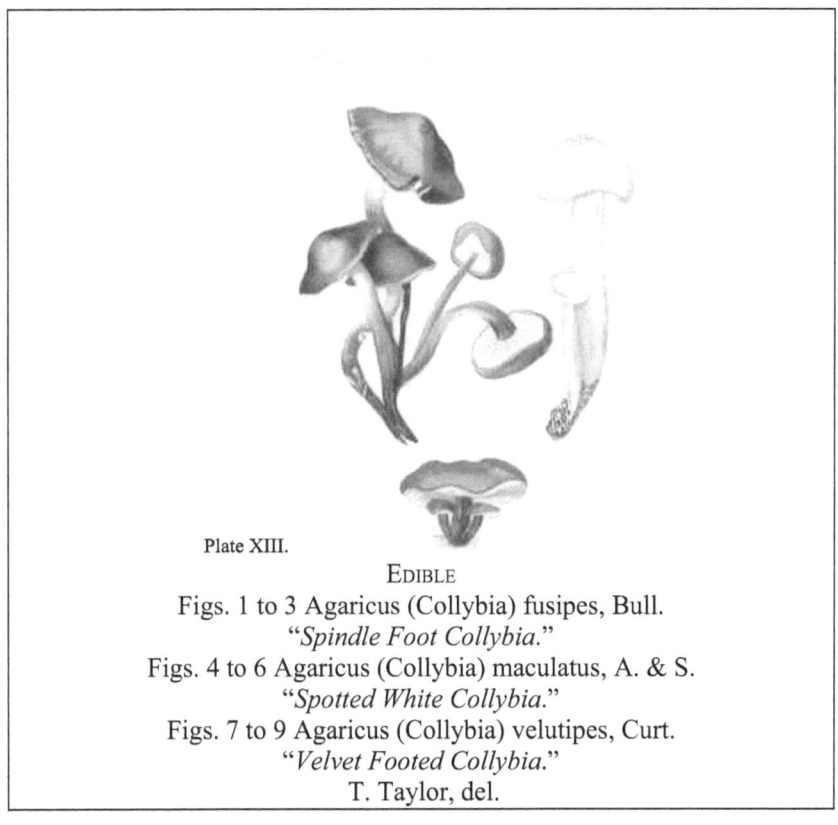

Plate XIII.

PLATE XIII.

FIGS. 1 to 3.—**Ag. (Collybia) fusipes** Bull. *"Spindle-Foot Collybia."*

EDIBLE.

Cap fleshy, somewhat tough, convex, then plane, smooth, even or slightly cracked in places, umbo evanescent, reddish brown; gills adnexed, nearly free, broad, distant, at length separating near the stem, firm, white, changing to fawn color, or pale brown often spotted; stem long, stuffed, then hollow, externally cartilaginous, contorted, swollen in the middle, cracking in longitudinal slits, fusiform, tapering narrowly to a rooted base, reddish brown. On stumps in woods in the autumn. Cap 1 to 2 inches broad; stem 2 to 6 inches long. This species is densely cæspitose. It is very generally recorded among authors as edible, although the flesh is somewhat tough. It requires long and slow cooking. An English author recommends it for pickling. Only the caps should be used for this purpose.

Figs. 4 to 6.—**Ag. (Collybia) maculatus** A. & S. (**Collybia maculata**).
"Spotted White Collybia."

Cap fleshy and compact, convexo-plane, obtuse, smooth, even, margin thin, at first involute, turned inwards, white; stem long and stout, externally cartilaginous, ventricose, sometimes striate, tapering towards the base; gills free, or nearly so, narrow, crowded, somewhat linear, white, becoming spotted. Taste slightly acid. The whole plant is creamy white, becoming spotted and stained throughout with rusty-brown or foxy-red tints. The plants are usually large, long stemmed, and grow in irregular clusters on decayed tree stumps in woods. Specimens of a large size have been gathered in the fir woods near Mattapoisett, Massachusetts. Cap 3 to 5 inches broad; stem 3 to 5 inches long. The variety *immaculatus* differs from the typical form in not becoming spotted and in the broader gills, which are serrated.

Figs. 7 to 9.—**Ag. (Collybia) velutipes** Curt. *"Velvet-Footed Collybia."*

Cap fleshy, thin, at first convex, then plane, obtuse, smooth, viscid, tawny or brownish yellow, turning dark; flesh yellowish and soft; gills slightly adnexed, pale yellow; stem tough, stuffed, externally cartilaginous, sometimes slender, but usually thick, covered with a brown velvety down, dark bay color. This is a very common species in some localities. It is densely cæspitose, growing in heavy clusters on old logs and tree trunks in parks, woods, and gardens. The plants are quite gelatinous when cooked. Group figured from illustration by M. C. Cooke.

Collybia *radicata* Rehl. is recorded as an edible species. The plants have a thin, slightly fleshy cap, slightly umbonate, wrinkled, and glutinous at maturity; distant, white, adnexed gills, and tall, slender, rigid stem. The latter is often twisted and usually attenuated upwards, color pale brown. It has a long tapering root entering deeply into the soil. This species is solitary in habit, and is commonly found in grass, or near decayed stumps. Cap from 2 to 3 inches in diameter, stem 6 inches to 10 inches in length.

Collybia *esculenta* Jacq., a small species found in pine woods as well as in pastures in the spring, is recorded as edible by a number of authors. In this species the cap is nearly plane, obtuse, and smooth, brownish; gills adnate, whitish; stem very slender, fistulose, equal, tough, smooth, reddish clay color, deeply rooting.

APPENDIX.

As Chief of the Division of Microscopy, U. S. Department of Agriculture, the author prepared for the World's Columbian Exposition at Chicago a collection of models of edible and poisonous mushrooms, for which a medal and diploma were there awarded. The same collection, which now belongs to the Museum of the Department of Agriculture, was exhibited at the Atlanta Cotton Exposition in 1895, where a diploma was again awarded for it, and has since been exhibited at the exposition of 1897 in Nashville, Tenn. The models composing this collection, about one thousand in number, were made from actual specimens and colored to nature, the same species being generally represented by numerous specimens so as to illustrate the various stages in the life of the plant, habit of growth, etc.

The following is a list of the mushrooms represented in this collection, among which there are types of most of the genera in which species recorded as edible occur:

Amanita *Cæsarea* Schaeff. "Orange Amanita." Edible.

Amanita *rubescens* Pers. "The Blusher." "Reddish-Brown Amanita." Edible.

Amanita *strobiliformis* Vitt. "Fir-Cone" or "Pine-Cone Amanita." Edible.

Amanita *pantherinus* D. C. "Panther Mushroom." Poisonous.

Amanita *phalloides* Fr. "Poison Amanita." Poisonous.

Amanita *muscaria* Linn. "Fly Amanita." "False Orange." Poisonous.

Amanita *verna* Bull. "Spring Mushroom." "Vernal Amanita." Poisonous.

Amanitopsis *vaginata* Roze. "The *Grizette.*" "Sheathed Amanitopsis." Edible.

Lepiota *procera* Scop. "Parasol Mushroom." "Tall Lepiota." Edible.

Lepiota *racodes* Vitt. "Ragged Lepiota." Edible.

Armillaria *mellea* Fr. "Honey Mushroom." Edible.

Tricholoma *terreum* Schaeff. "The Gray Cap." Edible.

Clitocybe *illudens* Schw. "Giant Clitocybe." Unwholesome.

Clitocybe *odora* Bull. "Odorous Clitocybe." Edible.

Clitocybe *laccata* Scop. Edible.

Collybia *fusipes* Bull. "Spindle-Foot Collybia." Edible.

Pleurotus *ostreatus* Jacq. "Oyster Mushroom." Edible.

Pleurotus *ulmarius* Jacq. "Elm Pleurotus." Edible.

Volvaria *bombycina* Schaeff. "Silky Volvaria." This species has been recorded by some authors as poisonous. Hays, after testing it, speaks well of it, and states that is eaten on the Continent.

Volvaria *speciosa* Fr. Not commended.

Pholiota *caperata* Pers. Edible.

Agaricus *campester*. "Field Mushroom." Edible.

Agaricus *arvensis* Schaeff. "Horse Mushroom." Edible.

Hypholoma *sublateritium*. "Brick Top." Edible.

Hypholoma *Candolliana*. Edible.

Coprinus *comatus* Fr. "Shaggy Mane Mushroom." Edible.

Coprinus *atramentarius*. "Inky Coprinus." Edible.

Cortinarius *turmalis* Fr. Edible.

Cortinarius *cærulescens* Fr. Edible.

Hygrophorus *conicus* Fr. Conical Mushroom. Has been recorded by a number of authors as poisonous. Some later writers speak of it as edible.

Hygrophorus *puniceus* Fr. "Purplish Hygrophorus." Edible.

Hygrophorus *ceraceus* Fr. "Waxen Hygrophorus." Edible.

Lactarius *deliciosus* Fr. "Delicious Lactarius." Edible.

Lactarius *volemus* Fr. "Orange-brown Lactarius." Edible.

Lactarius *torminosus* Fr. This mushroom is said to contain an acrid juice which acts seriously on the stomach and alimentary canal.

Lactarius *rufus* Fr. Intensely acrid.

Lactarius *vellereus* Fr. Extremely acrid.

Lactarius *piperatus*. "Fiery Milk Mushroom." Extremely acrid when raw. The Russians parboil it, throwing away the liquid, before preparing for pickling. A noted German chemist reports it "not very safe."

Russula *alutacea* Fr. Yellow-gilled Russula. Edible.

Russula *virescens* Fr. Edible.

Russula *cyanoxantha* Schaeff. "Variable Russula." Edible.

Russula *emetica* Fr. This mushroom is extremely acrid when raw; by some authors it is recorded as poisonous, by others as edible. Chemical analysis has shown that it contains a varying proportion of muscarin, as well as cholin, etc.

Cantharellus *cibarius* Fr. "The Chantarelle." Edible.

Marasmius *oreades* Bolt. "The Fairy Ring Mushroom." Edible.

Boletus *edulis* Bull. Edible.

Boletus *scaber* Fr. Edible.

Boletus *granulatus* Linn. Edible.

Boletus *brevipes* Pk. Edible.

Boletus *luteus* Linn. Edible.

Boletus *pachypus* Fr. Edible.

Boletus *Americanus* Pk. Edible.

Boletus *subtomentosus* Linn. Edible.

Boletus *castaneus* Bull. Edible.

Boletus *Satanus* Lenz. "White-topped Boletus." Recorded as poisonous.

Boletus *luridus* Schaeff. "Red-pored Boletus." Recorded as poisonous.

Strobilomyces *strobilaceus* Bull. Edible.

Fistulina *hepatica* Fr. "Beefsteak Fungus." Edible.

Polyporus *sulfureus* Bull. Edible.

Hydnum *repandum* Linn. Edible.

Hydnum *erinaceum* Bull. Edible.

Sparassis *crispa* Wulf. Edible.

Clavaria *cinerea* Bull. Edible.

Clavaria *rugosa*. Edible.

Lycoperdon *gemmatum* Fr. Edible.

Lycoperdon *giganteum* Fr. "Giant Puff-Ball." Edible.

Lycoperdon *pyriforme* Schaeff. "Pear-shaped Puff-Ball." Edible.

Scleroderma *vulgare* Fr.

Morchella *esculenta* Pers. Edible.

Morchella *conica* Bull. Edible.

Hirneola *auricula Judæ* Bull. Edible.

Ithyphallus *impudicus* Linn. Unwholesome.

Clathrus *cancellatus* Linn. Unwholesome.

NOTE.—In addition to the above there were also represented a number of coriaceous or woody species which grow upon trees, old stumps, etc.

STUDENT'S HAND-BOOK

OF

MUSHROOMS OF AMERICA

EDIBLE AND POISONOUS.

BY

THOMAS TAYLOR, M. D.

AUTHOR OF FOOD PRODUCTS, ETC.

Fellow of the A. A. A. S.; Hon. Member of the Mic. Section Royal Inst., Liverpool, England; Member of Honor of the International Medical Society of Hygiene, Brussels; Member of the American and Washington Chemical Societies; French Chemical Society, Paris; of the American Textile Society; Medical Society of Washington, D. C.; Cor. Member Academy of Arts and Sciences of Brooklyn, N. Y.; Cor. Member Mic. Societies of New York, Buffalo, etc., etc.

Published in Serial Form—**No. 5**—Price, 50c. per number.

WASHINGTON, D. C.:
A. R. TAYLOR, PUBLISHER, 238 MASS. AVE. N.E.
1897.

PUBLISHER'S NOTE.

It has not been possible to represent all the genera of mushrooms which contain species having value as esculents within the compass of this series of five pamphlets, but the demand for these promises to justify the publication, at a future date, of a second series, which the author now has in preparation.

A. R. T.

AGARICINI.

LEUCOSPORI—(Spores White).

Subgenus *Pleurotus* Fries. The Pleuroti are similar in some respects to the Tricholomas and Clitocybes, some of the species having notched gills near the stem, and others, again, having the gills decurrent, or running down the stem. Most of the species grow upon dead wood or from decaying portions of live trees. Very few grow upon the ground. The stem is mostly eccentric, lateral, or wanting; when present it is homogeneous or confluent with the substance of the cap; the substance may be compact, spongy, slightly fleshy, or membranaceous. Veil evanescent or absent. The spores are white or slightly tinted.

M. C. Cooke figures over thirty species of Pleurotus found in Great Britain, and describes 45 species found in Australia. With few exceptions, all of these grow upon wood. Very few have value as esculents.

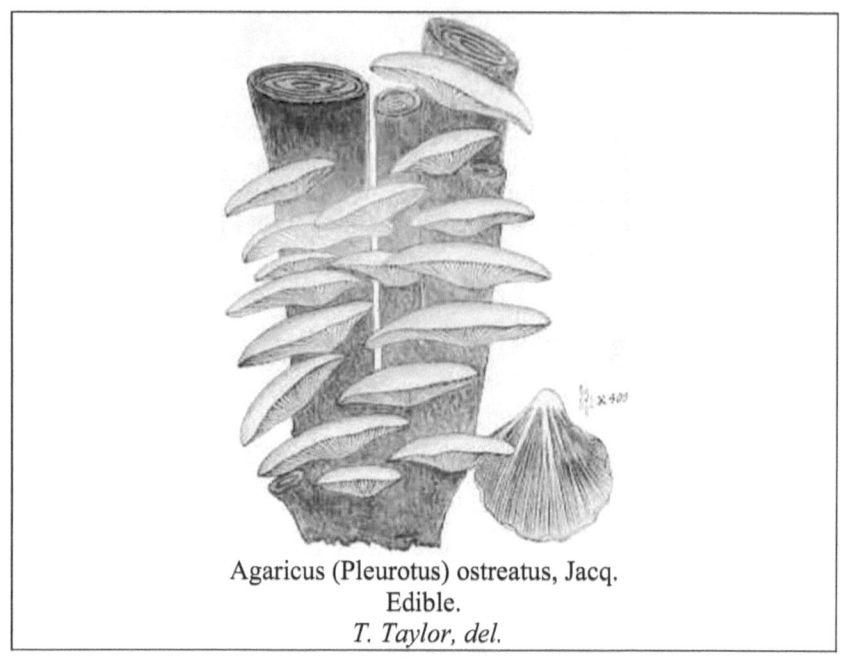

Agaricus (Pleurotus) ostreatus, Jacq.
Edible.
T. Taylor, del.

Ag. (Pleurotus) ostreatus Jacq. *"Oyster Mushroom."*

EDIBLE.

Cap soft, fleshy, smooth, shell-shaped, white or cinereous, turning brownish or yellowish with age. Flesh white, somewhat fibrous. Gills white, broad and decurrent, anastamosing at the base. Stem usually not well defined, lateral, or absent. Spores elliptical, white. The caps are sometimes thickly clustered and closely overlapping, and sometimes wide apart. This mushroom has long been known as edible both raw and cooked. It has a pleasant but not decided flavor and must be cooked slowly and carefully to be tender and easily digestible. Old specimens are apt to be tough. It is found on decaying wood and often on fallen logs in moist places or upon decaying tree-trunks. It is frequently recurrent on the same tree. I have gathered great quantities of the Oyster mushroom during several seasons past from a fallen birch tree which spanned a small stream. The lower end of the tree rested on the moist ground at the edge of the stream. Specimens have been found on the willow, ash and poplar trees, and upon the apple and the laburnum.

Pleurotus *sapidus* Kalchb. *Sapid Pleurotus.* Edible.

This species closely resembles the Oyster mushroom in form and habit of growth, and is by some considered only a variety of *P. ostreatus*. It grows usually in tufts with the caps closely overlapping, varying in color white, ashy, grayish or brownish. Flesh white. The stems are white, smooth and short, mostly springing from a common base. The gills are white and very broad, and decurrent. The spores assume a very pale lilac tint on exposure to the atmosphere.

Pleurotus *ulmarius* Bull. *"Elm Pleurotus."* Edible.

The Elm Pleurotus is quite conspicuous by reason of its large size and light color. The cap is smooth and compact, usually whitish with a dull yellowish tinge in the center. Flesh white. The skin cracks very easily, giving it a scaly appearance. The gills are broad, and toothed or notched near their point of attachment to the stem as in the Tricholomas, white in color, turning yellowish with age. The stem is firm and smooth, solid and rather eccentric, thick and sometimes slightly downy near the base, from two to four inches in length. Although this mushroom seems to prefer the elm and is most frequently found on trees of that species, it is found also upon other trees, but principally the maple, the ash, the willow, and the poplar. It grows upon live trees, usually where the branches have been cut away, and upon stumps as well. Most authors recommend it as an esculent, although it has not the rich flavor of some other mushrooms. It dries well and can be kept thus for winter use. This species has a wide range and grows most abundantly in the autumn. Its resistance to cold has been frequently remarked.

AGARICINI.

Subgenus *Amanita*. The Amanitas are usually large and somewhat watery, the flesh brittle rather than tough. The very young plants are enveloped in a membranous wrapper, which breaks apart with the expansion of the plant, leaving a more or less persistent sheath at the base of the stem. The universal veil is distinct and free from the cuticle of the cap. The cap is convex at first, then expanded; in some species naked and smooth; in others, clothed with membranaceous patches of the volva. The stem is distinct from the fleshy substance of the cap, ringed and furnished with a volva or sheath. In some of the species this sheath is connate with the base of the stem, firm and persistent. In others, it is friable, at length nearly obsolete.

The ring is usually persistent, deflexed, more or less prominent, in rare cases pressed close against the stem, and sometimes scarcely distinguishable from it. The gills in most of the species are free from the stems, but there are exceptions to this rule. Spores white. As to geographical distribution, according to M. C. Cooke, seven-eighths of the species are distinctly located in the temperate zone, one-twentieth at a temperate elevation, and only one-twentieth presumably tropical. Out of the eighty species, about sixty are North

American and European, and one species is found on the slopes of the Andes, in South America. As heretofore stated, this group among mushrooms is made responsible for most of the well authenticated cases of fatal poisoning by mushrooms. It would be judicious, therefore, for those who are not thoroughly familiar with the characteristics of the edible Amanitas to defer making experiments with them for table use until that familiarity is acquired.

Saccardo in his *Sylloge* describes no less than fifteen edible species of Amanita as found in different parts of the world. Of those I have personally been able to identify but three which are common in this country, and which have been well tested. Specimens of these three species are illustrated in Plates XIV and XIV½ of this pamphlet. They are each and all found in varying abundance in different parts of the United States.

EDIBLE AMANITAS.
Figs. 1 to 4 Ag. (Amanita) Cæsareus, Scop. (Amanita Cæsarea)
"Orange Amanita."
Figs. 5 to 9 Ag. (Amanita) rubescens. Pers. "The Blusher."
"Reddish Brown Amanita."
EDIBLE.
T. Taylor, del.

PLATE XIV.

FIGS. 1 to 4. **Ag. (Amanita) Cæsareus** Scop. (**Amanita Cæsarea**). *"Orange Amanita," "True Orange."*

Cap at first convex, afterwards well expanded; *smooth*, free from warts, striate on the margin; color orange-red or bright lemon-yellow, with red disk; gills lemon-yellow, rounded near the stem, and free from it; stem equal or slightly tapering upwards, stuffed with cottony fibrils, or hollow (color clear lemon-yellow), bearing a yellowish ring near the top and sheathed at the base with large, loose, membranous, white volva. Odor faint but agreeable. Spores white, elliptical.

The whole plant is symmetrical in form, brilliant in coloring, clean and attractive in appearance. The American plant seems to differ in some slight respects from the European as figured and described in European works. In Europe the pileus or cap is said to vary in color, being sometimes white, pale yellow, red or even copper color, although it is usually orange-yellow. My own observation of the American plant of this species agrees with that of Prof. Peck in that the cap is uniform in color, being at first bright reddish- orange or even brilliant red, fading with age to yellow, either wholly or only on the margin. No white specimens have been as yet recorded in this country. The red color disappears in the dried specimens. The striations of the margin are usually quite deep and long and almost as distant as in the edible species Amanitopsis *vaginata*. Some European writers have described the flesh or substance of the cap as yellowish. In our plant the flesh is white, but stained with yellow or red immediately under the cuticle. Amanita *Cæsarea* is the only one of the Amanitas which has yellow gills.

Berkeley, in his "Outlines of British Fungi," describes A. Cæsarea as it is found in some parts of Continental Europe, but states that up to the date of his writing it had not been found in Great Britain. It is not recorded in the more recent lists of British fungi by M. C. Cooke nor in that of Australian fungi by the same author. The species has a wide range in this country, and though not very common in the North, in some localities, as in the pine and oak woods of North Carolina, it is found in great abundance. Dufour states that it is much esteemed as an esculent in France, and though rare in the northern part of that country, it is common in the center and the south of France in autumn. It is well known in different portions of Continental Europe, and is frequently figured in contrast with its very poisonous congener, Amanita muscaria, or "False Orange," commonly known as the "Fly Amanita," or "Fly-Killer."

A careless observer might mistake one for the other, but with a little attention to well-defined details the edible form can be readily distinguished from the poisonous one.

In analyzing the species the attention should be directed to the following characteristics of the two mushrooms: In A. *Cæsarea* the cap is *smooth*, the stem, gills and ring *lemon-yellow*, and the cup-shaped wrapper or volva which sheathes the base of the stem is white and *persistently membranous.*

In A. *muscaria* the cap is *warty* or shows the traces or remains of warts; the gills *white*, stem *white*, or only very slightly yellowish, and the wrapper or volva is evanescent, breaking up into ridge-like patches adhering to the base of the stem.

The Amanita Cæsarea has long been esteemed as an esculent in foreign countries, and was known in ancient times to the Greeks and Romans. It is known under the following names: "Orange," "Cæsar's mushroom," "Imperial mushroom," "Yellow-egg," "Kaiserling," etc. Mycologists who have tested it agree as to its edibility and delicate flavor.

The specimens figured in Plate XIV represent the average size of those which I have gathered in the vicinity of the District of Columbia. Much larger ones have been gathered in the woody portions of Druid Hill Park, Baltimore, Md.

Dufour writes: "This mushroom, the "true oronge," is cooked in a variety of ways, and it always constitutes an exquisite dish." This author gives the following recipes for cooking the *Cæsarea*, which he calls the "Oronge:"

Oronge à la bordelaise.—The stem is minced with fine herbs, bread-crumbs, and garlic, and seasoned with pepper and salt. This hash is placed in the concavity of the caps, and all is put to bake with good oil in a pan steamed in a chafing dish.

Oronge à l'Italienne.—Stew gently with a little butter and salt, then serve with a sauce composed of oil seasoned with the juice of lemon, pepper, garlic, and extract of sweet almond.

The Spanish are fond of this mushroom, and it is said to enter into their national dish, olla podrida, a mixture of meat, vegetables, and spices, whenever it can be obtained.

It is sometimes fried in butter or olive oil and seasoned with sugar.

PLATE XIV.

FIGS. 5 to 9.—**Ag. (Amanita) rubescens** Pers. (**Amanita rubescens**). *"The Blusher,"* *"Reddish Brown Amanita."*

EDIBLE.

Cap at first convex then expanded, margin even or very slightly striated, usually reddish-brown or reddish-fawn color, covered with mealy, more or loss persistent warts; flesh white, changing to a reddish or pinkish tinge, where cut or bruised, the reddish tinge most intense in the bulbous portion of the base of the stem; *gills reaching the stem and forming decurrent lines upon it*, white, becoming spotted with rusty or wine red stains when bruised or attacked by insects; stem ringed, whitish or dingy white, becoming brownish or spotted, with reddish-brown stains. The base of the stem is usually bulbous, the bulb sometimes tapering to a point at the root, and in some instances ending abruptly.

The ring or collar which encircles the stem near the top is membranous, and usually well defined.

The volva which completely envelops the young plant is very friable and soon disappears. Fragments of the volva may be seen in the shape of scales or small particles upon the mushroom stem, and in wart-like patches upon the cap. In the representations of this mushroom which appear in European works the cap is a deeper reddish-brown tint than I have found it here. The color of the cap is usually a light reddish brown or reddish gray, sometimes almost white. This species is found usually in light open woods. In a warm moist climate it appears early in the season, and can be gathered until the frosts come. Taste very pleasant.

There is a poisonous species, Amanita *pantherinus*, rare, which has a viscid brown warted cap bearing a slight resemblance to that of the *rubescens*, but the gills do not turn red when bruised, and the volva at the base of the stem is well defined and persistent.

The *rubescens* is very plentiful in the woods of Maryland and Virginia, and specimens have been received from different parts of the country. I have frequently eaten it stewed with butter, and found it very good eating. Hay speaks of it as being eaten in England, where it is called the "Blusher." Cooke says it is pleasant both in taste and odor. It is spoken of by French authors as of delicate flavor, and as well known in some parts of France. In preparing for the table bring the mushroom to a quick boil and pour off the first water, then stew with flavoring to suit the taste.

The specimens of this species represented in Plate XIV were collected in the woods of Forest Glen, Maryland. They are often found of much larger size and much lighter in coloring, with the stains upon the gills redder in color. The very young plants as they burst through the surface of the soil show a distinct volva at the base of the stem. In the mature plant this disappears, often leaving the slightly bulbous base quite smooth.

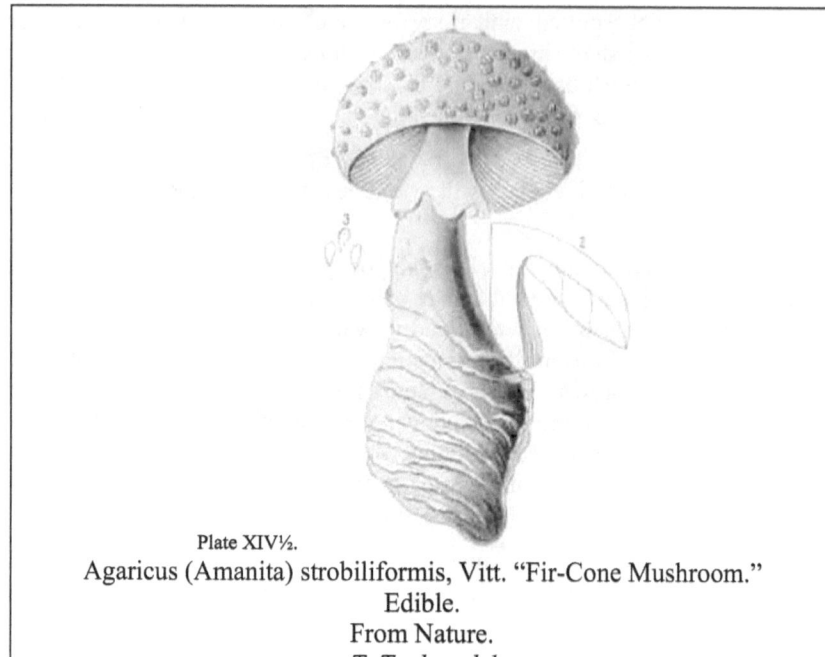

PLATE XIV½.

Ag. (Amanita) strobiliformis Fries (**Amanita strobiliformis**). *"Fir-cone Mushroom."*

EDIBLE.

Cap fleshy, convex at first, then expanded, covered with persistent white warts, margin even, white; flesh white, firm and compact; gills rounded behind and free from the stem, white; stem solid, the bulbous base tapering, furrowed with concentric and longitudinal channels at the root, and extending well into the ground, white; ring large, soon splitting; volva breaking up and appearing in concentric ridges upon the stem. Spores white.

This mushroom is very pleasant to the taste when raw as well as when cooked. It is found in light woods or on the borders of woods where the soil is somewhat friable, generally solitary, but sometimes two or three are found clustered together. The plants are sometimes so large that two or three of them would make a very good meal. Specimens have been found with the cap measuring 8 to 9 inches across when expanded, the stem varying from 6 to 8 inches in height, and from 1 to 3 inches in thickness. When young the plants are generally snowy white throughout, changing with age to a dingy white or cinereous hue. The specimens figured in the plate formed one of a cluster of three mushrooms of this species found growing in the fir woods of the District of Columbia.

During some seasons I have found the *strobiliformis*, or "Fir-cone mushroom," fairly plentiful in some parts of Maryland, and in other seasons it has been rare. The whole plant when young is enclosed in a white membranous wrapper.

Although this species is very generally recognized by mycologists as edible, I would advise great caution in selecting specimens for table use, since there is a dangerous species which might be mistaken for it by one not familiar with the characteristics of both species; I refer to a form of Amanita muscaria with ochraceous yellow cap which, when faded or bleached by the sun and rain, sometimes approaches, in tint, the dingy white of old or faded specimens of the *strobiliformis*. Both species have *white gills*, *white stems*, and *white flocculent veil*. The volva is evanescent in both, leaving traces of its existence in concentric ridges at the base, and part way up the stem.

In the species *strobiliformis*, the flesh of the cap is white throughout, as well as the cuticle.

In the yellowish *muscaria*, the flesh *immediately* beneath the cuticle of the upper surface of the cap is yellowish, frequently deepening at the disk to orange hue.

The cap of Amanita *muscaria* is very attractive to flies, but proves to them, as also to roaches and to some other insects, a deadly poison.

The juice of *strobiliformis* is not poisonous to flies. This fact may aid in identifying the species.

Subgenus *Amanitopsis* Roze. The species of this subgenus were formerly included in Amanita. The characteristic which separates it from Amanita is the *absence of a ring on the stem*. The gills are free from the stem, the spores are white, and the whole plant in youth is encased in an egg-shaped volva.[A]

[A] Although this subgenus is not included in M. C. Cooke's analytical key to the order of Agaricini, published with his kind permission in No. 3 of this series, he now includes it as one of the subgenera which should have a place in that list.

Amanitopsis *vaginata* Roze. Edible.

This species is very common in pine and oak forests. The plant, as a whole, has a graceful aspect and grows singly or scattered through open places in the woods. It is somewhat fragile and easily broken. The cap in this species is usually a mouse-gray, sometimes slaty gray or brownish, generally umbonate in the center and distinctly striated on the margin.

The stem is white, equal, and slender in proportion to the width of the cap, and sheathed quite far up with a loose white membranous wrapper. This sheath is so slightly attached to the base of the stem that it is often left in the ground if the plant is carelessly pulled. The gills are white, or whitish, free from the stem and rounded at the outer extremity.

There is a white variety, (variety *alba*) A. *nivalis*, in which the whole plant is white, and a tawny variety (A. *fulva* Schaeff.) in which the cap is a pale ochraceous yellow, with the gills and stem white or whitish. In the variety A. *livida* or A. *spadicea* Grcv. the cap is brown, while the stem and gills are tinged a smoky brown.

These are all edible and of fairly good flavor. Except in the absence of the ring upon the stem, the light varieties might be mistaken for small forms of the poisonous species Amanita *verna* or of *phalloides*. Great caution should therefore be observed, in gathering for the table, to be sure of the species.

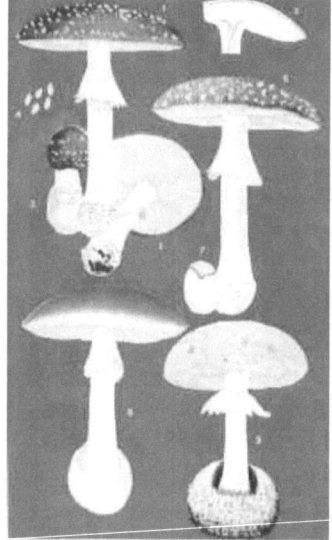

Figs. 1 to 7. Ag. (Amanita) muscarius, Linn. (Amanita muscaria)
"Fly Mushroom."
Fig. 8. Ag. (Amanita) phalloides,Fries.
Fig. 9. Ag. (Amanita) mappa Batsch.
POISONOUS.
T. Taylor, del.

PLATE XV.

Figs. 1 to 7.—**Ag. (Amanita) muscarius** Linn. (**Amanita muscaria**). "*Fly*

Mushroom," "*False Orange.*"

Cap warty, margin striate; gills white, reaching the stem, and often forming decurrent lines upon it; stem white, stuffed, annulate, bulbous at the base, concentrically ridged or scaly at the base, and sometimes part way up, with fragments of the ruptured wrapper. Spores widely elliptical, white, .0003 to .0004 of an inch in length.

The plants of this species vary very much in size and in the color of the cap. The latter is sometimes a bright scarlet and again it is orange color, more frequently ochraceous yellow, fading to a very pale yellow tint. In the variety *albus* it is white. The stem is stuffed with webby fibrils and varies very much in thickness: sometimes in young specimens it is very stout, with a thick ovate bulb reaching well up towards the cap, and again it is comparatively slender and nearly equal from the cap down to a very slight bulb at the base. The very young plant is completely enveloped in a white or yellowish egg-shaped wrapper or volva, which, being friable, generally breaks up into scales, forming warts upon the upper surface of the cap. When the plant is young and moist the cap is slightly sticky. A thickish white veil extends from the stem to the inner margin of the cap. This breaks away with the growth and expansion of the plant and falls in lax folds, forming a deflexed ring round the upper portion of the stem.

This mushroom is very common in woods and forests in summer and autumn, and has a wide geographical range. It is recorded by all mycologists as poisonous. One author states that when eaten in very small quantities it acts as a cathartic, but that it causes death when eaten freely. Flies find in it a deadly poison, and the poisonous alkaloids are not destroyed by drying.

Although cases are cited where this mushroom has been eaten without injury, its fatally poisonous effects have been too well and too often tested to allow of any doubt as to the danger of eating it, even in small quantities.

Amanita Frostiana, Frost's Amanita, is a much smaller species than A. muscaria. It bears a very close resemblance to the Fly Amanita, and might easily be taken for a small form of the same. The cap is yellowish and warted, and specimens occur in which the stem and gills are slightly tinged with yellow. It is poisonous.

PLATE XV.

FIG. 8.—**Ag. (Amanita) phalloides** Fries (**Amanita phalloides**) **A. vernalis** Bolt., **A. verrucosus** Curtis. "*Poisonous Amanita,*" "*Death Cup.*"

Cap bell-shaped or ovate at first, then expanded, smooth, obtuse, viscid, margin even, creamy-white, brown, or greenish, without warts; flesh white; stem white, hollow or stuffed, bulbous at the base, annulate; gills rounded and ventricose, coarse, and persistently white, free from the stem; volva conspicuous, large, loose, adhering to the base, but free from the stem at the top, with the margin irregularly notched. In the white forms there is frequently a greenish or yellow tinge at the disk or centre of the cap. The white form is most common, but the brownish is often found in this country. I have not yet found the green-capped variety sometimes figured in European works. In the brown variety the stem and ring are often tinged with brown, as also the volva. The cap is usually from 2 to 3 inches broad, and the stem from 3 to 5 inches long. The whole plant is symmetrical in shape and clean looking, though somewhat clammy to the touch when moist. It is very common in mixed woods, in some localities, and is universally considered as fatally poisonous.

The white form of A. *phalloides*, although in reality bearing very little resemblance to the common field mushroom, has been mistaken for it as also for the *Smooth white lepiota*, and in some instances has been eaten with fatal results by those who gathered it.

The distinction between this most poisonous Amanita and the common field mushroom is well marked. In the common mushroom the *gills* are *pink, becoming dark brown*, the *spores purplish brown*, and the whole mushroom is stout and short stemmed, the stem being shorter than the diameter of the cap, and having no volva, or wrapper at its base. In the species A. *phalloides* the *gills* are *persistently white* and the bulb is distinct and broad at the base, the white cup-shaped wrapper sheathing the base of the stem like the calyx of a flower. The *Smooth white lepiota* shows neither volva nor trace of one, and has other distinct characteristics which distinguish it from A. *phalloides*. See page 14, No. 4 of this series.

The specimen figured in Plate XV grew in Maryland, where it is quite common.

PLATE XV.

FIG. 9.—Ag. (Amanita) mappa (Amanita mappa) Linn., Amanita citrina, A. virosa.

POISONOUS.

Cap at first convex, then expanded, dry, without a separable cuticle, not warty but showing white, yellowish, or brownish scales or patches on its upper surface; gills white, adnexed; flesh white, sometimes slightly yellowish under the skin; stem stuffed, then hollow, cylindrical, yellowish white, nearly smooth, with a distinctly bulbous base; volva white or brownish. Odor pleasant. Spores spheroidal. The cap in this species is somewhat variable in color, but those having a white cap are most common. The plant is not so tall as those of the species *phalloides*. It is solitary in habit, and is found usually in open woods.

Curtis and Lowerby figure *mappa* and *phalloides* under the same name.

Fig. 1. Ag. (Amanita) vernus, Bull. (Amanita verna.) "Spring Mushroom."
Fig. 2. Represents section of mature plant.
Fig. 3. Spores; Fig. 4. Young plant.
POISONOUS.
T. Taylor, del.

PLATE XVI.

FIGS. 1 to 4.—**Ag. (Amanita) vernus** Bull. **(Amanita verna)** Linn., **Amanita bulbosa**, **Ag. solitarius.** *"Vernal Mushroom," "Spring Mushroom,"* etc.

POISONOUS.

Cap at first ovate, then expanded, becoming at length slightly depressed, viscid, white; margin smooth; flesh white; gills white, free; stem white, equal, stuffed or hollow, easily splitting, floccose, with bulbous base; volva white, closely embracing the stem, but free from it at the margin; ring reflexed; spores globose, .0003 in. broad. The plant is creamy white throughout and does not seem to be easily distinguishable from the white forms of A. *phalloides*. Fries and some others consider this species merely a variety of

Amanita *phalloides*, and it is regarded as equally poisonous, the poisonous principle being the same as that of A. *phalloides*. It is very common in mixed woods from early spring to frosty weather.

ALKALOIDS OF THE POISONOUS MUSHROOMS.

Schrader, after some experiments made in 1811, stated that the poisonous principle of the "Fly mushroom," Amanita muscaria, seemed to be combined with its red coloring matter and might be extracted by water or aqueous alcohol, but that it was not soluble in ether.

Vaquelin, as the result of more extended investigations made in 1813, expressed the opinion that this poison was not confined to the coloring matter of the mushroom, but that it was an integral part of the fatty constituents not only of *muscaria* but of several species of mushrooms. In 1826 and 1830, and again in 1867, important investigations were made and published by Letellier relating to the medical and poisonous properties of mushrooms growing around Paris. Letellier's early investigations led him to the conclusion that there were two poisons contained in certain fungi—(1) an acrid principle easily destroyed by drying or boiling or by maceration in alcohol or in alkaline solution, and (2) a peculiar poisonous alkaloid found only in certain of the Amanita group. Letellier in 1866 named this latter alkaloid *amanitin*. He then considered it to be the active poison of Amanita *muscaria*, Amanita *phalloides*, and Amanita *verna*, but a subsequent analysis by the German chemists Schmiedeberg and Koppe showed the *amanitin* of Letellier to be identical with *cholin*, a substance found in bile. Kobert says that *amanitin* is non-poisonous in itself, but states that it may be changed on decay of the mushroom to the muscarin-like acting *neurin*, which is highly poisonous. He thinks it highly probable that nearly all of the edible and non-edible mushrooms contain pure *amanitin* (cholin) partly in primitive condition and partly in a more intricate organic connection, as *lecithin*. It has been demonstrated that amanitin separates very readily from lecithin during the *decay or careless drying* of mushrooms and changes into the *poisonous neurin*; hence the necessity of using mushrooms only when *perfectly fresh* or when *quickly dried*.

MUSCARIN.[A]

[A] The earliest account of the separation of the poisonous principles of the mushrooms of the genus Amanita dates back to the experiments of Apoiger in 1851. Harnack's researches were published in 1876 and those of Huseman in 1882.

To the eminent German chemists Schmiedeberg and Koppe is due the credit of isolating the active poisonous principle of the Fly mushroom (*muscarin*). These authors published in 1869 a series of interesting experiments made with *muscarin*, having relation to its effect upon the heart, respiration, secretions and digestive organs, etc., and this was supplemented by other experiments made by their pupils, Prof. R. Boehm and E. Harnack. Schmiedeberg and Koppe's work relates to the effect of this poison on man as well as upon the lower animals. Dr. J. L. Prevost in 1874 reviewed the investigations made by Schmiedeberg and Koppe in a paper read before the Biological Society of Geneva, adding some confirmatory observations of his own relative to experiments made with muscarin upon the lower animals. The experiments made by these authors demonstrated "that muscarin arrests the action of a frog's heart, that a muscarined frog's heart began to beat immediately under the influence of atropin, and further that it was impossible to muscarine a frog's heart while under the influence of atropin."

Schmiedeberg subjected cats and dogs to doses of muscarin, large enough to produce death, and when the animals were about to succumb, injected hypodermically from one to two milligrams of sulphate of *atropin*, after which the toxic symptoms disappeared and the animals completely revived. Prof. Boehm found that *digitalin* likewise re-established heart action when suspended by the action of muscarin.

In man the fatal termination, in cases of mushroom poisoning, where the antidote is not used, may take place in from 5 to 12 hours or not for two or three days.

According to Prof. E. Kobert's recent chemical analysis, the "Fly mushroom," Amanita muscaria, contains not only the very poisonous alkaloid *muscarin* and the *amanitin* of Letellier (*cholin*), but also a third alkaloid, *pilz atropin*. The pilz-atropin (mushroom atropin) was discovered by Schmiedeberg in a *commercial* preparation of *muscarin*, and later Prof. Kobert discovered it in varying proportions in fresh mushrooms of different species. The effect of this third alkaloid, it is claimed, is to neutralize to a greater or less extent the effect of the poisonous one. Under its influence, when present in quantity, the poison is almost entirely neutralized. Contraction of the pupils changes to dilation, and slowing of the pulse may disappear. Only through the presence of this natural antidote in the Fly mushroom, says Kobert, is it possible, as in some parts of France and Russia, to eat without danger this mushroom, which contains 10% of sugar (trehalose or mycose) in a fermented and unfermented condition. He states also that delirium, intoxication, and other symptoms which, according to Prof. Dittmer of Kamschatka and various scientific travellers, are reported effects of the Fly mushroom in the extreme north, are not experienced in the same degree in southern Russia. This difference in action, he thinks, may be very properly attributed to the varying proportion of the above-mentioned atropin in the mushroom or to the presence of substances which develop only in the extreme north.

The symptoms of *muscarin* poisoning, apart from vomiting and purging, are slowing of the pulse, cerebral disturbance, contraction of the pupils, salivation and sweating. In case of death, which is caused by suffocation or a suspension of heart action, the lungs are found to be filled with air, and there is a transfusion of blood in the alimentary canal.

Prof. R. Kobert, in a lecture delivered before the University of Dorpat in 1891, states that *muscarin* is found equally in the Fly mushroom (A. muscaria), the Panther mushroom (A. pantherinus), Boletus luridus, and in varying quantities in Russula emetica. He states also that though highly poisonous to vertebrates, *muscarin* is not so to flies, and that the noxious principle in A. muscaria which kills the flies is not as yet determined.

It has been shown that the lower animals, such as sheep and geese, as well as man, have been severely poisoned by feeding on the "Fly mushroom," and that in the case of the horse, experiments have demonstrated that even 0.04 of a gramme, 0.62 of a grain, have caused marked symptoms of poisoning.

For *muscarin* as for *neurin* poisoning the antidote is atropin administered internally or by subcutaneous injection.

PHALLIN.

The toxic alkaloid of Amanita *phalloides* Fries (Amanita *bulbosa*) was examined by Boudier, who named it *"bulbosin,"* and by Oré, who named it *"phalloidin,"* but their examinations, it is claimed, proved little beyond the fact that it seemed to be in the nature of an alkaloid, identical neither with *muscarin* nor *helvellic* acid.

Oré affirmed that the *phalloidin* of the Amanita phalloides was very nearly related to, and perhaps identical with, strychnine. From this view Kobert and others dissent.

The poisonous principle of Amanita *phalloides* has recently been subjected to very careful analysis by Prof. Kobert. As a result of a large number of experiments and post-mortem examinations held on persons poisoned by A. *phalloides*, Kobert states that the symptoms can be explained uniformly by the action of a poison, to which he gives the provisional name of *"phallin."* This is an albuminous substance which dissolves the corpuscles of the blood, resembling in this and other respects in a remarkable degree the action of *helvellic* acid.

According to Kobert *phallin* has so far only been found in Amanita *phalloides* and in its varieties *verna, mappa,* etc. He finds also in this mushroom muscarin and an atropin-like alkaloid.

The symptoms of the phalloides poisoning are complex. Vomiting is accompanied by diarrhœa, cold sweats, fainting at times, convulsions, ending in coma. There is also fever and a quickening of the pulse. All these symptoms, which follow in succession, according to one author, are dependent on two different poisonous substances. The first may be an acrid and fixed poison, for it is found after repeated dryings, as well in the aqueous as in the alcoholic extract. The second acts by absorption, and is purely narcotic.

Phallin has some of the properties of the toxalbumin of poisonous spiders, and is a vegetable toxalbumin.

It has been remarked that in cases of poisoning by A. *phalloides,* the mushroom has tasted very good, and those poisoned felt well for several hours after eating.

Phalloides poisoning is said to bear a marked resemblance to phosphorus poisoning and to acute jaundice. There is no known antidote to the poisonous alkaloid *phallin.*

According to Prof. Kobert's analyses, the proportion of phallin in the dried mushroom amounts to less than 1%, but its effect on account of its concentration is the more intensive.

Extensive experiments made by Kobert with ox blood in regard to the comparative action of different substances in their power of dissolving the red blood corpuscles demonstrate that *phallin* in this respect exceeds all known substances. Kobert states that "If *phallin* be added to a mixture of blood with a 1% solution of common salt, using the blood of man, cattle, dogs, or pigeons, the blood corpuscles will be entirely dissolved by the poison diluted to 1-125,000."

Prof. Kobert states that he has examined the species Boletus edulis, Agaricus campester, and Amanita Cæsarea a number of times, but could never detect the action of phallin in them. Neither has he found it in A. muscaria.

THE POISONOUS ALKALOID OF GYROMITRA ESCULENTA FRIES (HELVELLA ESCULENTA PERS.)

HELVELLIC ACID.

Prof. Kobert writes of a number of cases of poisoning in the Baltic provinces of Russia by the mushroom Helvella *esculenta* Persoon, sometimes called the Lorchel. It should be here stated that the *Helvella esculenta* of Persoon is the *Gyromitra esculenta* of Fries. This mushroom is described as edible and placed in the edible lists by Dr. M. C. Cooke, Prof. Peck, and other distinguished mycologists, who have tested it and found it edible when perfectly fresh.

The poisonous principle of this mushroom was isolated and analyzed by Prof. R. Boehm, of Russia, in 1885. It was by him designated as *"helvellic acid,"* and found to be soluble in hot water. Profs. Eugene Bostroem and E. Ponfick, after giving some study to the effects of this mushroom poison, agreed in their report concerning it, which is to the effect that the *quickly dried* H. *esculenta* (Gyromitra *esculenta*) is not poisonous, and that the poisonous acid of the fresh ones may be extracted by means of hot water, so that while the decoction is poisonous the mushroom is not at all so, after the liquid is pressed out. Experiments with this mushroom were made by both authors on dogs, which ate them greedily, but without exception the dogs were very sick afterwards. The symptoms were nausea, vomiting, jaundice, stoppage of the kidneys, and hæmaglobinuria. The symptoms observed in man correspond to those manifested by the lower animals. Dissection showed the dissolution of innumerable blood corpuscles.

Prof. Kobert, commenting on the experiments made by Bostroem and Ponfick, states that he himself had been furnished yearly with fresh specimens of "H. *esculenta*" (G. *esculenta*) specially gathered for him at Dorpat, and after making various experiments with the freshly expressed juice he became convinced that the poisonous principle greatly varies, the juice sometimes operating as very poisonous, and sometimes as only slightly so. He states also that the proportion of poison in the mushroom varies with the weather, location, and age of the mushroom. The inhabitants of Russia do not eat this mushroom, but in Germany it is eaten dried or when perfectly fresh, after cooking, and after the first water in which it is boiled is removed.

Helvellic acid is not found in Morchella *esculenta* (the true Morel), nor is it known to exist in any other species except G. *esculenta*. It has been stated that there is no antidote for helvellic poisoning after the symptoms have appeared.

A specimen of Gyromitra esculenta was forwarded to me from Portland, Maine, by a member of a mycological club of that city, who stated that this mushroom was quite abundant in the early spring in the woods near Portland and that the plants were eaten by the members of the club, *care being taken to use them only when perfectly fresh.* Indigestion and nausea followed the eating of old specimens, but the general opinion was "favorable to the Gyromitra as an addition to the table." (See page 6, part 2, of this series.)

Prof. Chas. H. Peck, of Albany, while placing this mushroom in his edible list as one which he had repeatedly tested, advises that it should be eaten only when perfectly fresh, as nausea and sickness had been known to result from the eating of specimens which had been kept twenty-four hours before cooking.

I forwarded a number of drawings of the American species of G. *esculenta,* together with a dried specimen of the same received from Maine, to Prof. Kobert, who identified both drawings and specimen as the *Gyromitra esculenta* of Fries, synonymous with the *Helvella esculenta* of Persoon. Prof. Kobert also informs me that he finds the fresh G. *esculenta* perfectly harmless when freed of the water of the first boiling. He says: "My wife and I eat it very often, when in fresh condition, and after the first water in which it is boiled is poured off." The active poisonous principle of this mushroom is the *helvellic acid,* which is soluble in hot water. When the mushroom is gathered fresh and *quickly dried* it is then also innoxious. In this respect it differs from the species *A. muscaria,* in which the poisonous alkaloid *muscarin* is not destroyed in the drying, but remains unchanged for years in the dried mushroom.

The fact that there have been seemingly well-authenticated cases of fatal poisoning in the eating of this mushroom shows that if used at all it should be eaten *only when the conditions essential to safety are most carefully observed,* and as these mushrooms show varying qualities, according to local conditions of soil and climate, etc., amateurs finding it in localities where it has not been heretofore used should proceed tentatively and with much care before venturing to eat it freely.

POISONOUS AND DELETERIOUS MUSHROOMS OF THE LACTAR, RUSSULA, AND BOLETUS GROUPS.

Lactarius *torminosus* Fries contains in its milky juice an acrid resin which causes inflammation of the stomach and of the alimentary canal. When parboiled and the first water removed, it has been eaten without injurious effects. Lactarius *plumbeus* Bull., Lactarius *uvidus* Fries, Lactarius *turpis* Weinn., and Lactarius *pyrogalus* Bull., all acrid mushrooms, according to Kobert, are similarly poisonous.

Of the "Erdschieber" (Lactarius *vellereus*) and the "Pfefferling" (Lactarius piperatus Scop.) Kobert says they are eaten in parts of Russia and in some places in Germany, but that neither is very safe.

There is a species of *Russula* (R. *emetica*) very common in woods, easily recognized by its smooth scarlet top, white gills, and white stem and by its biting acridity, which, though recorded as poisonous by some authors, is considered edible by others. This mushroom, R. *emetica*, has been subjected to chemical analysis by Kobert, who finds in it *muscarin, cholin,* and *pilz-atropin* in varying proportions. Kobert states that in Germany it is "*rightly*" considered poisonous, though eaten in Russia, and ascribes the fact that it is not deemed poisonous in the latter country to the manner in which it is there prepared, the poisonous alkaloid being in greater part eliminated by parboiling the mushrooms, and not merely pouring off the water, but carefully squeezing it out of the parboiled fungi.

To the presence in this mushroom of the neutralizing alkaloid "pilz-atropin" in varying proportions may also be attributed in some measure the safety with which it has been eaten under certain conditions. R. fœtens and other acrid Russulas, as well as Lactars, have been known to produce severe gastro-enteritis.

Considering the foregoing, it would seem the part of prudence at least to avoid such of the Lactars and Russulas as have an acrid or peppery taste.

I think it would be a wise precaution to pour off the water of the first boiling in the case of all mushrooms about which there is a particle of doubt, whether *recorded* as poisonous or not.

Lactarius *torminosus* Fries. Cap fleshy, at first convex, then expanded, at length depressed in the center, slightly zoned, margin turned inwards, pale ochraceous yellow, with flesh-colored mottlings; *downy* or *hairy*; gills whitish, changing to pinkish yellow, narrow and close together; stem equal, stuffed or hollow, pallid or whitish; milk persistently *white and acrid.* In woods and fields. Specimens have been collected in New York, Massachusetts, Maryland, and Virginia. Cap 3 to 5 inches, stem 2½ to 4 inches.

Lactarius *pyrogalus.* Cap fleshy, slightly zoned, *smooth,* even, and moist, depressed in the center, grayish, or cinereous; gills white or yellowish, thin, not crowded; stem short, stout, stuffed, or hollow, sometimes slightly attenuated towards the root, pallid; flesh white or whitish; milk *white* and *extremely acrid,* copious. Borders of woods and meadows. This mushroom is sometimes called the "Fiery Milk Mushroom."

Lactarius *uvidus* Fries. Cap thin, convex, then plane, and slightly depressed in the center, sometimes showing slight umbo, viscid, *zoneless,* smooth, dingy gray or pallid brown, margin turned inwards; gills narrow and close together, white or yellowish, when cut or bruised turning a purplish hue; stem stuffed or hollow, viscid, smooth, equal or slightly tapering towards the cap, white; milk white, changing to lilac, acrid. Height 2 to 4 inches. Cap 2 to 4 inches broad. In woods.

Lactarius *turpis* Fries. Cap viscid, compact, *zoneless,* greenish umber, margin clothed with yellowish down; gills thin, paler than the cap; stem hollow or stuffed, stoutish, short, viscid, olive color, slightly attenuated towards the base; milk *white, acrid.* Fir woods.

Lactarius *plumbeus* Fries. Cap fleshy, firm, dry, somewhat hairy, varying in color, usually some shade of brown; gills yellowish, thin, and close together; stem solid, equal, lighter in color than the cap; flesh white; milk *white* and *acrid.*

Lactarius *vellereus* Fries. *Fleecy Lactarius.* Cap compact, convex or umbilicate, zoneless, *minutely downy*; margin reflexed, gills white, *distant,* arcuate; stem short, solid, pubescent; milk *white, acrid,* somewhat scanty. In woods. Whole plant white.

Lactarius *piperatus* Scop. *Peppery Lactarius.* Cap fleshy, compact, convex and slightly umbilicate, at last deeply depressed, becoming funnel-formed, smooth and even; gills decurrent, very narrow, thin, even and close together, dichotonous, white; flesh white; milk *white, extremely acrid,* copious; stem very short, stout, solid. Whole plant white.

Lactarius *blennius* Fries. Cap depressed, slimy or glutinous, greenish-gray; margin incurved and somewhat downy. Gills narrow, white or whitish; stem stuffed or hollow, viscid, and of same color as the cap or paler; milk white and very acrid.

M. C. Cooke divides the genus Lactarius into 4 "Tribes": (1) Piperites, in which the stem is central, gills *unchangeable*, naked, neither discolored nor *pruinose*, milk at first *white* and *commonly acrid*; (2) Dapetes, in which the stem is central, gills naked, *milk from the first deeply colored*; (3) Russulares, in which the stem is central, gills pallid, *then discolored*, becoming darker, changing when turned to the light, at length *pruinose*, with milk at *first white* and *mild* and *sometimes becoming acrid*; (4) Pleuropos, in which the stem is concentric or lateral.

To the first of these subdivisions, *Piperites*, belong all of the Lactars enumerated above. The Russians eat the Piperites only after the water of the first boiling has been taken off.

Lactarius *rufus* Scop., a very acrid species of large size, having reddish ochraceous gills and zoneless cap of reddish yellow with white milk, belongs to the subdivision Russulares. Common in fir woods. Dangerous.

Lactarius *volemus* Fries, a tawny yellow-capped mushroom with white gills changing to a yellowish hue, and copious *sweet* white milk, belongs also to the latter subdivision. Edible.

Russula (Fragiles) *emetica* Fries. Cap fleshy, at first convex, then expanded or depressed, smooth, polished, red, margin sulcate; gills free, equal and broad, white; stem solid but somewhat spongy in the center, smooth, short, stoutish, white or stained reddish; flesh white, sometimes slightly tinted red, under the thin red cuticle. The cap of this mushroom varies from a deep rich crimson to a pale pinkish red, being very subject to atmospheric changes. Specimens are often found with the cap washed almost white after heavy rains, or with but a slight red spot in the center. The gills and spores are pure white, and the flesh peppery to the taste. If tasted when raw the juice should not be swallowed.

The variety *Clusii* has a blood-red cap, pallid yellowish gills, adnexed, becoming adnate. Spores white. In woods. Acrid. The variety *fallax* is fragile, with dingy reddish pileus and adnexed, distant, whitish gills.

Besides the above mentioned, there are other acrid Russulas and Lactars which are regarded with suspicion, though not as yet satisfactorily tested.

POISONOUS BOLETI.

Several of the Boleti have the reputation of being poisonous or deleterious, among them Boletus *luridus*, Boletus *Satanas*, and Boletus *felleus*. Kobert's analysis of B. *luridus* shows the presence of the poisonous alkaloid muscarin in this mushroom, while the bitterness of B. *felleus* should make one chary of eating it in quantity, if at all. Schmiedeberg and Koppe describe experiments made with Boletus Satanas, in which the symptoms experienced closely resemble those of muscarin poisoning.

A correspondent living in Georgia, who is quite familiar with the species, writes that he has frequently eaten the yellow form of the *muscaria*, when cooked, without serious inconvenience. Another correspondent writes that he has eaten the species Boletus luridus and Boletus Satanas, as well as several other mushrooms of poisonous repute, with perfect impunity.

Without calling in question the testimony of persons who state that they have with impunity eaten mushrooms generally found to be poisonous, it must be said that even if, through local conditions of soil or climate, the poisonous constituents of such mushrooms sometimes exist in comparatively minute proportions, or are *neutralized* by an unusual proportion of *mushroom atropin* in the plant, or eliminated by some process used in its preparation for the table, or, finally, if constitutional idiosyncrasies should enable some persons safely to eat what is poisonous to others, the rule that such are to be avoided should never be disregarded by the ordinary collector, nor should it be departed from even by experts, except upon the clearest evidence that in the given case the departure is safe. It is certainly the part of discretion, when in doubt, to take no risks.

RECENT INSTANCES OF MUSHROOM POISONING.

About a year ago a physician in Vineland, New Jersey, furnished the following in regard to his personal experience of the effects of mushroom poisoning: "My wife, daughter, and self selected, according to an article in the Encyclopedia Britannica, what we thought were a nice lot of mushrooms, cooked them in milk, and ate them for dinner with relish. In a few hours we were vomiting, laughing, and staggering about the house. We could not control ourselves from the elbows to the finger tips, nor our legs from the knee to the ends of our toes. In other words, we were drunk on mushrooms. The mushrooms grew within the shade of Norway spruce and other ornamental trees on the lawn in front of our house. They were pure white inside and out; smooth shiny tops that easily peeled off. The caps were about two or three inches in diameter, and had a stem of the same length. On the day before, my wife and a friend ate some of these mushrooms raw and experienced no bad effects. The next day at noon we ate them cooked in milk with a little butter, and they were very good. About two o'clock our food did not seem to digest well, and soon my daughter, sixteen years of age, vomited all her dinner. Then my wife began to feel the effects, and took hot water freely, sweet oil, currant wine, and at last an overdose of tartar-emetic. Of course, she was the sickest of all. I was cool and happy and amused at the situation, and drunk from my head down. I did not vomit, and my mushrooms remained with me for at least 48 hours. I took nothing but hot water and sweet oil. A friend of my daughter's of her own age partook of the mess and had not a single bad symptom."

A physician from West Grove, Pennsylvania, writes: "I determined to risk a test of the Amanita muscaria. Accordingly, two good-sized specimens were steamed in butter. I ate one, and another member of my family ate the other, feeling that the consequences could not be serious from so small an amount. About an hour after eating, a sensation of nausea and faintness was experienced in both cases, followed by nervous tingling, some cold perspiration and accelerated and weakened action of the heart. Considerable prostration ensued within two hours. Knowing that sulphate of atropin has proved the most successful remedy for the active principle of the Fly agaric, Amanita muscaria, a small dose, one-sixtieth of a grain, was taken by each. Considerable relief was experienced within 30 minutes, and all unpleasant symptoms had disappeared within 6 hours, without repeating the medicine."

Another case, wherein the antagonism of atropin for muscarin was demonstrated, was brought to our notice during the month of September of the past year. An entire party of people were badly poisoned by eating mushrooms, and, although a doctor was called in very late, most of them were saved by the use of sulphate of atropin.

It would seem from the foregoing cases that the intensity and action of the mushroom poison must depend in some degree on the constitution of the individual, as well as on the quality and quantity of the mushrooms eaten. The first treatment should be to get rid of the poison immediately and by every possible means, so as to prevent or at least arrest the progress of inflammation of the alimentary canal, and at the same time to prevent the absorption of the poison. In a majority of cases the recovery of the victim depends solely upon the promptness with which vomiting is excited. Vertigo, convulsions, spasms, and other grave nervous symptoms, which ordinarily follow the cessation of the most important functions, yield, ordinarily, to the action of an emetic without the necessity of ulterior remedies, if taken in time, while the substance is yet in the stomach; when it has entered the lower bowels purgation is necessary. Sweet oil should always be taken in combination with castor oil, or such other purgatives as are used. Enemas of cassia, senna, and sulphate of magnesia have also been used with good effect.

The fatal poisoning of Count Achilles de Vecchj, in November, 1897, by eating the Amanita muscaria, is so fresh in the public recollection, and the details in regard to it were so widely published through the newspaper press, that it is unnecessary to take up space in recapitulating the circumstances.

The death of Chung Yu Ting, in 1894, was occasioned by eating mushrooms which he had collected in a patch of woods near Washington, D. C., and which I identified at the time as Amanita phalloides, sometimes called the "Death Cup." He had eaten very freely of this mushroom and died after great suffering, although ten hours had elapsed before the toxic effects began to show themselves.

Since it has been shown that vinegar and the solution of common salt have the power to dissolve the alkaloids of the poisonous mushrooms, it follows that the liquor thus formed must be extremely injurious. It should, therefore, be obvious that vinegar and salt should not be introduced into the stomach after poisonous mushrooms have been eaten. The result would only be to hasten death. Ether and volatile alkali are also attended with danger. A physician should in all cases be promptly called, and, if muscarin poisoning is suspected, hypodermic injections of the sulphate of atropin, the only chemical antidote known to be efficacious, should be administered, the dose being from $^1/_{180}$ up to $^1/_{35}$ of a grain. Small doses of atropin can also be taken internally, to accelerate heart action. To relieve the pains and irritation in the abdomen sweet oil and mucilaginous drinks should be given.

BIBLIOGRAPHY—FUNGI.

NORTH AMERICA.

Berkeley, M. J. "Fungi of Arctic Expedition, 1875-'76." Linn. Journ., xvii. 1880.

—— "Decades of Fungi," viii-x, in Hook. Journ., vol. iv. London. 1845.

—— "Decades of Fungi," xii-xiv. "Ohio Fungi," Hook. Journ., vol. vi. London. 1847.

—— "Decades of Fungi," xxi-xxii. "North and South Carolina." Hook. Journ., vol. i. 1849.

Berkeley, M. J., and Curtis, M. A. "North American Fungi" in *Grevillea*, vols. i-iv. London. 1871-'75.

Bessey, C. E. The Erysiphei. (Monograph.) Michigan.

Curtis, M. A. "Contributions to the Mycology of North America," Silliman Journal. 8vo. 1848.

—— "Catalogue of the Plants of North Carolina." 8vo. Raleigh. 1867.

Cooke, M. C. "Fungi of Texas." Linn. Journ., vol. xvii.

—— and Ellis, J. B. "New Jersey Fungi," in *Grevillea*. 1878-'80.

Ellis, J. B. "Canadian Fungi." Journ. Mycol., vol. 1. Manhattan. 1885.

Farlow, W. G. List of Fungi found in the vicinity of Boston. *Bulletin of the Bussey Inst.*, vol. 1.

Gibson, Hamilton Wm. Our Edible Toadstools and Mushrooms. Harper Bros., New York.

Harkness, H. W. Pacific Coast Fungi, i, iv. San Francisco. 1885-'87.

Peck, C. H. Reports of the New York Museum of Natural History. Albany. 1872-'97. Albany, N. Y.

Ravenel. "Fungi Carolinia," Fasc.: v. 90.

Schweinitz, L. de *Synopsis fungorum* in *Amer. boreali media degentium*. 4to. Philadelphia. 1831.

Taylor, Thomas. *Mildew of the Native Grape Vine. Peronospora viticola.*

—— *Erysiphei of the European Grape Vine.*

—— *Fungoid Diseases of the Peach Tree.*

—— *Mildew of the Lilac.* Illustrated. An. Report of the U. S. Dept. of Agriculture, 1871, pages 110 to 122, inclusive.

—— *Black-knot on Plum and Cherry Trees.* Illustrated.

—— *Blight and Rot of the Potato, "Peronospora infestans."* Illustrated.

—— *Blight and Smut in Onions.* Illustrated. An. Report of the U. S. Dept. of Agriculture, 1872, pages 175 to 198, inclusive.

—— *Potato Blight and Rot.* Pages 118 to 123 and 251-253.

—— *New Fungus of the Hawthorn. Rœstelia aurantiaca.* Pages 431-433. Illustrated.

—— *Rust of the Orange.* Pages 588-594. An. Report of Dept. of Agriculture, 1873.

Taylor, Thomas. *Fungoid Disease of the Cherry.* Page 173.

—— *Grape-vine Disease.* Page 175.

—— Cranberry Scald and Rot. Page 171. Illustrated. An. Report of Dept. of Agriculture, 1874.

—— *Fungoid Diseases of the Cranberry.* Page 206.

—— *Fungoid Diseases of the Plum and Cherry Trees.* Pages 119 and 413. An. Report Dept. of Agriculture, 1877.

—— Food Product Reports, Mushrooms, Edible and Poisonous. Annual Reports of U. S. Dept. Agriculture, 1885-1895.

—— Student's Handbook of Mushrooms of America, Edible and Poisonous.

Watt, D. A. P. Provisional Catalogue of Canadian Cryptogams.

Bulletins of the Boston, New York, and Philadelphia Mycological Societies. Published in Boston, Mass., New York, N. Y., and Philadelphia, Penn., respectively.

BIBLIOGRAPHY.

TOXICOLOGY OF MUSHROOMS.

Boudier, Emile. *Gazette des hop.* Paris. 1846.

—— Mushrooms Toxicologically Considered. Paris. 1869.

T. Husemann und A. Husemann. "Handb. der Toxicologie." Berlin. 1862.

Letellier and Speneux. "Experiences nouvelles sur les Champignons vénenéux etc." Paris. 1866.

McIlvaine, Chas. Article on Amanita poisonings, Therapeutic Mag. Philadelphia, 1893.

Schmiedeberg and Koppe. "Das Muscarin Das Giftige Alkaloid des Fliegenpilzes." Leipzig. Verlag von F. C. W. Vogel. 1869.

Kobert, Rudolph. "Sitzungsberichte der Naturforscher-Gesellschafft." Dorpat, Russia. 1891-'92.

—— Lehrbuch der Intoxication. Stuttgard, Germany.

INDEX TO ILLUSTRATIONS.

No. 1.

Plate A.   Agaricus (Psalliota) campester. Edible.

Plate B.   Types of the Six Orders ofHymenomycetes.

Plate I.   Russula virescens Fries. Edible.

Plate II.   Coprinus comatus Fries. Edible.

Plate III.   Marasmius oreades Fries. Edible.

No. 2.

Plate C.   Types of four of the leading genera of Discomycetes, in which occur edible species.

Plate D.   Four types of the genus Morchella. Edible.

Plate IV.   Outline sketches showing structure of the Agaricini.

Plate V.   Lactarius deliciosus Fries. Edible.

Plate VI.   Agaricus (Armillaria) melleus Vahl. Edible.

Plate VII.   Cantharellus cibarius Fries. Edible.

No. 3.

Plate E.   Outline sketches of various mushrooms.

Plate F.   Outline sketches showing characteristics of the lamellæ or gills of mushrooms.

Plate VIII.	Ag. (Hypholoma) sublateritius Fries. Edible.
Plate IX.	Ag. (Hypholoma) incertus (Hypholoma incertum) Peck. Edible.
Plate X.	Fistulina hepatica Bull. Edible.

No. 4.

Plate G.	Six types of the Puff-Ball Group. Edible.
Plate H.	Two types of the subdivision Phalloideæ. Unwholesome.
Plate XI.	Ag. (Lepiota) procerus Fries. (Lepiota procera.) Edible.
Plate XI.	Ag. (Lepiota) naucinoides Peck. Edible.
Plate XI½.	Ag. (Lepiota) cepæstipes—var. cretaceus Peck (Lepiota cretacea). Edible.
Plate XII.	Cortinarius (Inoloma) violaceus. Linn.
Plate XII.	Cortinarius (Phlegmacium) cærulescens Fries.
Plate XIII.	Figs. 1 to 3, Ag. (Collybia fusipes) Bull. Edible.
Plate XIII.	Figs. 4 to 6, Ag. (Collybia maculatus) A. & S. (Collybia maculata). (After Cooke.) Edible.
Plate XIII.	Figs. 7 to 9, Ag. (Collybia) velutipes Curt. (After Cooke.)

No. 5.

Plate J.	Ag. (Pleurotus) ostreatus Jacq. Edible.
Plate XIV.	Figs. 1 to 4, Ag. (Amanita) Cæsareus Scop. (Amanita Cæsarea). Edible.
Plate XIV.	Figs. 5 to 9, Ag. (Amanita) rubescens Pers. Edible.
Plate XIV½.	Ag. (Amanita) strobiliformis Vitt. Edible.
Plate XV.	Figs. 1 to 7, Ag. (Amanita) muscarius Linn. (Amanita muscaria). Poisonous.
Plate XV.	Fig. 8, Ag. (Amanita) phalloides Fries. Poisonous.
Plate XV.	Fig. 9, Ag. (Amanita) mappa Batsch. Poisonous.

CORRECTION OF PLATES.

No. 1.

Plate B.	Fig. 4 should read Fig. 5, Fig. 5 should read Fig. 4.

No. 2.

177

Plate D.	Fig. 3, the exposed inner surface of the cap, should be *smooth*, not *ridged*, as the straight lines in the engraving might suggest.
Plate V.	For Lactarious read Lactarius.

No. 3.

Plate VIII.	The red on the upper surface of the cap is too bright in tint. It should be a dull brick-red.
Plate IX.	Fig. 6. The spores should be a deeper tint or brownish purple.

The spores as delineated on the plates represent a magnification of from 400 to 500 diameters.

www.ingramcontent.com/pod-product-compliance
Lightning Source LLC
Chambersburg PA
CBHW021231020726
47498CB00008B/2796